THEY KNOW HOW
THEY KNOW WHY
THEY JUST DON'T KNOW WHO'S NEXT

KEY MAN

_____

A NOVEL

BY
ALLEN K. HUFFSTUTTER

CROSS
CREEK
BOOKS

Hardback: 978-1-7369004-0-6
Paperback: 978-1-7369004-1-3
Ebook: 978-1-7369004-2-0

Dedication

To Sandra
Best wife, best friend, and best editor

Chapter 1

Strolling out of the elevator, Henry took his time crossing the lobby. He thought of his wife and smiled. He'd be home from work before 8:00 pm and, even though it was New Year's Eve, Molly would think that his coming home this early meant something was wrong.

"Evenin' Mr. Watson," called Manny, the security guard, from behind the reception desk. "Good evening Manny," Henry responded, proud that he was still able to remember every one of his employees' names down to the last clerk and janitor. "Hope you have a happy New Year," replied Manny. "To you as well" said Henry, adding "Let's all hope 1999 is as good a year for Watson

Enterprises as 1998 has been." "I'll drink to that," answered Manny, "... but not 'til I finish my shift."

As he did every evening, Henry exited the building, turned, and briefly scanned the Watson Towers. After all these years, Henry still hadn't decided what he loved best, the sheer substance of the structure, the rosewood and hunter-green lobby that stated in no uncertain terms that "men work here," or his office, which was clearly where the "Big Dog" kept watch.

As always, his nearly new Mercedes was the only car left in the executive lot, just off to the side of the main entrance to Watson Towers. Even though he reserved other choice spaces for the up-and-comers in his organization ... the number 1 space was his daily reward.

He lowered his six-foot-four-inch frame into the driver's seat, closed the door, inhaled the leather fragrance, and paused in the stillness. Not a creak, not a rattle, not a sound.

Normally, everything in Henry's life hummed. He was keenly aware of sounds. Once the work-day started, his building was a Babylon of noise. When he was alone at work, there was the background buzz of the fluorescent lights, the soft whir of his computer.

At home there was the constant racket his two boys generated. Even in bed, Henry Watson was enveloped in a cacophony of sounds, the beating of his heart, the ringing in his ears left over from those damn earaches he had as a kid, the rustle of the sheets as Molly shifted from her back to her side.

But in his tightly engineered, sound-proofed Mercedes, it was as quiet and still as a coffin. Henry settled into the stiff leather seat, leaned over to check his hair in the rear-view mirror, turned the key, and ceased to exist.

II

Samuel Siemen and Askeia Johnson had only been working cases together for a couple of months. While they got along fine, there were still a few kinks to work out in their relationship. Then again, with Samuel, there were always a few kinks.

Sam to his friends, Sperm behind his back, Samuel Siemen was the veteran of the two-man team. Sam fancied himself a Bogart look-alike but, in reality, he was just short ... a rather plain-looking man in his late forties whose most distinguishing characteristic was an unsuccessful attempt to cover his bald spot with a classic comb-over.

Sam was the kind of guy who reminded people of someone they had met before. Later, if he wasn't in the room, he became almost impossible to describe.

Sam had been a detective for as long as anyone could remember, but his career to date had been uneven and undistinguished.

On the other hand, Askeia Johnson — Ski — was a black twenty-something whiz-kid who seemed to have made detective right out of the academy. Ski could have been the poster child for an anti-stereotype campaign. Over six-foot-five and weighing in at a slim 185 pounds, Ski didn't get his growth spurt until he was in junior college and, while he was somewhat athletic, couldn't play basketball worth a damn.

In keeping with his name, Ski liked to ski. Downhill, cross country, anything up in the mountains, out in the snow. In fact, Ski once had visions of becoming the first black to compete in the Nordic-combined in the Winter Olympics. But his late seven-inch growth spurt took care of that.

Ski had grown up in a sheltered environment in Grass Valley, California, not far from the recreational areas surrounding Lake Tahoe. The only child of the local postmaster and an elementary school teacher, Ski enjoyed an uneventful childhood. But, being the only black man on the ski slopes, Ski realized that racism was still alive and well. Nothing overt, but the whispers, lack of eye contact, and the wide swath cut around him gave constant reminders that he was different from the "normal" ski crowd.

Maybe it was the subtle racism he experienced on the slopes, maybe it was just his quiet nature, but Ski preferred on-line conversations to face-to-face interaction. On-line, it's intelligence that counts, not the color of your skin, how tall you are or aren't, or the accent you bring to the conversation. Ski loved almost everything on-line, but most of all he loved chatting with people he knew he'd never, ever, meet.

Soft spoken and articulate, Ski, without fail, surprised people who had only talked to him on-line or by phone, when they met in person. But once people met Ski, they had no doubt that, unlike Sam, they had just met someone who was unforgettable.

III

Because of Sam's seniority, Sam and Ski didn't normally pull the swing shift. But, Joey and Bill, Mel and Frank — the night shift teams — had all requested shift swaps so that they could drink themselves silly at this year's version of Joey's infamous New Year's Eve extravaganza. Neither Sam nor Ski were party animals, especially with other cops, so they were filling in for the night.

The homicide load was usually light at the beginning of the New Year's Eve shift since the shootings and stabbings that spawned from parties gone bad usually occurred well after midnight, and they were not classified as homicides until the next morning. The extra pay was nice. And for a day or two after the shift, no one at work, or at home, expected much.

So Sam was reading the *Thin Man* for the umpteenth time and Ski was on-line, chatting, when the call came in. As was his habit, Sam carefully marked his place and reached for a scratch pad and pencil before he picked up the receiver.

"Homicide, Detective Siemen, what's up? ... When? ... Where? ... How many hurt? ... How many dead? ... Bomb squad's already dispatched? ... How big a blast? ... Give me that address again ... OK, we're on our way."

Sam started to set down the receiver but had a second thought. "Hey, one more thing. Could you get a message to the bomb sweepers? Ask them to try and not disturb the crime scene any more than they need to ... Hey, I hear ya, I wouldn't be in their shoes for a million bucks. But I'm the one who has to reconstruct the crime ... Yeah, tell 'em I asked, just as a reminder."

Turning towards Ski's desk, Sam hung up the phone and reached for his coat, "Grab your note pad, detective. Big-time car bombing downtown. At least one dead and four injured. Bomb squad hasn't hit the scene yet, so we don't know if there are any more explosives on site."

As they quickly made their way to the parking garage, Ski rattled off a string of questions. Sam, having already shared all the information he had, just answered with his own string of "Don't know ... don't know ... don't know."

It was quiet on the streets, with most parties already underway. Traffic was light so Sam decided not to use the siren. That was fine with Ski, who still hated the sound and had come up with even more questions that Sam couldn't answer.

Turning the corner from Mill Street onto 4th Avenue, the detectives were greeted with a night sky illuminated by pulsating orange and red strobe lights from the dozen or so police and emergency vehicles that had descended on Watson Towers. Sam eased his vehicle into the first available parking space and turned off the engine.

The blast that had instantly consumed Henry Watson was so powerful that it shattered nearly every pane of glass on the first three floors of Watson Towers. The two mammoth plate glass doors that marked the entrance to the building, while still intact, had been blown completely off their hinges. In the parking lot, near the entrance to the building, in the center of what looked like the remains of a giant collegiate homecoming bonfire, were the twisted remains of Henry's Mercedes.

Still trying to impress his new partner with his powers of deduction, Sam turned to Ski and stated flatly, "Going to be a bitch piecing this puppy back together after all these folks get done traipsing through the crime scene. I see one big footprint after another on every piece of evidence out there."

Without much field experience or the slightest idea of what Sam expected to find at a blast scene, all Ski could say was, "Yeah, footprints ... all over our evidence!"

Despite the vehicles, personnel, and pulsating orange and red lights, Sam and Ski emerged from their squad car into an almost surrealistically quiet night. There was the occasional crackle of a police radio, but otherwise everything was still. Everyone was standing quietly, eyes glued on the office building.

Sam led Ski to the command car and, in a whisper, asked "Bomb squad inside?"

Officer Mitchell whispered back, "Yeah, cleared the car and the lot but just entered the building. Looks like they'll be in there for a while."

"Did forensics beat us to the scene?" Sam asked.

"Yeah" Mitchell replied. "They picked up a few scraps of possible bomb material from the blast site. Not much to work with. They said they'd tackle the building tomorrow."

Sam indicated with a gesture that he and Ski were going to take a look at what remained of the Mercedes. Officer Mitchell nodded his OK and added in a still, soft voice, "You'll have to come back tomorrow if you want to poke around inside the building. I can leave a note for tomorrow's duty officer to let you know when forensics signs off on the building if you want."

Ski whispered his thanks and Sam just nodded as they turned and headed toward the smoldering hulk. Sam, with Ski following, approached the remains of the car through a series of tighter and tighter concentric circles, Sam on the lookout for any shred of evidence.

Ski had quickly concluded that nothing useful could be found outside the car itself. After participating in Sam's slow dance for a couple of minutes, he started to head for what could have been the driver's side of the pile of wreckage.

"Don't touch anything!" shouted Sam, shattering the silence.

"Don't touch anything," Sam reiterated in a loud whisper as heads that had been focused on the office building turned to see why their bomb squad vigil had been interrupted.

With all eyes now on him, Ski tried to look cool, and, with a wide sweep of his hand, gestured around the parking lot and said to Sam in a reserved voice, "Nothing here but broken glass. If we're going to find anything useful, it'll be in the car."

"What's in the car, will still be in the car ten minutes from now," retorted Sam flatly. "What's out here, if there is anything out here, will be gone as soon as more people start working the scene. Maybe there's something out here, maybe not. But I can guarantee you we'll never know unless we take the time to look. So, slow down. Show a little patience. And, let me finish out here before you start yanking things out of the car. OK?"

With all eyes now back on the building and all thoughts on the bomb squad, Ski was able to slowly back away from the car without embarrassment.

Sam painstakingly completed his investigation of the area surrounding the smoldering wreckage. "Nothing," he finally declared.

"Nothing," repeated Ski, who added, "But, at least we know."

"Yeah," replied Sam, "At least we know."

It was impossible to tell that the charred remains were once a luxury automobile. It would have been hard to tell it had been an automobile at all, if it weren't for the tell-tale wheels and axles that had survived almost intact. Everything else was just charred, twisted, jagged metal and a fine dust of blistered paint and pulverized safety glass.

Every stitch of the luxurious leather interior had been consumed in the inferno that followed the blast ... a fire so intense that there wasn't a crematorium in the city that could have done a more thorough job of reducing Henry Watson's remains to ashes.

"Jesus, Sam" whimpered Ski as he got his first look inside the remains of the Mercedes.

"This guy must have really pissed somebody off," mumbled Sam, as much an observation to himself as a reply to Ski.

As Sam was about to begin a new slow dance immediately around the Mercedes, which had become its own junk yard, he instructed Ski to check back with Officer Mitchell and see what information he had about the bombing.

"I think his first name is John, but it could be Jim," offered Sam. "Can't remember for sure, been a long time since we shared a shift."

Ski hustled back toward John Mitchell, or Jim Mitchell, glad to retreat from the gruesome wreckage that was once Henry Watson and his new Mercedes. As it turned out, Officer Mitchell introduced himself as Jack.

Jack Mitchell was born to be a crime scene officer. A large, fit man, he had a distinct bearing. Jack projected a gravity that was inappropriate for most circumstances but created an anchor for a crew forced to deal with death and destruction.

As the senior officer at the crime scene, it was Jack Mitchell's responsibility to appear bored and in-charge, at the same time. The appearance of boredom was the signal that everything was under control. No need for panic. No need for alarm. See, everything's so calm here that those of us in the know are already bored.

The appearance of being "in charge" saved everyone else from having to deal with the end-less unanswerable questions that swirled around a crime scene. Best to have all the babble directed at one individual instead of scattered around, in-terfering with the real work that was required to secure the site.

As he approached the command car, Ski in-troduced himself. "Detective Johnson, everyone calls me Ski."

"Jack Mitchell ... see you got teamed up with Sperm."

"Sperm? Oh yeah, Sam," responded Ski, somewhat surprised at the irreverence, given the situation.

"Yeah, Sam ... Sperm, whatever ... little guy gets pretty dramatic around a crime scene," yawned Officer Mitchell.

"Yeah, he's a little intense. Just doesn't want to overlook anything that might be helpful later," replied Ski, in defense of his partner.

"Well there must be about ten billion pieces of evidence blown to bits around here, so he ought to be in hog heaven tonight," said Officer Mitchell, punctuating his statement with a broad sweep of his hand.

To move off the subject of his partner's quirky behavior, Ski asked, "Do we know anything about what went down here?"

With that opening, Jack Mitchell took a couple of steps to his right, reached through the side window of his patrol car, and retrieved a note pad.

"Here's what we got so far. Dead guy's Henry Watson."

"How did we get an identity so quickly?" asked Ski.

"Night watchman, make that 'Building Security,' saw Watson leave the building and head for his car just before the blast."

"Did this guy see the explosion?"

"No, had his back turned."

"Did he see Watson get in the car?"

"No, but Watson was the last guy in the building, other than the janitorial staff. His car was the only one left in the parking lot. The night watchman, make that 'Building Security,' watched him exit the lobby and head toward his car. And the next thing he knows, he's been blown off his feet by the blast. Now there's a dead guy in the burned-out hulk over there and my best guess is that it's Watson."

Starting his own notes, Ski asked flatly, "But Building Security didn't actually see Watson get in the car?"

"Right ... Building Security, make that the night watchman, didn't actually see Watson get in the car," Mitchell replied sarcastically.

"What else do we know at this point?"

"Watson must be some big shot 'cause he owned all this." offered Mitchell, with another prolonged hand-sweep.

"Owned what?" asked Ski.

"Building, business," answered Mitchell matter-of-factly. "This is ... was ... Watson Enterprises. Everyone we interviewed from the building confirmed that Watson was the big cheese."

"Do we know anything about Watson Enterprises?"

"Nope, just that the dead guy's name was on the building and the survivors said it was his business they worked for," answered Mitchell, getting a little annoyed at being treated more like a witness than the duty officer.

With his eyes still focused on his note pad, Ski charged on, "How many survivors?"

"Four. Night watchman, a janitor and two cleaning ladies."

"And where are they now?" asked Ski.

Officer Mitchell's tone improved as he decided he might as well be helpful. "Sent them all to Good Samaritan. The night watchman was pretty nicked up ... took a lot of flying glass in the back. Looked like he'd been run over by a rototiller."

"Is he going to make it?" asked Ski with genuine concern.

"Oh sure," replied Mitchell, "Cut up pretty bad. But he took the brunt of the shards in the back. Had on one of those thick cotton, you know, canvas-type jackets, which helped. No arteries cut and his bleeding was starting to coagulate by the time the ambulance made it to the scene. From what I saw, I'm sure he'll be OK."

Ski steadied himself after his knees buckled slightly at the thought of being sprayed with flying glass. He took a deep breath then continued. "What about the others?"

"We were already on the scene when the janitor comes strolling out of the emergency exit. Said he was up on the eighth floor cleaning, when the blast went off. He's almost deaf, so he didn't hear the explosion, but said the building shivered. Said he thought it was an earthquake ... lived through his share of earthquakes ... didn't see any reason to survive a major earthquake and then die of a heart attack trying to rush down eight flights of stairs, so he'd taken his time.

"Both of the cleaning women had been knocked around by the blast, but as far as we could tell, beyond a few bumps and bruises, they were fine physically. I think one was heading into shock after hearing that Watson was at ground zero. But by the time her breath went shallow and she started to turn white, the medics were on the scene. I'm sure she'll be fine as soon as they get her calmed down and warmed up. To be safe, I sent them all off to Good Sam."

Ski finished a shorthand note and asked, "Did we get statements?"

"Just briefs about where each one was when the explosion hit, what they did following the blast, and the little we found out about Watson. I sent officer Dominguez along with the ambulance to take additional statements as soon as they're all cleared by the emergency room staff."

"Any witnesses other than the four in the building?" Ski asked, making direct eye contact with Jack Mitchell for the first time since they began talking.

Looking up to Ski, Mitchell replied, "Lots of calls to 911 to report the blast or the fire. But, so far, no one's stepped forward to say they'd seen anything. You know, commercial area, New Year's

Eve, not a lot of traffic in this part of town. Now that there's cops and firefighters crawling all over the place ... my guess is that if anyone witnessed what went down here and was going to come forward, they'd be talking to you by now."

As Ski was finishing up with Mitchell, the four spacemen from the bomb squad began to emerge from the building. Ski noticed that, while the entire front of the building had been blown into the lobby, creating a giant entrance, the bomb squad, one by one, made sure to exit through what had been the lobby doorway. At first he thought that might be a safety precaution, but then decided it was probably superstition.

As they made their way out into the fresh air and began to strip off their protective suits, one of them announced that there were no other victims or survivors in the building. No additional explosives had been uncovered. And that, while the building needed further structural inspection, it seemed sound.

In Ski's opinion, the bomb squad had just performed a heroic act, and he felt like applauding. But, since everyone else was being cool, he stifled his cheer and headed towards the Mercedes' skeleton to share with Sam the little he had learned from Officer Mitchell.

Sam was down on all fours trying to peer under the twisted metal that had been the Mercedes' chassis. It was impossible to see anything, since the body of the car had come to rest only inches off the ground.

The explosives experts would be able to determine the force and direction of the blast and probably the major components and design of the device that had reduced the Mercedes to its present state. That kind of analysis was way beyond Sam's ability.

Sam would leave the technical analysis for the experts. All he was looking for was that one clue, that abbreviated version of "ah ha" that would enable him and Ski to solve this crime. But he quickly realized, if that clue existed, he wasn't going to find it under the car.

Dusting the pulverized glass and charred auto body paint off his hands and knees as he rose to his feet, Sam asked Ski what he'd learned from officer Mitchell.

"Not much," Ski offered half-heartedly.

He then went on to fill Sam in on the four survivors who had been taken to the hospital, Henry Watson's identity, and the fact that Watson owned the building that now looked like it belonged in Beirut. He added the tidbit that the hunk of metal that Sam was hovering over had, earlier in the evening, been a nearly new, top of the line Mercedes sedan.

"Listen, Ski," started Sam. "I hate to dump the grunt work on you, but how 'bout you start canvassing the neighborhood. See if anyone in any of the office buildings or parking garages saw anything unusual around here tonight. I want to try and track down the forensic team that was out here. See if they have any guesses on what caused this mess."

"No problem," Ski offered as he turned and headed for the street. Ski would have volunteered for a hundred canvasses if it meant he didn't have to hang around while Sam talked with the forensic guys to see if they had recovered anything from the dust and gristle that had been Henry Watson and his Mercedes. But that was information Ski decided he really didn't need to share with Sam.

After about an hour, Ski made his way back to the crime scene. He hadn't turned up a single witness, or even anyone who admitted to seeing anything unusual in the neighborhood, anytime that evening.

Sam hadn't been much more productive. The forensic team had gathered up what little evidence they could scrape together. Teeth, charred bones, the contents of the glove compartment that had amazingly survived the fire, charred bits and pieces of paper that hadn't fared so well, and the frame of what had been a briefcase.

Sam knew the explosives experts would piece together enough fragments from the site to eventually tell just what kind of explosive material was used, approximately how much, and what type of triggering mechanism had set the whole thing off. Now that the forensics team had gathered what they wanted from the burnt out car and the immediate area around the car, Sam felt free to dig in and look for the clues that forensics might have overlooked.

If that singular clue was there, Sam hadn't found it by the time Ski returned from the canvas. At Sam's insistence, they went straight to the hospital to see if they could re-interview the four survivors before they were discharged.

Chapter 2

Molly Watson was devastated by the news that her husband had been killed. It was hard to tell what hit her the hardest. The fact that her Henry was dead. The fact that he had been murdered. Or, the fact that he had been viciously car bombed. Every piece of information was overwhelming.

Informing a victim's next of kin was a part of the job that was still new to Ski. And, even after all these years, it was the one aspect of homicide work Sam detested.

"Just what are you supposed to say?" asked Ski, wanting, but not getting, an answer from Sam. It had already been a long night that had stretched into a grim morning. Sam didn't need any more rookie questions.

Molly was attractive, but in a way that didn't say 'trophy wife.' Sitting in the Watson's family room, it was soon clear to Sam and Ski that the Watsons had been together for a long time. A faded wedding portrait, baby pictures, school photos, family sittings marking the passage of time, all spoke silently of a long, stable marriage.

After completely breaking down upon first hearing the horrible news, Molly tried very hard to regain her composure. She needed someone to be strong for her. But Henry had always been her strength. She needed someone to hold her and stroke her hair and tell her everything was going to be all right. But there was no one but the two detectives.

So she willed herself to stop crying. She willed herself to stop shaking. She willed herself to stop thinking and to concentrate, instead, on the questions. No, she had no idea of who would want her husband dead ... No, she wasn't aware of anyone holding a grudge, having fought with, or, in even the slightest way, having been upset with Henry.

In Molly's eyes, Henry had no enemies. He was a great boss. A good husband. A reliable friend.

Oh, Molly admitted that she and the kids had had to share Henry with his work. But she had reconciled herself to that reality years ago.

Henry worked a lot, more than she would have liked. But when he wasn't working, he was with his family. He didn't golf. He didn't fish. He didn't carouse with the guys.

Molly offered that while Henry worked long hours, he had built a successful business that had allowed her and the boys a very comfortable lifestyle. Henry's success also allowed the family to enjoy fabulous vacations the two weeks each year they could drag Henry away from the office.

Henry had his work and he had his family. He was happy with both, and both were happy with him.

Molly added that there were a lot of other people besides herself and the boys who relied on Henry Watson. Henry had to run his business because it wouldn't run without him. As far as Molly was concerned, Henry Watson was Watson Enterprises.

Ski had been silent throughout the entire interview. Now Sam was out of questions.

Molly sat for a minute and then said without emotion, "If we're finished here, I need to talk with my sons. Please excuse me."

"Is there anything we can do to help?" Ski asked, with a sincerity in his voice that caught both Molly and Sam off guard.

"No, but thanks," answered Molly as she rose and led the detectives from the family room, through the kitchen, across the living room, to the front door.

"Thank you for being so helpful," offered Sam. "Please call us at any time if you think of anything that might help with our investigation." Handing Molly a business card, Sam finished with, "Home and work numbers are here for both detective Johnson and myself. Call us anytime."

As he passed through the front door, Ski turned, looked at his feet, and almost whispered, "Sorry for your loss."

Chapter 3

Karl thought he was going to explode. Was it the heat? The air-less, window-less room? The humidity? The seven, or was it eight, blue drinks he'd inhaled the night before? The random patterns of the 'aloha' shorts and tops? Or the varicose veins laying out a road map on the legs of the fat lady from Iowa, seated in the first row? Whatever it was, he couldn't decide whether he should pass out or throw up.

What was he doing here? This had to be a horrible mistake.

But mistake or not, Karl had his pitch and his pitch just went on and on. "... investment potential ... tax advantages ... swaps with owners in other, exclusive, resort properties ..."

Timeshares, what a scam.

Take a condo that's really a hotel room, wave a wand over it, and call it a timeshare. Take a condo that's worth maybe $200,000, tops, wave a wand over it, call it a timeshare, and now it's worth $650,000.

Do the math. Christ, you buy a timeshare for $12,500 and now you can use a hotel room for a week. Two weeks? Sure, that'll be $25,000.

Do the math. $12,500 per week times fifty-two weeks, that's $650,000. Who are they kidding?

$12,500. Add taxes and homeowner's fees, stick the money in the bank, and you could afford to stay at the Four Seasons one week a year, every year, for the rest of your life. Do the math.

But there they were. Tourists, mostly from the Midwest and Canada, listening to a canned pitch.

"Scott, what do you want? A unit facing the golf course or one with an ocean view? Come on Scott, you must have a preference ... or do you let the little missus make all the decisions?

"Ellen, it is Ellen isn't it? Wouldn't you just love to have a place to call home for at least two weeks each year ... other than Sioux Falls?

"I know you could just write me a check for one of the units Fred, but let me tell you about our low down and easy monthly payments."

Karl had a new appreciation for the phrase, "Ugly American." He looked around the room and wanted to puke.

II

Avarice molded Karl Heulenberg. It made him what he was ... successful. It kept him from being what he wanted to be ... happy.

In Karl's world, there was always a greener valley just over the next ridge. Then another ridge and another, even greener valley, just beyond reach.

Karl had a wonderful wife. He wanted a better one.

Karl had a gifted daughter. He wanted a brilliant son.

Karl would buy a beautiful 3,000 square foot house – then see a 4,000-square-foot house he coveted.

Karl would move and then despair when he heard about a new 4,500-square-foot house under construction. A larger house, always on a larger lot. A newer house, always with a better view.

Karl had a good job, but he wanted a better one. When Karl got the better job, he wanted to make partner. When Karl made partner, he wanted to own his own company.

Motivated by his constant desire for something more, something better, Karl drove everyone around him. Oblivious to the wants, needs, or fears of others, Karl bullied his family, staff, and those he thought were his friends in the single-minded pursuit of his latest obsession.

Karl was a success in spite of himself. He had long since passed his level of competency, but his strong suit was intimidation. And, at the end of the day, intimidation shouts down competency every time.

III

The only time Karl Heulenberg looked backwards was when he fantasized about what it must have been like to grow up in the Territories during the early 1800's, when half a continent of ridges and green valleys lay to the West. Opportunities to be explored. Opportunities to be exploited.

But Karl was born and raised in Sacramento, California, and his westward trek could only take him as far as San Francisco. There he staked his claim in the investment banking industry and set about mining riches from small companies that desperately needed capital for growth.

Karl started as an associate at Sunrise Securities, where he brought in clients like Lock & Store, North Coast Fabrication, and Transbay Yachts. He moved to Jade Investment Bankers, where he managed private placements for companies like Star Electronics and American Filters, and for investors like Walter Blodget and Red Rock Venture Funds.

When Crocker Securities wanted to establish a beachhead on the West Coast, they brought in Karl Heulenberg. As Managing Director, Karl used his new position to expand his reach beyond the Bay area and explore the green valleys of underwriting opportunities from Los Angeles to Seattle.

Karl did very well during his stint at Crocker Securities. He moved his second ... better ... family into a new ... better ... home in Mill Valley. He leased a new ... better ... car and shopped for a new ... better ... wardrobe.

While he was doing very well financially, it was clear to Karl, that the firm was doing even better. After he'd brought in the likes of Metallurgica, Noir Films, and Watson Enterprises, Karl knew he deserved a bigger slice of the pie.

Karl wanted it all. But starting a new investment banking concern isn't quite like opening up a pet grooming salon. An investment banking firm's inventory is capital, and it takes a lot to be a player.

Karl had to borrow heavily just to put his first deal together. But he pulled it off, and the fees from the private placement for Jetway Services set him up for his next deal.

Karl bludgeoned his way through deal after deal. Soon the fees weren't enough. Karl wanted ... Karl deserved ... a piece of the action.

Lacking the creativity to ever conceive of a new product or service on his own, Karl Heulenberg was determined to horn his way into equity positions in the firms he was helping finance. Karl began bullying options, warrants, and even outright share allocations from the businesses that came to him for underwriting services.

It was a whole new ball game for Karl, with clients like Mossberg Inc., Redmond Resources, and Zebron Industries. Once they went forward with big public offerings, Karl was positioned to ride the surge in share values.

Cash flow suffered under Karl's new strategy, as did the quality of the firms he was able to underwrite. But the play was on. A couple of wins and Karl would have scaled a whole new series of ridges.

Chapter 4

Most of her friends and acquaintances considered Katherine Newberry ... well, complicated. A rich bitch when she wanted to be, Katherine was old money, well-traveled, and finishing-school educated.

"Kate," on the other hand, played soccer and volleyball with the abandon of a hormonal teenage boy, could drink like a frat rat, and was outspokenly Republican, unlike most of her wealthy friends who could easily afford the tax deductible contributions to the charitable causes that allowed them to consider themselves liberals.

And then there was "Kat." Kat didn't come out to play very often, but when she did you could bet there was going to be some eye-popping, head-banging, sweat-dripping sex in some lucky buck's immediate future.

It took some work to keep Katherine, and especially Kat, in check, but Kate was Katherine Newberry's most comfortable persona. That's where she was most of the time. That's where she best connected with her friends.

With a little work, Katherine could be stunning, but most of the time Kate just looked wholesome. Her five-foot ten-inch height made her noticeable in most any crowd, but her slender frame and brownish hair kept her from really standing out.

If she'd had blond hair and large breasts, Kat would have been a conversation-stopper. Kate was grounded enough to be grateful not to have those "gifts."

Against everyone's wishes, Kate had entered the MBA program at UCLA after being "finished" at Brown. Newberry women were supposed to look good; carry on a cocktail party conversation about art, politics, and current events; engage in charity fundraising; and never, ever, be threatening to Newberry men, past, present, or future.

Katherine's parents had pleaded with her to give up on the idea of a professional career. Marriages of equals were for the nouveau, not for the circles in which the Newberrys traveled. Even worse, they saw no grandchildren springing from their only child, since Katherine showed no interest, whatsoever, in the eligible bachelors they tried to match her with at every conceivable social occasion.

Jonathan Newberry, Katherine's grandfather and the patriarch of the family, had protested long and publicly about her decision to study business. But in private, Jonathan had told her, "Sweetheart, don't pay any attention to anyone who tries to tell you what to do with your life, especially your father. What the hell has he ever done that was original, or even interesting? Follow your heart. You know what's best for Katherine Newberry. No one else does."

It was Kate's turn to give her grandfather some advice when he was first diagnosed with a pre-cancerous colon. "The death watch is on, isn't it Kate?" Jonathan had whispered from his hospital bed after the exploratory surgery. "Big time, grandpa," Kate had answered. "But here's the plan. Act really ill for the next couple of days. Do what you want when no one is here, but lie there and moan when anyone is around. The more you ham it up, the better. Then, in about a week, when the family is about to call for last rites, jump out of bed and declare yourself cured. They'll be devastated. It'll be great."

"Kate, I really <u>am</u> ill. I don't <u>need</u> to act. All I <u>can</u> do is lie here and moan. I don't think I'm going to make it ... I don't know if I want to make it.

"Kate, I'm tired of being old. I'm tired of watching the buzzards circle. Knowing, that, to my family, I'm only a piece of tough old meat standing between them and the inheritance they can't wait to get their hands on."

Kate never did tolerate Jonathan's self-pity. "I know it's hard, but you've got to get better. You can't leave me here to deal with 'this family.' I need my silent partner. You've got to get better. If for no other reason than to piss everyone off."

Knowing there was one person who wanted him to live, Jonathan made up his mind to recover. He did. And it did piss everyone off. Everyone but Kate.

As is often the case, love and respect had jumped a generation, and Kate always felt closer to her grandfather than to her own parents. So it was a devastating shock when her father called to tell her that Jonathan had been killed in what appeared to be a car bombing.

II

When the phone rang, Sam was finishing the report on the drive-by they'd either solve in the next forty-eight hours, or never. Ski was online trying to trace ownership of a handgun used with fatal results in a liquor store heist gone bad.

Sam was up, so he took the call. After a brief exchange he put the receiver down and let Ski know that the call was for him.

"Who is it?" whispered Ski to Sam, not knowing whether Sam actually put the call on hold or just set the phone down.

"Katherine Newberry."

"The old guy's granddaughter?"

"That's the one."

"What's she want?"

"Why don't you ask her. She asked for you, didn't want to talk to me, I guess."

"Why'd she want to talk to me?"

"Christ, Ski. Stop asking me questions I can't answer and just pick up the fucking phone."

"Detective Johnson, can I help you? ... Certainly I remember you Ms. Newberry ... Well there really aren't any new developments ... Actually, Ms. Newberry, that case is being handled by detectives Martin and Sizemore ... Yes, we did interview you concerning your grandfather's death, but as we told you, our interview was in connection with another case we are working ... No ma'am, I don't think Martin and Sizemore are incompetent ... No ma'am, I'm sure they do care about the case ... I know you're upset, it's just that sometimes these cases take a long time. And, while it may not be apparent to you, I'm sure that detectives Martin and Sizemore are giving your grandfather's murder the attention it deserves ... I can't really do that, ma'am ... Ma'am, Martin and Sizemore ... Yes, ma'am ... Yes, ma'am ... I understand, ma'am ... All right, ma'am ... That'll be fine, ma'am ... 2:30 this afternoon, let me check. Yes, ma'am, 2:30 will be OK ... You're welcome. See you at 2:30."

Sam, who tried to eavesdrop on every conversation in the precinct, couldn't wait for Ski to hang up the receiver they shared. "What in the world was that all about? You got a date?"

"I wish," replied Ski with a wistfulness he immediately hoped wasn't noticed. Quickly, Ski added, "She thinks Martin and Sizemore don't care about her grandfather's case. She thinks they're either lazy or incompetent, and said they both just shine her off when she tries to get any information out of them."

"So? Martin and Sizemore are lazy!" Sam responded. "If they weren't so lazy it'd be easier to tell if they're incompetent. But as it is, that's a hard call. I'd say your Ms. Newberry's pretty perceptive."

Then Sam asked in a teasing voice, "So what's she want from you?"

"She said that out of all the cops she's talked to, I'm the only one who seems to care. She just wants to talk to me, us, about her grandfather and our Watson case."

Sam wanted to tease Ski about coming on to Katherine with a 90's kind of warm-and-fuzzy-guy line, but Ski really was so damn sincere that it wouldn't have been funny. So Sam let that thought pass. "You know you can't talk to her about Watson. Anyway, we haven't come up with anything that even remotely links Watson to her grandfather's murder, except the fact that both these guys were rich and that somewhat similar

— but very common — explosive devices were used. What're you going to tell her?"

"I don't know. All I know is that she really needs someone to be as concerned about her grandfather's murder as she is. No one's stepping up to the plate. So, I guess I will." Ski hesitated for a moment and then added, "Listen, she's coming by at 2:30. I'd really like for you to be here."

"Why?" asked Sam with some confusion in his voice.

"Because," Ski replied, "I'm better talking online, or two-on-one, than I am one-on-one. It'd just be easier for me if you're around. Besides, we're not getting anywhere on Watson fast and, if there is some connection between Newberry and Watson we've missed, maybe talking to Katherine could help us."

III

At 2:30 sharp Kate exited the elevator and located the reception area at the entrance to the sea of cubicles that was home for the LAPD detective squad. She had expected more of an open bull pen, like the ones on all the TV cop shows, so she was a little disoriented at first.

Following the receptionist's directions, she made her way back to the cubicle that Sam and Ski shared. As she negotiated the narrow aisle, she realized she was traversing a space that was as metal-desk-gray, dingy, and depressing as the set of any police drama and that, except for the partitions, the scene really was exactly what she expected.

Sam and Ski both looked up from the paperwork they were shuffling and then rose to greet Kate after she knocked gently on the partition defining their space. Ski gestured to the gray-metal-chair nearest to his gray-metal-desk. "It's a little cramped. We can talk here, or, if you'd be more comfortable, I can see if one of the interview rooms is available."

Taking the seat Ski had offered, Kate indicated that the detective's space was adequate for talking.

The two detectives shared a cubicle that was the size of a small bedroom. They had arranged their desks at the back of the cubicle so that they faced each other. Each officer had a small file cabinet next to his desk and there were two chairs pushed back against the side partitions.

There was a computer monitor on the top of each desk, along with the obligatory pile of case files. The phone they shared was strategically placed where both detectives could reach it.

After taking a seat, Kate scanned the surroundings and realized that the heaviness of the space was accentuated by the complete absence of any sign of life beyond the police force for either of the detectives. There were no pictures of girlfriends or families on the desks or walls. No softball or bowling trophies. Not even a pennant, poster, or snapshot that would indicate either of the men who shared the cubicle had a favorite team, actress, sports car, or fishing hole.

The weight of the absence of life in Sam and Ski's space caused Kate to slump slightly forward in her chair. Ski broke the silence just as the clouds of depression were gathering again in her head.

"You remember detective Siemens don't you?" asked Ski, looking from Kate over to Sam.

"Certainly," answered Kate.

"I asked Detective Siemens to join us because we always work cases as a team. Is that all right with you?"

"Certainly."

Using the most conciliatory tone he could muster, Sam leaned slightly toward Kate and began, "Ms. Newberry."

Kate raised her eyes and interrupted, "Please call me Kate."

"OK, Kate," Sam continued, "But only if you call me Sam and Detective Johnson Ski."

"Ski?" Kate again interrupted, this time turning toward Ski.

"Yes, ma'am, Ski. My first name's Askeia, but everyone calls me Ski."

Sam tried again, "Kate, we know you're upset," looking over toward Ski, Sam added, "Very upset, over your grandfather's death."

"Murder!" interjected Kate.

"Murder," Sam continued, "We're sorry for your loss, but there's not much that we can add.

It's not our case. Detectives Martin and Sizemore are working your grandfather's case. They're the ones who can tell you where the investigation is heading."

Kat's eye's flashed, "Sizemore and Martin don't know dick!"

Kate looked at her feet, took a deep breath, regained her composure and continued, "Sorry, but detectives Sizemore and Martin are nowhere. They've as much as said they've given up already. I don't know if they've got too much work, easier cases, or ... " Kat added, "just don't give a shit!" Kate continued, "They're not putting any effort into my grandfather's murder, and they're about to file it away in the unsolved, do not disturb, department."

Uncomfortable with the silence that followed, Sam felt obliged to speak, "I'm really sorry Kate, but sometimes we are handed crimes we just can't solve. Ski and me, Martin and Sizemore, none of us bats a thousand."

Kate turned to Ski as she responded to Sam, "I know that, but you've got to try. I've got to try. No one much liked my grandfather. Most of the family is glad he's gone so they can get to the inheritance a little sooner. But, he was my grandpa. He cared about me. And while he could be a real pain in the ass in public, he was my best friend.

"Christ, Jonathan was in his seventies. He wasn't in great health. I knew he'd die someday. I think I was ready for that. But to be blown up! Nobody deserves that. Somebody did that to grandpa. Somebody has to be held accountable."

Sam started to speak but Ski cut him off, "Kate," Ski almost whispered. "Kate, I wish we could help. But,"

Kate interrupted Ski this time, "I know, it's not your case."

Ski started to continue, but was again cut off by Kate, "But you have an identical case."

"Not identical," Sam squeezed into the conversation.

Ski continued, "We thought there were similarities. Our victim and your grandfather were both rich and the explosive devices were similar. But beyond that, we haven't been able to come up with one single thing that really ties the two cases together."

Speaking as much to himself as to Kate, Ski added, "Watson's family probably feels the same about Sam and me as you feel about Martin and Sizemore. We've been on our case for over three months now and haven't gotten anywhere." Realizing he was talking out of school, Ski felt slightly flushed and vowed to shut up.

"Tell me everything you know about your case, and I'll tell you everything I know about my grandfather. There's got to be some connection," pleaded Kate.

"We really can't do that," Sam stated. Adding, "Guidelines don't allow us to divulge information on an open investigation outside the force."

Kat snapped, "Now you sound like those pricks, Sizemore and Martin!" Kate continued, "Look, you got a dead guy. I got a murdered grandfather."

"So you can just go fuck your guidelines!" interjected Kat.

"Maybe," Kate added, trying to control her emotions, "if we take a fresh look at things together, we'll get somewhere."

"OK ... OK," Sam uttered in an almost conspiratorial whisper. Punctuating his acquiescence with a palms-down, arms-outstretched, slightly downward patting motion, Sam added, "OK, you're right, just calm down. It can't hurt to come at this from a new angle ... see if we can deduce some connections we might have missed."

"OK by me," chimed Ski.

"OK by me too," added Kate, with a slight smile.

IV

For the next two-and-a-half hours the detectives told Kate everything they knew about the Watson car bombing, and Kate told them everything about her grandfather that she thought might be helpful.

Sam started it off with one of his first thoughts at the bombing scene. Maybe it wasn't really Henry Watson who got blown to bits. After all, there were no eyewitnesses to the explosion. Sure, the night watchman had seen Watson leave the building, but he didn't actually see him get in the Mercedes. Maybe the car bombing was some kind of insurance fraud and some poor junkie bought the farm so that this Watson guy could collect on a big policy.

But when the forensic reports came back, they confirmed that the teeth taken from the crime scene were in fact Watson's. So that theory was out the window.

There hadn't been any question of the victim's identity in the Newberry case. Jonathan had been at a Trustee's meeting at the Getty Museum. It was after normal hours when the meeting broke up but, even though Jonathan had been one of the first to leave, there were still at least half-a-dozen people who watched him get into his Bentley just before the explosion.

Then Sam figured they'd run into drugs, money laundering, or organized crime as they investigated Watson's murder. But that hadn't happened either.

Aside from being a workaholic, Henry Watson was a choir boy. Actually, more an Eagle Scout. Everybody loved Henry. His wife, family, neighbors, staff, business partners, bankers, you name 'em, they loved, trusted, and relied on Henry.

Sam returned to his insurance fraud theory, this time sure that someone had knocked Henry off for an insurance windfall. Henry Watson was covered by a life policy that would help take care of Molly and the boys, as well as an insurance policy that paid a small benefit to Watson Enterprises. But, if anything, Henry Watson was underinsured. He had been worth far more alive than dead.

Every path that Sam and Ski took led nowhere. No drugs. No kinky sex. No girlfriends on the side. No boyfriends on the side. No jilted lovers. No gambling debts. No massive business obligations. No cheated partners. No union problems. No big insurance policies. Nothing. Nada. Zilch.

No one wanted Henry Watson dead. No one stood to profit from his death. In fact, Henry Watson was so loved by his family and friends and was such a key figure in his business, that when he died, everyone lost.

"Well, Jonathan wasn't so well-loved," Kate explained. "Jonathan never was a happy person, and he grew into more of a bully with age. He wielded his wealth as power. And he turned almost every encounter into a test of wills ... a test he always won."

According to Kate, lots of people disliked, even hated, Jonathan Newberry. Lots of people stood to profit financially or emotionally from his death.

But the Newberry fortune was old enough that everyone in the family was already more than comfortable. They could wait for Jonathan to go naturally. Everyone, including Kate, assumed that, given Jonathan's litany of ailments, his passing would take place in the next few years, at the latest.

"Isn't there anybody else who stood to profit from your Grandfather's death?" Ski asked.

"Not really," Kate answered. "Jonathan was fond of using little adjustments to his will for punishments and rewards. But everyone in the family knew that, even if they were in Jonathan's doghouse, they'd be well taken care of."

"Anyone outside the family?"

"No. The lawyers took care of that."

"How so?"

"Well, certain members of the family haven't always been sexually discreet, so there are some seeds that didn't fall far from the Newberry family tree. But, with all the legal advice this family has had over the years, those unpleasant situations have been weeded out before they could take root."

"So, nobody outside of the immediate family stood to financially benefit from Jonathan's death?"

"Nobody."

"And Martin and Sizemore interviewed all of the immediate family members?"

"We had a family meeting after the funeral. Everyone had already been interviewed."

"I don't remember any weak alibis in Martin and Sizemore's file."

"No, I know everyone in the family was accounted for," Kate concluded.

Kate was sure her grandfather had had business dealings during his life that probably left those on the short end fit to kill. But neither Jonathan, nor any of the Newberry family, had been active in the business that created their wealth for more than twenty years. Nobody carried a business grudge that long.

As Kate, Sam, and Ski wound down, it again became clear that there were really no significant similarities between Henry Watson's and Jonathan Newberry's murders Except for the explosives. The explosives experts had determined that both car bombs were of the same crude design. Both involved a large amount of gasoline and fertilizer placed under the cars. The explosives had not even been attached to the chassis, just shoved under the driver's side.

Both explosions were triggered by a simple detonator. So simple, in fact, that, while remote, the detonator required the assailant to have an unobstructed sight line between the triggering mechanism and the detonating device.

Unfortunately, the recipe for the explosives and the design for the detonating device were readily available on the Internet or in any number of survivalist's or paranoid-anti-government -conspiratorialist's publications. The guys down in explosives couldn't say for sure whether or not the bombs used to kill Henry Watson and Jonathan Newberry were made by the same person, or whether they just happened to have been made using similarly crude designs.

V

"I'll tell you where we are on our case, Kate, and it's exactly where Martin and Sizemore are on your Grandfather's case," Sam concluded. "These two murders may or may not be connected. But whether they are or not, they are both the type of homicides we may never be able to solve. No witnesses, no apparent motives, no obvious suspects, no money trails, none of the connections we normally use to direct our investigation and build a case."

"So that's it?" asked Kate. "If you aren't a usual suspect, you can blow someone up and get away with murder?"

"That's not what I'm saying," Sam continued. "What I'm saying is that most homicides give us a lot more to work with. Most are surprisingly easy to solve because there is a bad business deal or a jilted lover, drug connection, witness, informant, or accomplice who can't keep his mouth shut. One of these gets us looking in the right direction. But we don't have that here."

"Is it hopeless?"

"No, but it's going to be more difficult. We may develop some new leads, but at this time we're left with the possibility that these two murders could be random acts.

"We're looking at known pyromaniacs who could be headed on a path toward this kind of violence. You know, guys who have moved from playing with matches, to setting small fires, to destroying property, to putting lives at risk. We're concentrating on pyro's who have some history of other violent behavior. Killing dogs or cats, fights at school, that sort of thing.

"But, this is a hard group to investigate. We know what they've done in the past, but we don't have any way of tracking them down to interview. They're not like child molesters. Their movements aren't monitored."

Now that Sam had opened the door by divulging some information about the investigation, Ski felt free to add more. "We're also looking at the 'lunatic fringe.'" Ski punctuated this by making circles around his ear with his index finger, an action he immediately regretted.

"Either one or both of the bombings could have been carried out by some group with a political or religious agenda. But no one has claimed credit for the bombings.

"And, unfortunately," Sam concluded, "We can't rule out the possibility that some wacko heard voices telling him to blow up cars. Without an eyewitness, the lone psychopath is the toughest to track down."

Ian Proctor had certainly taught Sam that lesson. Sam hoped this case wouldn't force him to face another psycho like Ian.

"We just don't have much to work with. That doesn't mean it's hopeless, or that we won't continue to work to develop leads," Sam finished, standing to indicate their discussion of these cases was over.

"You know we could be just one phone call away from solving both these homicides," Ski added hopefully. "One tip, one suspicious wife who thinks her husband is up to something strange, one slip-up, and we could be on our way. You have to trust us Kate. We <u>will</u> keep working on our case, and we'll also make sure Martin and Sizemore don't drop the ball on your Grandfather's investigation."

VI

Kate couldn't tell whether she felt better or worse after her meeting with Ski and Sam. She knew that the news of her grandfather's death had drained away all the possibilities that just weeks before had been her future.

She had come to realize that <u>her</u> strength had been Jonathan's strength. Her fire had been Jonathan's fire. Her willingness to take risks and be her own person was grounded in the knowledge that Jonathan was always there to provide unconditional love, support, and understanding, if not publicly, at least privately.

And now he was gone. How could she possibly let go of her grandfather if his case wasn't solved?

For his part, Ski realized he liked being around Kate. He liked her determination to not let her grandfather's murder get swept aside. He was also taken by the sparkle in Kate's eyes whenever she talked about the conspiratorial relationship she and her grandfather had developed over the years.

Outwardly, the set-in-his-ways, sexist patriarch and the free-spirited, independent young woman had nothing in common. But privately, they clearly shared a deep love and uncommon respect. Ski hoped he would find that kind of love and respect sometime in his life.

As for Sam, he felt a renewed drive to work the Watson case, even though the tell-all session hadn't resulted in any new information or fresh leads. Still, Sam was ready to not only hit the streets again on the Watson case, he was willing to go to the lieutenant to see if he could get the Newberry murder reassigned. He was sure that Martin and Sizemore would be thrilled to dump the case. And he felt in his gut that, while the three of them hadn't come up with anything connecting Watson to Newberry, there had to be a connection somewhere.

Chapter 5

He never really thought it worked that way. You know, the inspiration, the action, the revelation that changes your life. The single defining moment when your focus clears. The moment that truly separates the past from the future.

Terrance Newberry had just had his moment. It took his breath away.

The instant the thought was fully formed, Terrance knew he'd have to make a choice. Already on a fast track, should he take the leap? Could he take the leap?

It took surprisingly little time, or reflection, for him to decide that yes, Terrance Newberry could, and yes, Terrance Newberry would, act.

He'd worked long and hard and made lots of money ... for everyone else. Now it was his turn.

If he didn't act, if he cowered from the risk, he'd be a wage slave for the rest of his life. Good wages, mind you, but wages nonetheless.

Just a couple of key moves and he'd be on his way. He'd have to be cautious. He'd have to cover his tracks. That'd be the easy part. Those were skills he'd already polished.

Terrance now knew how to create his own opportunities. He knew the profits could be his. He knew he could pull it off.

He'd had his epiphany. He knew it was his turn.

II

Nothing had ever come easy for Terrance. He'd been tested at every turn of his life. With grim determination, he'd persevered and had achieved nearly every goal he'd set for himself. Then he just walked away from it all.

The money, the status, and especially the adrenaline rush that came with being a star-on-the-rise. The women. Christ, the women who were drawn to the action the way prepubescent girls are drawn to androgynous rock stars. The need and excuse to relax using any physical or chemical means necessary. All that, and he just walked away.

It hadn't made sense to anyone at the firm. But then, after a couple of days everyone agreed that Terrance had always been a little strange. Couldn't afford to let deviant behavior fester ... like just walking away from the opportunities that were clearly in his career path — where the really big money was — couldn't let that kind of thing seem acceptable.

So, in short order, Terrance had been mentally marginalized. After a week or so, he was forgotten altogether.

Deals to do. Got to move on.

Besides Terrance didn't have any real friends to start with. Shallow friendships have short memories.

So, Terrance, who had come from nowhere special, returned.

Chapter 6

Ski was the first to arrive at work the day after Kate's visit to the precinct house. Eyes focused on the non-dairy creamer he was stirring into his first cup of coffee, Ski was startled to find Kate seated in his cubicle. "Kate?" came out as a pointless question.

The day before, dressed in slacks, blazer, and silk blouse, Kate sat in the same chair and at times looked quite vulnerable. Today, dressed in jeans, and UCLA sweatshirt, with her hair pulled back into a ponytail, Kate surprisingly looked all business.

"I hope I didn't startle you," Kate offered as Ski caught his breath.

"No, well yes, I guess a little," Ski fumbled as he reached to set his coffee down on the edge of his desk. "I just didn't expect to ever see you again. I mean see you ... here again ... I mean ..." Ski began to explain until his voice just trailed off.

"Look," Kate started, motioning for Ski to take his seat, at his desk, in his cubicle. "When I left here yesterday I felt like I had closure on this whole thing. I wanted answers, but there are no answers. I did what I felt like I needed to do. I felt like there was nothing left to do besides keeping grandpa alive in my heart." Ski watched Kate gently clasp both her hands together and unconsciously raise them to her chest as she spoke.

"I realized that there wasn't going to be an answer as to why grandpa had to die the way he died," Kate continued, "It was what it was, and I needed to get over it."

"I understand," Ski tried to interject.

"No you don't," Kate whispered, looking for the first time like she might cry. Regaining her composure, Kate rose, crossed the cubicle and took both of Ski's hands in hers, "No, you don't understand!"

Staring into Ski's eyes she continued, "When I left here yesterday, I really thought my grandfather's murder was behind me. I'd let it go.

"Then last night I couldn't sleep. I couldn't sit still.

"I got really mad at the world for being the kind of place where old men just get blown up. I got really mad at you and Sam for not having the answers I needed. I got really mad at myself for being mad at everyone else."

Finally breaking eye contact with Ski, Kate began in an almost apologetic tone, "Then I recognized a familiar feeling. The kind of disappointment I feel whenever I do a superficial job on something that could be done well, if I'd just taken the time and put in the effort."

Increasing her grip on Ski's hands, Kate again stared into his eyes and in a more matter-of-fact voice continued, "Ski, if this was a term project, I'd have to give myself a 'D.' I mean what kind of research had I done? Talked to you and Sam. Talked to those other two clowns. Followed the story in the newspaper. Superficial crap that's not even up to the level of copying out of an encyclopedia for a middle school term paper.

"Ski, I'm better than that. I can do a better job of following this through. I have to do a better job. I have to try harder or this thing is going to drive me nuts.

"You've got to help me Ski. I can't let it go. I can't just let it go. I've got to do a better job."

There was a slight crack in Kate's voice and, for a moment, Ski thought she might start to cry. But the fierceness and determination in her stare told him otherwise.

After a moment it was clear that it was Ski's turn to talk. "Kate, you know I'd like to help. I'll do whatever I can. But I really don't know what else to do."

Kate let go of Ski's hands and returned to her seat. It was Ski who took the next turn at standing, but he quickly realized that the difference between his standing eye level and Kate's sitting eye level was too great, so he returned to his chair.

Kate picked up the conversation, "Ski, I'm really good at research. Really good. I can help you do your research. And you can help me gain access to the places where my research might be productive."

Somewhat lost in the conversation, Ski started to fumble with his tie, "I'm not sure I follow you. We interviewed everyone who might have any connection with Watson. And while you might not be satisfied with their work, both Sam and I have reviewed Martin's and Sizemore's file on your grandfather, and we didn't see any gaping holes in their investigation."

Kate's eyes started to sparkle as she launched into her proposal, "I'm not saying you or Sam or anyone else, for that matter, missed something in your investigation. What I'm saying is that at first you looked at the Watson murder as an isolated incident and talked with everyone who had an obvious connection with Watson and who might figure in his death.

"You looked into my grandfather's death because of the similarity in the car bombs, but didn't find a common denominator. What if there's a bigger picture? What if there's more to this than just my grandpa's and Watson's deaths?"

As she warmed to the subject, Kate rose and started to pace around the cubicle. "I've studied just enough Chaos Theory to believe that patterns may exist even though they aren't always apparent. You just need big enough databases and the willingness to keep sifting through the data, testing all kinds of combinations, and sooner or later a pattern will emerge.

"You looked at two murders and found two common elements. Both victims were rich, and both car bombs were of a similar design. Maybe if you look at three murders, or thirty murders, or three hundred murders you'll find more common characteristics.

"Then, maybe you find a pattern. Then, maybe that pattern leads you to a motive. And with a motive, you find the bad guy.

Kate stopped pacing and pleaded with Ski, "Help me find the right databases. Let me find the patterns."

"But, what if there aren't any other cases that are even remotely similar to our two? Even if we find some other cases, what if there's no pattern? What if there's no common thread?" Ski asked in an almost pleading voice.

Kate looked straight into Ski's eyes again. "Then at least we'll know. At least I'll feel like I really tried. At least I'll be able to get rid of this incomplete feeling. This guilty, incomplete feeling that I haven't put in the kind of effort grandpa would have expected from me."

Just then Sam strolled into the cubicle. Ski was glad that Sam hadn't been there to interfere with the moment he had just shared with Kate, but was uncertain as to how he was going to explain all that had transpired.

With Kate sitting quietly by, only interrupting to clarify a point on occasion, Ski proceeded to describe the situation to Sam. He must have done a credible job, because when he finished, Kate just smiled and Sam said, "OK."

After a minute, Sam cleared his throat and said, "OK, I'm not sure I followed much of what you were saying, Ski. But I'm all for keeping Watson and Newberry out of the un-solved file cabinet. If that takes doing something we haven't done yet, I'm all for it. Sign me up. Just don't tell the lieutenant. He's a little sensitive about having civilians work homicide cases."

"It'll be just our little secret," Kate whispered as she extended her hand to shake Sam's. A wink sealed the deal with Ski.

Chapter 7

Foley's Fish Market! Some fish market, thought Tex. This evening could be full of surprises, or it could just be expensive. But Tex, a bull of a man who'd made a fortune in a bull market for premium bull semen, had time to kill, and he could certainly afford to amuse himself.

Far from being a fish market, Foley's was an elegant restaurant on the second floor of New York's Renaissance Hotel. Strategically situated at the north end of Times Square, Foley's didn't just offer a view ... no, with floor to ceiling glass windows on three sides of the restaurant, Foley's put you right in the middle of the action. Dining at Foley's was like dining in the middle of a postcard.

Once Tex began exporting bull semen to the Orient he found he couldn't avoid meetings in New York. He didn't really care for the city, but that's where the deals were made. Tex rationalized that, if he had to be in New York, the least he could do was have some fun.

When Tex first began doing business in New York, he found the whole Broadway scene exciting. But after he'd been to the city more times than he could remember, it began to be a bore.

Tonight, however, he had Mary Louise for company. She'd suggested Foley's. She'd probably want to see a damn show.

But they were on his nickel, so she could just forget the show. They'd be going straight to what Tex had on his mind.

Tex had been introduced to Mary Louise by a friend of a friend. Now here he was at Foley's Fish Market with Mary Louise Richter, and she really was as gorgeous as everyone had said. Nothing could go wrong tonight.

"Prix fixe?" Mary Louise responded to Tex's question. "It means fixed price. You get to choose certain portions of the meal, but basically it's a meal of complementary courses at a set price."

"You mean this is all there is to the menu?" Tex huffed. "I hate all this fru-fru crap. I just want a steak, a well-done steak, and a baked potato.

"The poached salmon in mousseline sauce is quite good here."

"Can't you get an honest to God meal in a place like this?" Tex grumbled to no one in particular.

Mary Louise smiled and changed the subject. After the appetizer and a glass of the very nice wine she had selected, Mary Louise steered the conversation, if you could call Tex's one-sided, self-centered rantings a conversation, around to Tex's plans for the rest of the evening.

Tex leaned back in his chair and broke out his most self-satisfied smile as he outlined his intentions. Mary Louise had heard enough, so she just smiled back.

This could be a humdinger of an evening after all, thought Tex.

But before he could add any more details to his plan, Mary Louise smiled again, softly slid her chair back, took a one-hundred-dollar bill from her wallet, placed the bill neatly under the edge of her appetizer plate, and said softly, "For the wine and the tip,"

Tex's huge frame slumped and he sat in stunned silence as Mary Louise rose from her chair with true elegance and style, turned on her heels and made an almost unnoticed exit. The short elevator ride down to the street level entrance of the Renaissance gave Mary Louise a chance to collect her thoughts.

She nodded to the doorman when he asked if she needed a cab. Seventh Avenue, half a block from Broadway, an available taxi was at the curb before Mary Louise could cross the sidewalk.

Harry Chapin's rueful voice and Michael Masters' haunting cello were fading to a close on the once-upon-a-time hit song 'Taxi,' as the doorman at her luxury apartment building opened the cab door. She smiled to think of the irony. That song always seemed to be playing at the most appropriate and inappropriate times.

How could one golden oldie sum up her life? *"She was going to be an actress and I was going to learn to fly ... And here she's acting happy inside her handsome walls. And me, I'm flying in my taxi. Taking tips and getting stoned. I go flying, so high, when I'm stoned."*

Mary Louise used to hate that song. But like so many things in her life, once she learned to take things as they were, Taxi became one of her favorites.

She was an actress, in a sense. She'd hated the work. She'd hated herself. At least for a time.

But once she accepted who she was. What she was. Once she took control of her life, she realized everything was OK.

Besides, she'd learned some lessons from those rich and powerful men. She had plans.

Chapter 8

It didn't take long for Sam, Ski, and Kate to work out a routine. After the first few days of their new collaboration, Kate had exhausted all of the databases she could locate on the Internet. She couldn't access confidential police records on her own, so every morning she'd e-mail Ski a list of records she wanted him to search. He'd do her bidding and then download the results to a disk, which he delivered when the three of them met for a drink every evening.

Sam quickly became bored with the regime because he wasn't a contributing player, got lost whenever Kate and Ski slipped into geek-speak, and frankly didn't see the additional effort going anywhere.

Besides, Sam finally had a lead on a creep named Jules Jewel. Jules had become the number one contender on Sam's pyro-sicko rankings. So while Ski and Kate compiled their database, Sam set off to track down Jules.

What kind of parents with the last name of Jewel would name their child Jules and not expect him to be fucked-up?

Well, Jules didn't disappoint on that score. He was a real piece of work.

Jules had amassed quite a police record. Sam could only guess what his sealed juvenile record looked like.

If there was a profile for a lone wacko capable of random car bombings, Jules had to fit. He had been implicated in more than three dozen arsons ranging from small open field fires to one industrial fire that had completely destroyed a large warehouse. The warehouse fire came close to claiming the lives of three stevedores who managed to escape, but only after using a forklift to crash through a wall of flames, suffering extensive burns in the process.

Jules also appeared to have a bad habit of befriending and then abusing mildly dysfunctional street people. And there were indications he may have participated in the sacrifices of live chickens and goats.

But nothing ever stuck. Not that Jules was a clever psychopath. It just turned out that none of the cases against Jules ever contained that one irrefutable piece of evidence that could lead to a conviction. Dumb luck kept Jules on the street.

So the file on Jules Jewel continued to grow. And Jules Jewel continued to be a free man.

Sam finally tracked Jules to a dilapidated travel trailer, set up on blocks and virtually hidden by weeds, at the back of a vacant lot in San Pedro. The trailer reeked of marijuana but, as Sam entered, he didn't see any visible signs of pot or drug paraphernalia that could give him probable cause for an arrest that would hold up in court.

"Detective Sam Siemens, LAPD," Sam announced as he shoved his way through the trailer's screen door. "Jules, you're a hard man to find."

"Not hard enough ... you found me."

"Jules, I'm investigating a couple of incidents and I need to find out where you were on the evening of Thursday, December thirty-first and also on the evening of Tuesday, April sixth."

"I was here, man. Here alone in my trailer reading my Bible, man."

"That's a pretty quick and easy answer don't you think? It's been months since those particular dates. Don't you need to look at a calendar or do a little thinking before you give me such a definitive answer?"

"No, I'm certain I was here in my trailer ... reading my Bible."

"Come on Jules. Don't pull my chain. You'll give me a reason to haul your ass down to the station and get a warrant to search this dump for the drugs you can smell a mile away."

"Listen man, I'm not jerking you around. I don't need any trouble with you guys, but I know I was here 'cause I ain't been anywhere else for the past two years."

"You expect me to believe you haven't been outside this trailer in two years?"

"That's not what I said, man. I ain't been anywhere else in the evenings for the past two years. That's what I said."

"And why am I supposed to believe that?"

"'cause it's true, man. I get up in the morning ... walk to work at the shit job I got parking cars at the Marina ... walk home ... eat dinner ... read my Bible ... go to bed. The next day, I get up and do it all over again. That's it, man, that's my life."

"So that's it? You expect me to believe that all you have done the past two years is sleep, work, and read your Bible? Didn't even go out on New Year's Eve?"

"Been longer than two years, man. Been forever. 'Cept for Friday nights. Get paid on Fridays, so I stop on the way home and buy food for the week. If I've gotten any tips during the week ... and the fuckers down here don't tip much, even at the Marina ... if I've got some spare change I might get a couple of beers for Friday night."

"And the smoke?"

"Ain't sayin' nothing about no smoke."

"You don't go dancin'? You don't party? You're not out playin' cards with your buds or scorin' chicks?"

"I wish."

"So you don't have any way of confirming you were here, in this trailer, on the nights in question?"

"I don't have any way of confirming shit."

"Then you don't have a real alibi for the nights in question?"

"Alibi? Shit, you're a cop, right? You've seen my file. I'm not a real likable guy. I ain't got no buds. Ain't scorin' no chicks. I work. I read my Bible. I sleep. Alibi, got to have a life before you can have an alibi. You tell me how to get a life, I'll be happy to run right out and get an alibi.

"So you can haul me wherever you need to haul me. And you can hassle me all you want for not having some airtight alibi for whatever night you have 'in question.' But the truth is, you pick a night, any night, and I was here in this sorry-ass trailer. And I was either eating, sleeping, or reading my Bible, 'cause that's all I ever do."

II

Kate dove into the mass of information she and Ski generated as though it was a make-or-break graduate school project. They had organized their research into two distinct searches.

The first covered unsolved, apparently random homicides. Their thought was that possibly either Jonathan or Watson could have been the victim of a serial killer who used a variety of methods to kill his targets. Maybe there was some pattern that would surface if they looked at enough seemingly isolated crimes.

Ski also felt that Jonathan's murder could have been a copycat crime since it had taken place a few months after the Watson car bombing, which had made quite a splash in the newspapers. Maybe by looking at a larger cross-section of murders they would find other matching pairs of homicides and that would reinforce Ski's copycat theory.

The second line of inquiry was other car bombings. That was, after all, the one common link they had so far. Car bombings were actually few and far between in Los Angeles, but maybe if they expanded their search until they found a large enough sample, some pattern might emerge.

Starting with city records for the past year, their effort expanded to include the county, then the state, adjacent states, and then the entire country. The search of unsolved, apparently random homicides yielded so many cases that Ski and Kate decided to limit that search to California, Oregon, Washington, and Nevada. The search of car bombings yielded far fewer results so they decided to continue to gather data on car bombings nationally.

The time frame of the data search was also expanded. First by a year. Then a second year. Then ten.

When they were through, Kate and Ski had searched computerized police records covering every random homicide that had gone unsolved in the four-state region and every car bombing that had occurred in the United States during the previous ten years. From the information they compiled, they developed a matrix of facts typically reported on each case. Then they subjected the matrix to statistical analysis, looking for any and all common characteristics.

In the end they refined their search down to two lists. The first covered 714 unsolved murders that, at least on the surface, appeared to be random acts of violence. The second list contained thirty-five car bombings that had at least three "knowns" in common: unsolved case, single driver killed, simple explosive device used.

The 714 seemingly random murders was still an overwhelming sample, so Ski and Kate set about devising additional ways of analyzing the information they had available in an effort to narrow their search.

The car bombing results were, if not more promising, at least more manageable. With thirty-five cases, Kate and Ski felt confident they could develop additional details on the bombings and narrow that search even further.

Even Sam renewed his interest in the process at this point. Sam knew that in his whole career he'd never be able to investigate 714 random murders. But, he could wrap his arms around the possibility of finding clues in thirty-five cases.

Detailed case files were ordered on all thirty-five. More information was extracted from each case and entered into a new matrix. And while Kate and Ski continued to look for a means of analyzing their huge database of random murders, they began to statistically slice and dice the new car-bombing matrix, hoping to extract additional common characteristics.

Expecting this final analysis to produce maybe a couple of cases with some common characteristics, they were surprised to discover that thirty-three of the thirty-five cases involved victims who were between forty and fifty-five years old. All thirty-three of these victims were also up-and-coming entrepreneurial business leaders.

Kate's grandfather, who was in his seventies and no longer either up-and-coming or a business leader, was one exception. The other was Vic Bacilly. Vic was a twenty-eight-year-old with apparent ties to organized crime. It was thought that Vic was a driver for Tommy, the Pie Man, Piazza. Tommy was a known contract killer and, in Vic's case file, there was speculation that the bomb that took out Vic was intended for Tommy.

The case file further noted that, within three weeks of Vic's death, three henchmen in the

Piscatti Family had taken fatal shotgun blasts to the face. These three murders, like Vic's car bombing, remained unsolved.

The initial thrill of having thirty-three cases survive their latest analysis quickly subsided, and Kate and Ski realized that their list of victims had nothing in common beyond age, executive positions, and the cause of death. Kate reanalyzed the data time and again, looking for other statistical matches, but there were none to be found. The car bombing list looked to be no more promising than the unmanageable random murder list.

"Now's the time for some real police work," Sam finally offered as Kate and Ski were about to abandon their search.

"What do you mean, real police work?" asked Ski. "What do you think we've been doing?"

Sam, Kate, and Ski were engaged in their nightly "drink and discuss" ritual at the bar in Ted's, a local hangout that was tastelessly decorated with drunken-escapades-memorabilia involving Ted Kennedy. "Don't get me wrong," Sam continued. "What you guys have been doing is impressive. But at some point, you've got to turn off the computer and do real police work."

It was Kate's turn to be mildly offended, "Such as?"

Sensing his opportunity to finally contribute, Sam picked up steam, "Such as re-interviewing witnesses, developing new leads, reanalyzing physical evidence, using your brain, intuition, and common sense ... not a computer ... to find the common threads you're looking for."

So it was decided. Ski and Kate would concentrate on narrowing their list of random murders, and Sam would begin the re-investigation of the thirty-three car bombings.

III

Sam's effort was often frustrating and unproductive. Many of the cases were old, and all the interviews had to be done on the phone, rather than in person.

Sam hated phone interviews because he was convinced he could learn more from a person's eyes and body language than anything he could discover from what was said. But there was no way they were going to be able to personally interview witnesses all across the country, even if they took Kate up on her offer to draw on her trust fund and foot the bill.

As it was, the Lieutenant was already making noises about how much time they were spending on the Watson and Newberry cases. Sam and Ski were working them as much as they could in their off hours, but they still had to fudge their weekly activity reports to keep the lieutenant from realizing how much time and energy the cases were consuming.

As he proceeded with his re-investigation, Sam's mantra was, "Follow the money! Sex, drugs, gambling debts ... those are the things that get you blown up ... but the money trail leads to the perp."

Sam's 'real police work' generated new information on almost every case. He learned a lot about the victims and their individual business enterprises and even began to feel like he knew them.

As he 'followed the money,' he ran across a few minor gambling debts, a few allegations of drug or alcohol problems, a few marriages that seemed to be on the rocks. But most of the new information Sam uncovered appeared to be specific to one victim and totally unrelated to the others.

When all was said and done, he had uncovered only two new, tantalizing leads.

Sam identified an investment banker, Karl Heulenberg, who had helped at least four of the West Coast victims raise capital as they were growing their businesses. When looking into the finances of these four companies, Karl's name came up frequently, and usually in a negative context.

The second lead was more mysterious. Looking into appointment schedules for the time period preceding each bombing, Sam had discovered that the initials 'ML' and 'MLR' appeared repeatedly in the day-timers of three of the East Coast victims. What was intriguing about these initials was that there wasn't a single assistant, secretary, co-worker, or wife who could identify 'ML' or 'MLR.'

'ML' and 'MLR' could have been two separate individuals, but one of the victims had initially used 'MLR' as a notation and then switched to 'ML.' Taking this as his Rosetta Stone, Sam believed 'ML' and 'MLR' were the same person. Also, all the appointments scheduled with either 'ML' or 'MLR' were for an evening or weekend, further indicating that the notations referred to a single individual.

Maybe he was on to something. Maybe not. But tie two or three of these cases together, and he might uncover the key to solving Watson's murder.

Sam knew one thing about 'ML/MLR.' Whatever connection there was to the car bombings, if any, only pertained to the East Coast victims. Not their jurisdiction. But, Karl Heulenberg had been associated with Henry Watson. Their open investigation. Their jurisdiction.

Sam knew there wasn't going to be any budget for investigating cases outside their jurisdiction. But, if he could tie Karl Heulenberg more closely to Henry Watson, the lieutenant would cut him some slack.

Sam decided he'd start by tracking down Karl Heulenberg. He'd work on 'ML/MLR' later.

It took Sam only half-a-dozen phone calls to confirm the connection between Karl Heulenberg, Henry Watson, and three other West Coast victims. Initially, Sam liked where the trail was leading.

Unfortunately, it had been over three years since anyone he talked to had had any contact with Karl. Karl's business had gone bust, and Karl had disappeared into the ether.

Chapter 9

Arnie Nugent and Fletcher Pound — at least that's what Fletcher called himself now — had actually gone to school together. Monte Vista High, Spring Valley, east San Diego County. But Arnie and Fletch, or Bruce Boswick as he was known back then, didn't travel in intersecting circles.

Not so long ago, Spring Valley was pretty nearly the end of the earth. But it became just another trolley stop, non-descript bedroom community of San Diego, after the city evolved from a back-water navel-port-of-call into a Mediterranean-like Mecca.

Arnie was the older of the two. He was a good looking, tall, slender kid who took life seriously.

Active in Youth for Christ, the glee club, and the science club, Arnie was a good student whose studies and after school commitments left no time for a social life.

Since Arnie's family barely survived on his father's modest income as an auto mechanic, Arnie wasn't guaranteed a college education. He needed good SAT scores, a solid GPA, and a record of community involvement if he was going to become the first in his extended family to reach beyond a high school education.

Fletch traveled a different road. Short and square, Fletch didn't take much of anything seriously. Except being tough. Fletch concentrated on, and excelled at, being tough.

Pound for pound the most feared individual at Monte Vista, Fletch never let a good fight pass him by. Even when the sheer size of an adversary, or the numbers against him, put Fletch at a disadvantage, he was still up for a rumble.

Right next to kicking the livin' shit out of some poor bastard, Fletch seemed to enjoy getting the crap kicked out of himself. Maybe a good ass-whippin' reminded him of home. Home after his mother ran away when he was six, leaving him alone to contend with an abusive, alcoholic stepfather. Home, before he ran away to live on his own at age 14.

Fletch only stayed in school because it provided him a cadre of other misfits who were more than happy to kowtow to any tough guy. Within his crowd, Fletch was as much a leader as any class president. Besides, the small subset of the student population he led had a far greater impact on the school and its surrounding community than the mainstream student government.

Fletch discovered drugs long before they spread into the cowboy culture of east San Diego. And he discovered guns before the rural phenomena had spread to the big city.

After some wild experimentation, Fletch relegated drugs to a commodity for commerce, not personal consumption. Fletch had his own highs, and for God's sake he didn't want to be mellowed out.

But guns were a different story. With guns you were talking Fletch's language. The betting line started when Fletch was a junior in high school and continued until he finally went underground. Would Fletch gun someone down before he got shot?

Fletch played a 'winner take all' game. He wasn't the right person to bet against.

II

Neither Arnie nor Fletch made it to their five or ten-year high school reunions. That was a shame because they would have spiced up what were otherwise dull evenings.

Arnie had graduated from Monte Vista in the top 5% of his class, and even though there was some chance for scholarships to more prestigious colleges, he enrolled at San Diego State. Still living at home, Arnie hadn't even made it through his general education requirements when he first heard the whispers. He'd picked up a part-time job, moved out on his own, and taken his first upper division psychology classes by the time the whispers became voices. After the voices began screaming at him day and night, Arnie lost his job, dropped out of school, and began living under a bridge.

Teen schizophrenia is an equal opportunity horror. It strikes across all the races, religions, incomes, and educational levels that typically segregate society. Some families are able to throw more money at it. But all are devastated by the sight of a child, sibling, friend, or lover transformed into a non-functioning vessel that ebbs and flows to the tides of a separate reality.

Arnie couldn't or wouldn't tell his family or his doctor what the voices were saying. But one thing was for sure. They told Arnie not to stay on his medication.

By the time the Nugents finally lost all contact with him, Arnie had become hyper-agitated, paranoid, and sometimes violent. The Nugents grieved as if Arnie had died. It would have been easier if he had. Because they knew that Arnie was still out there somewhere. And there was no telling where his tortured soul was going to lead him.

III

Fletch wouldn't have gone to his high school re-unions even if he'd been invited. But he wasn't invited because he never graduated.

Working as a freelance drug and gun dealer, it wasn't long before Fletch fell in with the Mexican Mafia. As a kid in a border town, Fletch grew up thinking of Mexicans as Chicolet-hawking street urchins, bribable federales, and two-dollar whores.

Needless to say, those early encounters didn't foster a lot of respect. But as he began developing his supply lines, Fletch found that the soldiers in the Mexican Mafia were just as tough as he was. The leaders were as ruthless as he wanted to be. And the organization provided a structure to his life that he needed.

Fletch rose quickly through the 'gringo' side of the organization. His abilities to move freely across the border and to blend into the scenery anywhere in the states were assets that were fully exploited.

It wasn't long before Fletch moved into man-agement. And while his new authority and the accompanying perks were great, Fletch missed the action. His body churned out more adrenaline when he was out on the street providing muscle than it did from negotiating a drug deal, pool side, at one of the local resorts. And while Fletch had long ago sworn off drugs, he had certainly become an adrenaline junkie.

As in any organization, the Peter Principle had moved Fletch beyond his level of maximum competence, yet he was smart enough to recognize the situation. So Fletch eased himself out of his management responsibilities by developing an expertise that was equally valuable to the organization.

It wasn't long before Fletch cemented his reputation on the West Coast. His move was good for the organization and good for Fletch. It had taken some time, but Fletcher Pound finally felt like he'd found his place.

Chapter 10

Jules moved out of the shadows and stood quietly watching the flames. It was a magnificent sight. But the show he hoped for was still to come.

When Jules first started setting fires, he'd run away as soon as they were lit, listen for the sirens from a distant hiding spot, and not return to inspect his handiwork for days. As time went by, Jules found he could only satisfy himself by being closer and closer to the action. Now he needed to be in direct sight of the inferno before he could slip back into the darkness and finish his personal business.

The fire he'd set was beautiful in its own right, but the response had been too efficient and the fire crew was already at the scene. This wasn't going to turn out the way he had planned.

The market that was now engulfed in flames wasn't Jules' real target. He had his sights set on the fireworks booth that had been set up just outside. Jules wanted to see that baby blow.

No matter how much Jules yearned for big explosions, in 1994 California law allowed only the most pathetic fireworks to be sold to the public for Fourth of July celebrations. Even so, Jules had figured that even those puny pyrotechnics would put on a show worth watching if they all went up at once.

But the damned fire department already had the situation in hand. Now Jules needed more stimulation if he was going to make himself explode.

He'd been sleeping in an empty shed at the back of a vacant lot that sported a weathered 'coming soon' sign for a discount store that clearly wasn't. Just beyond the chain link fence that marked the rear of the property was the back side of a large warehouse where paints and industrial solvents were stored.

He'd had his eye on the warehouse but held back, because it wasn't that easy to find free housing in the Bay Area and he didn't want to lose his. But it was time to move on. The police knew Jules and he was now getting hauled in for questioning on a regular basis.

Yes, it was time to move on. Maybe someplace warmer.

But first there was the warehouse. Then some personal business. Then maybe a shot at another fireworks booth. Then maybe some more personal business. And then on his way out of town, who knows what. Jules could hardly wait to see what the night would bring.

II

After twenty minutes of fitful tossing, Sam decided he'd wasted enough time trying to get to sleep. He knew the drill. No sandman leading him down the path to quiet and peaceful sleep. It would take two hours of walking and half a bottle of scotch, or, a full bottle of scotch without the walk, before he'd be able to keep his eyes closed. He dressed and headed out for the walk. Tonight might take both exhaustion and excess.

Sam, on a whim, had jumped in his car and headed to San Francisco to celebrate losing another partner _and_ the end of yet another failed marriage. The pattern was now pretty well established. Sam could deal with a partner, make that, his partners could tolerate Sam — for three to four years. His marriages lasted about half that long.

Brock had requested the transfer. He said he wanted to pursue an interest in white collar crime, but everyone knew he just wanted to get away from Sam. Betty said she had 'issues' she needed to resolve, but everyone knew the issue was Sam.

When his relationship failures overlapped, Sam would disappear for a few days to reassess his life. Excessive drinking helped him rationalize that it wasn't his fault. So, on that 4th of July evening in 1994, Sam headed out for a stroll, hoping it would help moderate his desire for self-medication.

III

While Jules Jewel was watching his first fire of the evening, Mary Louise Richter was exiting the United flight she had just taken from New York. Even in July, San Francisco flights are often delayed due to fog, so both Mary Louise and Jonathan were surprised that her flight was on time.

Jonathan had invited Mary Louise to join him on a week's cruise from San Francisco to Alaska. They were planning to rendezvous at the Airport, spend the evening at the Mark Hopkins, and board the ship the following day. That evening, the liner would begin a leisurely departure, allowing its passengers an unmatched view the city and its Fourth of July fireworks.

Mary Louise was first introduced to Jonathan during a charity fund raiser at the Kennedy Center a few years back. They 'dated' whenever Jonathan had occasion to be in New York and had 'vacationed' the three previous summers.

Mary Louise 'vacationed' with a few other older gentlemen and Jonathan, frankly, wasn't her favorite. But anything beat Manhattan in the summer, and Jonathan could be kind of cute, sometimes even tender, once they were alone.

IV

Karl Heulenberg was so wrapped up in his own thoughts that he didn't realize Independence Day was just around the corner. Independence ... a concept that was slipping further and further from Karl's grasp.

Where did all this independent thinking come from? Karl was the financial expert. He knew when it was time for his clients to sell equity or take on a new debt load. He knew what it meant to his future for his clients to unquestioningly follow his advice.

So what was the story with all this independent thinking? "Now's not the right time for us, Karl." "It'll be better for our company if we wait until after the Christmas selling season before we look at a public offering, Karl." "We're just three or four months away from filing two new patents. We'd be selling ourselves short if we brought in a venture capitalist now, Karl."

Well ... what about Karl? He needed the deals now. He needed the cash flow now. He couldn't just sit around and enjoy the sights and sounds of San Francisco while these upstarts ruined his business by waiting for their pissant little companies to turn some magical corner.

Karl had his own agenda. He had his own timetable. He'd make something happen. He always did.

V

"You look quite elegant in that dinner jacket Mr. Newberry," the tailor offered, stepping back to admire his handiwork.

"Well, I liked the cut when I bought the first one last year. It does fit nicely doesn't it? I hated to have to throw that first jacket out, but after what that old blue-hair did to it, I had no choice but to toss it."

"Excuse me Sir, you've rounded your shoulders a bit. If you could just straighten your back for a moment, I can make sure there's no bunching below the collar."

"What a tedious evening. We were having dinner at Chantells, a fund-raiser for the Symphony, and Tilly Pruet, sweet old girl's got to be 92 years old, keeps leaning across me to eavesdrop on the conversation that's going on between Peter and his wife, who are seated on my other side. Peter's the head of the Symphony Board and Tilly must think she's going to miss out on some juicy gossip if she doesn't catch his every word.

Each time Tilly leans over she grabs my sleeve to steady herself.

"We were served a very nice duck in cranberry sauce that evening and the old girl must have been eating with her fingers, because when I got home I saw the greasy fingerprints up and down my sleeve. Sent the jacket to the dry cleaners three times, but they couldn't salvage it."

"What a shame. To ruin such a fine article."

"I was just happy to see that you still carried the style. Most fashions come and go faster than my tastes change. I prefer to stick with what I already know I like, but I often find I can't replace an item in my wardrobe."

"That can be a real problem. But as you know, here at Barnaby's, we don't change very quickly either."

"That's exactly why I shop here."

Terrance was on one of his twice-yearly shopping excursions to the Bay Area. He couldn't stand the shops in L.A. They all tried to be so trendy that it made it impossible to find even the simplest evening wear. Try to be elegant, and classic, and just a little bit different from the rest of the crowd ... well you could forget that in L.A.

No, San Francisco was the only place to shop. Outside of maybe Boston or London. And in San Francisco, on occasion, Terrance could get a little work done when he wasn't replenishing his wardrobe.

VI

Life is full of coincidences, and so Fletcher Pound and Arnie Nugent, who had gone to the same bordertown high school together, but weren't acquainted, both ended up spending time in the Bay area that 4th of July evening in 1994, without ever meeting. But then, it's not like San Diego or San Francisco are small towns where everyone's paths will eventually cross.

Once Fletch had found his niche in the organization, it was clear that he'd found his true calling ... like he'd been born and bred for this new line of work.

In his youth, Fletch liked the company of his hangers-on. He enjoyed the notoriety, even the celebrity, that his status as the numero uno misfit created. And he reveled in the fury of his encounters.

Now he liked the solitude. He mastered blending into the crowd. He reveled in the meticulous planning, the precision, the sheer poetry that marked his work.

Fletch had interned throughout Mexico. He'd marveled at the cultural differences between the U.S. and Mexico, but in the end saw the beauty of the Latin approach.

North Americans are always in too big of a hurry. Always focused only on immediate results.

South of the border, the pace is more relaxed. And the message is more important than expediency.

Fletch learned that mañana doesn't always imply procrastination. Mañana can mean waiting for the right time. Waiting for the right place. Waiting for the opportunity to send the intended message.

Fletch was biding his time. He knew the set-up. He'd done his homework. The play was on and it didn't bother him in the slightest that he'd have to wait. He'd learned to savor the anticipation.

So for now, Fletcher Pound was content to stroll through Golden Gate Park. Enjoy the summer afternoon. He might even head down to the wharf to watch the fireworks.

VII

Arnie Nugent enjoyed Golden Gate Park to the extent he could enjoy anything. Arnie would lie for hours on the grass, listening to the saxophonist who mastered the acoustics of the tunnel under the stone footbridge, at the center of the park. When Sax Man was playing, the voices were always quiet.

Within the currents of foot traffic that coursed through the Park, Arnie often found himself in a backwater or eddy. He'd know where he was, but didn't know how he got there. Or he'd know where he'd been, but couldn't figure out where he was.

No matter how lost or agitated he was, however, Arnie always found Sax Man's melodies comforting. He couldn't say the same thing about the rollerbladers who'd commandeer an intersection, set up their boom boxes, and rollerdance to reggae and hip-hop for hours. Too much noise. Too much color. Too much movement.

In the summer, when the days were long, the rollerbladers made it hard for Arnie to get any sleep. The girls in their tight shorts and tank tops. The boys with their fearless moves and tightly wound bodies.

On the days when the rollerbladers chose to stake out a spot near the park bench where Arnie was sleeping, he'd have to get up and move. There was already too much going on inside of Arnie's head. He just couldn't tolerate the additional stimulation.

While Arnie spent his days in the park, he spent most of his evenings keeping himself fed. Arnie would panhandle and dumpster dive like the rest of the transients. But the voices that had led him on the circuitous trek that landed him in San Francisco also led him to the meetings where he could always get a cup of coffee, with tons of cream and sugar, and a handful of cookies.

Arnie wandered into and out of any number of gatherings during the course of a week. Religious services, PTA meetings, various 12-step programs, civic forums, you name it and Arnie was likely to drop by for refreshments. Arnie couldn't keep track of much in his life, but he always made it to the Aryan Cell meetings and the White Wings of Vengeance gatherings because he liked them the best.

At those meetings Arnie even tried to follow the discussions. These people knew that the Jews and the blacks were out to subjugate white men and deflower white women. These people knew that the government spied on those who had stumbled onto the conspiracy to hand over our great and beautiful country to the Chinese. These people knew.

These people heard the voices. They knew the voices spoke God's truth.

And besides, the Aryans and the White Wings didn't just serve snacks. They always had sandwiches and those little bags of potato chips. Arnie loved the little bags of potato chips.

Plus, there was always a bottle or two being passed around. They'd let Arnie drink as much as he wanted, not like those skanks back at the park who always bitched about Arnie hogging the bottle.

Arnie felt comfortable with the Aryans and the White Wings and would spend hours at any meeting he could find. They seemed to like him as well. The leaders of the groups would even take time to personally talk to Arnie to make sure he understood the importance of their work.

Arnie always tried to concentrate on what they told him. He tried to do what they asked. But it was hard to remember from one minute to the next, so he was never quite sure if he understood what they wanted from him or if he ever did what they requested.

But whenever Arnie stumbled onto an Aryan or White Wings meeting, he was greeted with smiles, handed a sandwich and two bags of chips, and offered a long draw on the bottle that was being circulated. Arnie always slept well the day after one of these encounters.

Arnie must have found a meeting, because even though the park was teeming with Fourth of July picnickers, Arnie was out like a light. Sprawled out on a bench, Arnie finally woke up to find himself half-way between Sax Man's tunnel and a gaggle of rollerdance kings that was starting to assemble.

VIII

During that Fourth of July weekend back in 1994, while Sam slept off three hours of walking and a bottle of Johnny Walker Black, San Francisco witnessed an unusual amount of unauthorized fireworks. All of the city's emergency crews put in plenty of overtime.

Over the course of the weekend, there were four fires of suspicious origin and three definite arsons. The worst: a warehouse where three workers were nearly trapped in the massive blaze.

And then there were the murders. Even for a city that averages nearly a homicide a day, the weekend body count was abnormally high.

An anonymous tip Saturday evening led the police to a nice home near the Coit Tower, where they discovered five dead Colombians. The three men, one woman, and one young boy had apparently been stripped, gagged, and lined up in the living room of the house where they were executed. They had then been shot, one-by-one, in the back of the head. The three males had then been rolled over and sliced open, from chin to pelvis. Each of the adult males also had a syringe stuck in his jugular, and it appeared they had been injected with what later would be confirmed as black tar heroin.

A black male, who later died, was shot outside a North Beach strip joint. A fight had broken out over either drugs or a prostitute, or possibly both, and the victim lost.

There was a car accident on the 101 resulting in three fatalities. The one positive side of bumper-to-bumper congestion is that most traffic accidents are mere fender benders. But not that evening. The traffic into the city to watch the fireworks had thinned, turning the freeway into a racetrack, with fatal results.

The body of a wealthy businessman was discovered in the study of his Sausalito estate. He had been bound, gagged, and duct-taped to his maroon leather, high-backed, executive chair. His wallet, full of cash and credit cards, his check-book, and a current issue of *Fortune* magazine had been placed in his lap. One wrist was surgically slit, and he had been allowed to slowly bleed to death. It must have taken hours.

A small boy, who had been rollerblading with friends, disappeared from Golden Gate Park. His violated body was later found stuffed into a trash can outside the Presidio.

The carnage finally ended with a car bombing, down at the Marina, in the Transbay Yachts park-ing lot. Lev Wassermann, Transbay's charismatic CEO, was killed.

Chapter 11

Karl Heulenberg never realized how loosely the fabric of his life was woven until it began to unravel. When trouble hit, Karl tried to rally those around him for his protection. Rally they did all right, but not <u>for</u> Karl ... more like a pack of wolves rallying around a wounded caribou. He didn't stand a chance.

Karl had misjudged his ability to rush his clients into their next round of financing, the point in their company's life cycle when he planned to make his killing.

Months went by. And while he sat on a potential gold mine, Karl's business plowed through its cash reserves at an alarming rate.

Karl couldn't unload the equity positions he'd stockpiled. He hadn't had time to create the public market he needed for that exit strategy.

He couldn't service the debt he'd already accumulated. So additional borrowing was out of the question.

He tried to generate business from former clients, clients like Blodget, Watson, and Star. But he'd always stepped on one client to get to the next, and no one was anxious to feel Karl's shoe leather a second time.

Karl Heulenberg's fall was swift and complete. He lost everything, personally and professionally. He was back where he started. Without fortune, friends, family, or even gainful employment.

The word pariah must have been invented for those who fall from grace in the financial world. Who wants investment advice from a chump who just went bankrupt? No one, as far as Karl could tell.

He hit bottom when he learned that his accountant, in an effort to maximize Karl's draws, had excluded Karl from payroll tax calculations so he couldn't even draw unemployment. For the first time in his life, Karl felt that, with his $2,000 of gold bridgework, he was worth more dead than alive.

Desperate, Karl hocked the few personal possessions his wife left behind when she finally walked out on him. A couple of grand, not much of a stake.

II

To his credit, Karl Heulenberg eventually picked himself up and moved on to a new life.

With nothing left to lose, Karl realized there was a whole new world of green valleys for him to plunder. He had no ties. He had no roots. He had every reason to move on, and not a single reason to stay.

But where to go and what to do? He knew he could sell, so using the last of his cash, Karl boarded a plane and headed to Kauai. If you can go anywhere, why not paradise? And even though he'd never been there, he was sure Kauai would be paradise. As he settled in, Karl Heulenberg vowed to build a new life ... and to balance the ledgers with those who had turned their backs on him.

Karl had thought that no job could be too difficult after raising cash for chronically under-capitalized start-up companies. That had to be the hardest sell in the world. But then he'd never tried selling timeshare condos to couples from the Midwest.

Who would have guessed that those kindly couples from Kansas would play their free round of golf, drink their free Mai-Tai, and then yawn their way through Karl's canned spiel? Who would have guessed that Princeville's most prominent attribute was an annual rainfall that rivaled that of Washington's Olympic Peninsula?

Who would have guessed that Karl would struggle to make a living in paradise? Hating every fucking rainy day. Hating trying to make a living in fucking paradise. Slipping further and further back into depression every fucking rainy day he spent trying to sell those lousy, fucking timeshares, in that lousy fucking resort, on that rainy fucking island, in the middle of lousy, fucking, nowhere.

Chapter 12

Terrance Newberry had grown up as Terrance McKulvey in what would normally be considered a very middle class environment. But given the expectations of the McKulvey Family, you would have thought they lived in abject poverty.

Mary McKulvey, Terrance's mother, was a women so obsessed with the past, or at least the past she chose to believe in, that the perceived injustices of that past colored every aspect of her life. Mary saw the black side of every situation. She spiced her bitterness with the uncanny ability to convert psychosomatic symptoms into very real ailments. It seemed that her primary reason for being was to drain the life out of everyone and everything she encountered.

Alan McKulvey probably would have been an OK guy if it weren't for the glacial wear of Mary's nagging and the McKulvey family's weakness for substance abuse. Terrance was only eleven when Alan finally finished the job of drinking himself into an early grave.

Terrance was a terribly bright child. He would have excelled at school under any circumstances, but long hours of studying provided an acceptable excuse to remove himself from his mother's ranting, so above all else, Terrance studied.

II

Mary was obsessed with the heritage and fortune she considered her just due. Convinced by family lore that her roots came from a severed limb of the Newberry family tree, Mary brooded endlessly, conjuring up elaborate scenarios that involved everything from the discovery of stolen wills to angelic intervention. Each scenario ended with a change in heart by the Newberrys that resulted in Mary's debut into "society" and receipt of her rightful inheritance.

Mary went so far as to use every last dime of the proceeds from Alan's life insurance policy to sue the Newberry family. She actually managed to prove that some Newberry blood, or at least Newberry sperm, had migrated over to the bastard lineage that eventually spawned Mary Blackwell, later to become Mary McKulvey.

Unfortunately for Mary, the Newberrys had always employed excellent counsel, and the wills, trusts, and estate plans they had drawn were iron clad. While Mary proved her link to the past wasn't a total fabrication, her lifelong efforts didn't result in any cash.

Having squandered what little capital Alan had left them, Mary found some victory — hollow, but still a victory — in legally changing their last names to Newberry. Terrance, she vowed, would carry on the fight to reclaim the wealth and status that were rightfully hers.

Terrance was determined not to grow bitter like his mother or be weak like his father. He managed for a while, but the roots of the Newberry obsession went deep, as was the genetic disposition toward mood altering substances.

A large part of his upbringing had been built on the premise that, after high school, Terrance would matriculate at Stanford. All the Newberry men attended Stanford. And, even if Terrance wasn't admitted with open arms as a legacy, he'd surely be accepted based on his academic accomplishments ... or, at least, that was his mother's reasoning.

So when Stanford rejected him, Terrance's disappointment was overwhelming. He'd been so conditioned to think a Stanford degree was his destiny that he hadn't even bothered to apply to any other college. The Stanford rejection not only rocked the foundation of Terrance's self-image, it set him back a full quarter.

The full-ride he eventually received from USC did little to quell Terrance's anger. Rather than enjoy any part of his college experience, he plowed through a grueling class load to graduate early. He'd get the jump on those Stanford bastards.

The dogged determination and research skills Terrance Newberry displayed set him apart from his contemporaries at USC as much as did his lack of interest in the fortunes of the football team or the cheerleaders. To say that Terrance was a loner implied that he was even noticed.

That was until the recruiters hit campus. Then Terrance was, for the first time in his life, in demand. Now it was his turn.

Chapter 13

July 4th, 1999. Kate, Sam and Ski met up at Ted's for beers and burgers because, to be honest, they didn't have anywhere else to go. It had been six months since the Watson car bombing and the trio still hadn't been able to link that case to Kate's grandfather's murder.

After swallowing a large bite of her cheeseburger, Kate asked rhetorically "Is this the worst 4th of July ever or what?"

Ski immediately responded, "Not even close. My worst 4th was when I was nine years old and was called the 'N' word to my face for the first time. What made it worse was that the person spewing racial slurs at me was an otherwise kindly looking older white lady whose face was contorted with rage. And my sin? I was sitting on the curb in front of her house watching the parade of bunting-decorated golf carts in the annual Glenbrook community parade with a couple of 'white boy' friends. While the few of us who were blacks were tolerated in the wider Tahoe community, the very rich white folks who came up to the Glenbrook enclave from San Francisco or Sacramento for weekends or retirement didn't bother to hide their bigotry."

"I'm so sorry" said Kate. "I wish I could say that I'm sure things are much better these days. But I imagine that where rich whites gather, things haven't changed much."

Kate went on, "My worst 4th was when I was a sophomore in high school. Johnny Jenkins asked me out on a date. He was a good-looking senior: left-handed quarterback, captain of the football team. Sitting in the front seat of Johnny's dad's car, apparently Johnny's throwing hand thought it had license to wander wherever it pleased. On his third attempt to feel me up, I grabbed three fingers and bent them back until he screamed. I think he was about to call me either the 'b' word or the 'c' word when I drove my left elbow into his face. I don't think I broke any fingers but, guessing by the blood streaming down his face and the angle of his nose, I probably broke that. I also guessed that our date had ended and that I was going to be walking home. Fortunately, the fireworks helped light up the night sky."

All Sam said was, "My worst 4th was 1994." He wouldn't elaborate and, when pressed, just stated flatly that he was starting to feel the beer ... Sam never acknowledged feeling the beer ... excused himself, got up, and headed for home.

Kate and Ski had another drink and talked about maybe heading over to Santa Monica to watch the fireworks off the pier. When they couldn't generate much enthusiasm for that idea, they instead decided to each head home to get a good night's sleep; then they'd be ready to renew their search for the connection between Watson's and Jonathan's murders the next day.

Chapter 14

Mary Louise Richter was the only child of Dr. Louis Richter, renowned Chapel Hill cardiologist, and Maria Richter, Louis' socialite wife. Louis had brought brains to the relationship. Maria brought money. Mary Louise had enjoyed both.

She couldn't have asked for a more enjoyable childhood. Private schools, private piano lessons, private riding lessons, summers at the Richter family's very private villa in Provence.

If she had asked for anything more while growing up, it might have been for a few close friendships. But there had never been the time for close friends.

Until Mary Louise came along, Southmont High had never graduated a salutatorian who was also the head cheerleader. Blond, blue-eyed, and perfectly proportioned, Mary Louise was that rare combination of drop-dead good looks, genuine enthusiasm, and exceptional intelligence that only comes along once in a great while. Sure, she was a little standoffish. But she had been asked to carry a lot of water during her adolescence, and she was just so gorgeous that, when it came to socializing, people cut her a lot of slack.

Mary Louise could have attended any college in the country, but when you grow up in the shadow of Duke, why aspire to be anything other than a Blue Devil? Besides, Duke offered everything she wanted. The chance to lead cheers for a consistently NCAA-bound, always nationally-ranked basketball team, as well as to double major in Art History and French, her two passions.

Having vacationed in France her entire life, Mary Louise thought she was fluent in both the French language and French culture. Her junior year spent at the Sorbonne taught her that, when it comes to France, Paris is as different from Provence as Provence is from Chapel Hill.

Mary Louise polished her French and refined her appreciation of art while in Paris. But it was what she learned outside the classroom that really anchored her career.

After graduating from Duke, Mary Louise moved to New York. She had planned to work as an interpreter at the UN. And, Mary Louise Richter, daughter of Louis and Marie Richter, head cheerleader, Duke graduate, conversation stopper, was used to having her life unfold just as she planned.

But New York kills just as many dreams as it fulfills. At first, Mary Louise had difficulty accepting that all the good jobs, the important jobs she wanted at the UN, would go to French nationals. Wasn't her French just as good as theirs? Didn't she have an advantage in understanding how things were done in the US?

Over time she came to appreciate that the French could care less about how things are done in the US. The French way was all that counted. French norms, like French conversation, would always be her second language.

Mary Louise quickly learned that her Chapel Hill upbringing provided less preparation for dealing with life in New York than the cultural life-lessons her Parisian counterparts brought to the table. But if Mary Louise Richter was anything, she was a quick study ... not to mention ambitious, independent, and pretty damn resilient.

Chapter 15

Jackee inhaled another gulp of cooking wine – the wine she drank while cooking, as opposed to the wine she added to her fancier recipes. She was on her second glass, or was it her third, when the phone rang. She instantly froze. God, how she had learned to hate the phone.

She'd just let it ring. Maybe whoever it was would give up.

But the calls kept coming. By the time she finally decided to answer, Jackee had moved on from cooking wine, to dinner wine, to her one glass of after-dinner wine. Jackee allowed herself only one glass of after-dinner wine. To Jackee, that exhibition of self restraint meant she didn't really have a drinking problem.

Answering the phone, Jackee immediately asked for the caller's name and phone number. She then promised to return the call and promptly hung up. She wasn't just being rude. She was just being cautious.

She didn't mind returning long distance calls, even at her expense. She just liked to make sure she knew the caller's real identity.

Return the call and you know if someone is really who they say they are. Otherwise it could be just another bill collector.

They had all these tricks, those bastard bill collectors, pretending to be someone or something they weren't, just to harass you some more. Even after all these years they'd still surface every once in a while. It was only smart to be cautious.

So Jackee took down his name and number and the next morning returned the call. After they had talked for a while it was clear that the officer was just trying to do his job. But why couldn't this ever stop? It had been years.

She was still trying to get over the whole mess. But the phone calls made it so damned hard ... forcing her to reach back into the past ... a past she was trying desperately to forget.

II

As soon as Jackee hung up the phone with Detective Siemens, she called Helen. When she finished that call, she rang up Teresa. She repeated the story of her conversation with Detective Siemens to Teresa, word for word, just as she had for Helen. Teresa had just as much right to know.

Besides, Jackee wanted to assure Teresa she hadn't given Detective Siemens either Teresa's or Helen's phone numbers. If he called them, it was because he somehow dug up their numbers himself.

She hadn't compromised their trust. She wouldn't ever do that.

Teresa and Helen were her friends now. Her only friends in fact. Detective Siemens might find them. But it wouldn't be her doing. She'd played dumb.

Besides, what could they tell Detective Siemens that she hadn't already told him. Karl Heulenberg was gone. Just gone. No one knew where. No one really cared. If fact, the more gone the better.

Hadn't Teresa and Helen spent an incredible amount of time and gone to extremes just to ensure Karl couldn't find them? Why would they want to know where he was?

Jackee had explained all that to Detective Siemens. She explained that anything and everything to do with Karl Heulenberg was painful. Maybe now Siemens would leave them alone.

Chapter 16

Mary Louise Richter had always been a beauty. But there were lots of other stunning women in the city. In the urban montage of beautiful people, it was Mary Louise's Southern accent with a French twist that first caught people's attention. Then it was her interest in art and politics that carried any evening.

Mary Louise had moved to New York. She'd gotten a job at the UN. Not the one she wanted, but a job at the UN nonetheless.

Even though she held a very minor position at UNESCO, it wasn't long before she was being introduced to an assortment of visiting politicians and dignitaries. It wasn't long before she was being invited to attend the opera, the latest

Broadway premier, or the newest 'A' list bistro. It wasn't long before she was invited up to someone's Ritz Hotel room for a nightcap. It wasn't long before there was a thousand dollars in cash accompanying the room service coffee and croissant the next morning.

The sex, Mary Louise discovered, was the easy part. The older men didn't want or require much. And when it came to the younger men, well, interesting men got her adrenaline going and besides, there wasn't anything wrong with a good fuck to work off the calories from an intimate up-town dinner.

The hard part for Mary Louise was finding the spark that would lead to an evening of lively conversation. It sometimes took a while for her 'dates' to realize they needed to entertain as well as be entertained.

The evening with Tex at Foley's wasn't the first time Mary Louise Richter paid for her own dinner and left a 'date' sitting speechless as she escorted herself out of a restaurant, into a taxi, and then home, when it became clear the evening was just going to be about sex. Mary Louise offered and expected mental as well as physical stimulation.

If a client just wanted sex there were plenty of other subcontractors for that service. When it came to the total package, there weren't many in Mary Louise Richter's league.

At first Mary Louise was schizophrenic about her new life. She enjoyed the parties, the evenings at the theater, the cruises, the shopping sprees. But she thought she hated the work. She thought she hated herself because of the work.

Actually, she didn't mind the work. She was an actress. Well, an actress like in the Harry Chapin song. She was good at what she did. She just wished people didn't think of her as a prostitute.

Mind you, Mary Louise Richter wasn't the stereotypical prostitute. She was the 'creme de la creme.' She worked at the highest echelons of her profession. She was a consummate professional and provided an unmatched quality of service. She was as high class as her clientele. A true companion for an evening or a three-week cruise. Not just a piece of meat beneath the sheet.

II

Mary Louise held onto her job at UNESCO for a couple of years. It provided both a constant stream of clients and a good cover when it came to her parents.

Louis and Marie could be proud of a daughter who was working for children's causes around the world. Even though she was one of the best, Mary Louise wasn't so sure they'd be quite as proud of a daughter who was a prostitute.

After a while, the dichotomy between watching bureaucrats proselytize endlessly over "doing what's good for the children, given limited resources," and then watching them curry her favor with gifts and nights on the town, just came to be too much. So, Mary Louise retired from UNESCO and became a consultant.

Her parents seemed happy to have a daughter who was an international consultant. Interestingly, never once did they ask what she consulted on.

After freeing up her days, Mary Louise also broadened her client base. Soon she added businessmen to the list of diplomats and politicians who had been her core clientele.

Mary Louise was an independent contractor. No manager needed. No madam. No pimp. No co-workers. Word of mouth her only advertising.

She 'dated' whomever she pleased. She never had to negotiate 'price.' In fact, 'price' was surprisingly never discussed. After a 'date' there would always be compensation. It was usually far more than Mary Louise considered book value.

After striking out on her own, the scope of Mary Louise's business spread to include a handful of West Coast regulars who would enjoy her company when visiting New York. Victor, the Russian nightclub impresario; Paulo, the Chilean vintner; Michael, the sheep rancher from New Zealand; and Jonathan. Each of them invited Mary Louise to accompany them on cruises or extended holidays abroad.

Mary Louise always enjoyed these extended 'dates.' Parading through Europe or the Caribbean as a 'trophy wife' for a week or two, these were her only real vacations.

III

John Baxter was a member of Mary Louise's new clientele. An overly enthusiastic talk-a-holic, John was the principal deal maker of Back Side Sports, the marketing agency he had founded in Stamford, Connecticut's sports marketing corridor.

Back Side Sports had developed a very profitable niche negotiating endorsement contracts for Division I coaches. They were also head and shoulders above their competition when it came to extracting large sums of cash and equipment from sports apparel companies for Division I schools, in exchange for placing logos on team uniforms.

John's agency was well positioned. After the initial public offering, it was just a question of whether Back Side Sports would be acquiring smaller agencies or whether they'd be gobbled up by one of the handful of huge international firms.

John could have cared less about his future. He was living large and intent on having a good time.

John Baxter was less cultured but often more interesting than most of Mary Louise's other clientele. Getting John to talk was never a problem. Getting him to stop could be.

Mary Louise hadn't been south of Newark since leaving UNESCO, so it was with some trepidation that she agreed to travel with John to attend the Kentucky v.s. Duke basketball game. She knew she couldn't go back to Chapel Hill, but she reasoned that no one would recognize her in Lexington. She couldn't have been more mistaken.

Of course, John got great seats. He already represented the University of Kentucky, and he hoped to add Duke to his client list. So there was John and Mary Louise, the lovely couple, seated second row, center court.

Of course, they got invited to the after-game reception. John and Mary Louise, the lovely couple, mixing with the other Wildcat and Blue Devil alums.

Of course, she was recognized. They were, after all, John, the sports agent, and Mary Louise, the ex-cheerleader.

Of course, they had to be an item.

Of course, John had to have too much to drink.

Of course, he had to let slip some graphic details as to the lovely couple's true relationship.

Of course, that would become a topic of conversation back in Chapel Hill.

Of course, some genuinely concerned soul would have to inform Louis and Marie.

Of course, Marie would have a breakdown.

Of course, Mary Louise would be devastated.

Of course, John Baxter would barely remember the entire episode.

IV

Marie Louise Richter and John Baxter never 'dated' after that. Mary Louise didn't 'date' anyone for a while. But she had developed a very comfortable lifestyle, there were bills to pay, and a consultant needs to work. So, Mary Louise Richter went back to work. Only now there was no joy, no amusement, no entertainment, no excitement.

Mary Louise Richter was no longer an actress. She was what she was, a prostitute.

Not long after she'd returned to work, not long after she'd stopped receiving the hysterical calls from her mother, not long after she was informed that she was no longer considered Louis and Marie Richter's daughter ... not long after all of that, Mary Louise read in the *Times* that John Baxter had been murdered. Blown up in his car.

Served the fucker right.

Chapter 17

Ski and Kate had run out of ways to analyze the massive database they had compiled on the seventeen hundred and fourteen apparently random homicides. But before giving up they decided to enlist the help of Dr. Randolf English.

Ski had begun visiting a variety of chat rooms on the Internet, looking for anything that might lead him to pyromaniacs, sadomasochists, and fringe organizations. He also sought out help on database analysis.

It was during one of his visits to an ultra-nerd chat room that Ski first ran into Professor English. With a little research, Ski soon confirmed what he had guessed from his first on-line encounter. The man was brilliant and was considered, at least on-line, to be the ultimate resource for massaging meaning out of apparently meaningless data.

Ski arranged a direct contact with Dr. English and explained his dilemma. The Professor was intrigued with the challenge and arranged for a secure connection so that Ski could transfer the database to the professor's computer, where Dr. English could manipulate the information looking for patterns Ski and Kate had been unable to find.

Dr. English told Ski that, given his schedule, it would be at least a week before he could hope to finish his analysis. In reality, Dr. English confessed, there was really no way to tell how long it might take him to make some sense out of the data.

Sam was still busy tracking down Karl Heulenberg when Ski turned over the random homicide data to Dr. English. Taking advantage of the pause in Ski's data analysis, Sam asked for some help. Ski was more than happy to take on a new challenge and agreed to try and find out who or what 'ML and 'MLR' referred to and what, if any, connection 'ML' or 'MLR' might have to Sam's car bombing investigation.

Most of the mysterious notations in the Daytimers of the three East Coast victims appeared to involve appointments that had taken place in New York. So Ski began an on-line search of New York phone listings, compiling a list of every entry in the 'R's' that began with an 'M' or included an 'M' and an 'L.'

He sorted his list to break out businesses from individuals and to prioritize any entry of a business with an 'L' in the business name or an individual with a middle initial of 'L.'

After staring at the overwhelming list for a while, Ski decided to ask Kate for help. She was happy to pitch in and even invited Ski over to her place. "I've got an extra receiver we can hook up to the line I use for my computer, and then we'll each have a phone. It'll be fun."

As a bonus, Kate didn't mind footing the long distance charges. That was a big plus as they tried to keep the lieutenant in the dark about the expanded scope of their investigation. Nothing got the lieutenant's attention faster than a bulge in the department's phone expense.

This was the first time Ski had been to Kate's home and he assumed that, given her family fortune, she would be living in an exclusive, spacious, expensively decorated property. When he arrived, he was surprised to find Kate living in a tidy and comfortable – but ordinary – place. It was certainly several steps up from his humble quarters, but nothing more impressive than the homes of a few of his acquaintances who enjoyed the spoils of two incomes.

After a quick tour of her digs, they set up a phone in a nook that Kate had turned into a study area. Kate laid claim to this workspace because it's where she felt most comfortable. Ski was relegated to the kitchen.

As they launched their search, Ski took the business listings. Kate took the individuals.

"Good afternoon," Ski would start. "Could I please speak to the manager? ... Sir, I'm trying to track down a former client of yours, John Baxter. I wonder if you could help me with his address?"

Ski and Kate had decided that the only way they could find the real 'ML/MLR' was to throw out Baxter's name, the first of the East Coast victims, and hope for a reaction. Ski, who was unaccustomed to dealing with New Yorkers, was unprepared for the reactions he received. He had no idea New Yorkers could be that busy or that rude. Ski got nowhere fast.

Kate had better luck. There, near the top of her list of 'M's and 'L's and 'R's,' was Mary Louise Richter.

"This is Mary Louise," the answering machine started. "If it's between 8:00 and 6:00, you can reach me at the American Art Investors Gallery. The number there is 359-1212. If you're calling between 6:00 and 9:00, I'm probably home and just not answering the phone. If you're calling after 9:00 I'm definitely in bed and not answering the phone. So just leave a message or please call back tomorrow."

Kate rang up the American Art Investors Gallery. "Mary Louise?" the voice on the phone responded after Kate indicated that Mary Louise's answering machine had directed her to call this number. "Mary Louise isn't here," the voice yawned.

"Can you tell me when she'll be in, so I can call back?" Kate inquired.

"Well you can try back next week ... but she hardly ever comes into this gallery anymore," the voice drifted.

"Can you tell me how I might get a hold of Mary Louise before next week?" Kate asked in her most solicitous voice.

"You could try her over at Musée de Lumière. That's where she hangs out most of the time these days," the voice huffed, hanging up the phone before Kate could ask any further questions.

Kate called information and got the number for the Musée de Lumière. She dialed the number and was greeted by a thick French, "Bonjoir. Musée de Lumière, en quoi pourrais-je vous servir?"

"Uh ... "mumbled Kate.

"En quoi pourrais-je vous servir?"

From somewhere in the recesses of her memory of high school French, Kate dredged up, "Parlez-vous anglais? Do you speak English?"

"Certainly, can I help you?" came the response, with just a hint of a Southern accent.

"I'm looking for Mary Richter. Is she available?"

"This is Mary Louise, and you are?"

"Kate Newberry."

"Well Kate, what can I do for you?"

"I'm trying to reach John Baxter. A friend of mine gave me your name and said you might know how to contact John."

Mary Louise hesitated for a moment. "The last time I saw John was six, maybe seven, years ago. I'm sorry, I haven't got the slightest idea how to reach him these days." No need to be the bearer of bad news. Besides, that was a true statement. Mary Louise didn't know how John could be reached in the hereafter.

"I'm sorry I couldn't be of some help," Mary Louise offered.

"Oh, that's all right," Kate sighed. "I'm sure I'll be able to track him down somehow."

"Good luck," Mary Louise concluded sarcastically, and with an "Au revoir," hung up.

II

Kate was so excited that, as soon as she hung up the phone, she leaped to her feet, ran across her living room into the kitchen where Ski was using her other phone, grabbed him from behind, and gave him a big hug.

"Same to you, asshole!" Ski muttered as he hung up the phone and then slowly turned in Kate's arms until the two were facing each other. "I didn't mean you ... that you're the asshole ... the guy on the phone ... I meant he was an asshole ..." stammered Ski.

"Shouldn't be calling your partner in 'real police work' an asshole," Kate teased.

"I didn't mean you ..." his voice trailing off as he began to blush.

Peering up into Ski's eyes, Kate wanted to continue the moment. But Ski had tensed, so she gave him one quick squeeze, released her grip, and stepped back. He was going to take some work.

After an awkward moment, Kate in a sing-song offered, "I got an 'MLR' who knew John Baxter." With that, Kate began to dance around her kitchen continuing her song, "I got an 'MLR' who knew John Baxter."

"Take it easy," Ski stated, feigning concern, but in reality wishing that Kate's embrace hadn't startled him. "Let's back up and try that hug once again," Ski was thinking to himself, but instead said to Kate, "Take it easy and tell me what happened."

Kate was so excited that she could hardly stand still as she recounted her brief conversation with Mary Louise Richter. "Mary Louise, 'ML.' Mary Louise Richter, 'MLR.' Even Musée de Lumière, another 'ML.' Coincidence? I think not!

"She definitely knew John Baxter," Kate exclaimed as she resumed her dance around her kitchen table. "She pretended like she'd just lost touch with him or something, but I think she knows more than she was letting on."

"And just why do you think that, Detective Newberry?" queried Ski.

Now it was Kate's turn to blush. "Cause," was the only response she could muster.

Chapter 18

Helen was Karl's first wife. She bore him a daughter. He bore her a grudge.

Karl and Helen's marriage lasted just long enough for him to batter her into a state of fear and self-loathing that she harbored, still. Helen and her daughter, Sara, escaped from Karl in the middle of the night and were housed by a series of battered women's shelters as they slowly moved east.

Finally settling in Maine, Helen and Sara began to rebuild a life. But it was a Spartan existence compared to the life they had known in San Francisco.

Gone were the fancy parties. Gone were the nice clothes. Gone were the gifts Karl would lavish on his wife and daughter.

Also gone were the screaming fits that followed every party. The rampages that shredded the nice clothes. The beatings that preceded the lavish gifts, which were somehow supposed to make everything OK.

No, Helen wasn't interested in where Karl was these days, much less what he was up to. Let the cops figure that out.

II

Teresa married Karl after a whirlwind romance. They had only known each other for six weeks when they tied the knot. Teresa regretted not waiting longer.

Teresa was a very pretty girl, of average intelligence, who just happened to come from very simple surroundings. Growing up in Sparks, Nevada, Teresa had been average at everything. Everything except for boys. Teresa and boys got along just fine.

When it was time to stake out new territory beyond the Sparks, Nevada homestead, Teresa headed for San Francisco. Her experience with boys had given her a plan. That plan now called for a man.

Teresa's plan was simple enough. Move to the big city. Marry a rich man. No fuss, no muss.

Karl first spotted Teresa at the neighborhood park, half-a-block from his office. Teresa had found a filing job at a nearby bank. A job that paid about half her rent. She figured that her job, along with her life savings, would allow her to husband-hunt for close to eight months, as long as she controlled expenses, like brown bagging her lunch.

Karl used a noon hour sprint around the block to blow off steam. He'd burst from his office, snarling, and storm out of the building.

Karl usually hit the streets because some dumb fuck hadn't followed up a sales lead the way Karl thought he should. He was always sure that botched lead would have made him some money. And Karl wasn't pleased when those around him weren't maximizing his returns.

Fatefully, Teresa smiled at Karl during one of his death marches. Karl knew good breeding stock when he saw it. And six weeks later, as they say, all that, and everything in between, was history.

The new Mrs. Heulenberg made the leap from Sparks, Nevada to San Francisco. She'd executed her plan. What could possibly be wrong?

Teresa might have wished for a happy, or contented, or secure life. Instead, her focus had been solely to marry a rich man. As she was to learn, you can't confuse a step toward a goal with the goal itself. She shot too low.

At first it was all a grand adventure for Teresa ... for a while. She'd grown up with a pa who had his mood swings. She knew that roller coaster. She could live with that.

But soon, the giddy excitement of living in a luxurious home, traveling in exclusive circles, shopping in fancy stores, dining in fine restaurants began to wear thin. What was left was Karl Heulenberg.

Teresa had been married for nearly a year before she learned Karl had been previously married and divorced. It was several more months before she found out Karl had a daughter. What kind of man wouldn't tell his wife he already had a daughter?

Especially since, right from the start, Karl began pressuring Teresa to have a child. He was obsessed with having a son and described to Teresa, in intricate detail, his plan for her pregnancy, ultrasound exams, in vivo testing, and if necessary, abortion — before starting the process all over again — to ensure that he would have a perfect son.

At first, nature blocked Karl's grand scheme, as Teresa was too nervous to ovulate on a regular basis. After trying for a year, Karl had his doctor prescribe fertility and mood-altering drugs for Teresa ... to fix that little problem and speed things up.

But by that time, Teresa had seen enough of the real Karl to know she didn't want to bear him a child. He threw her out the night he found the birth control pills.

The next time Teresa saw Karl, he gave her two choices. She could sign the divorce papers he had had drawn up and take a thousand dollar cash settlement. Or, she could just go fuck herself.

Teresa signed the papers, took the grand, and headed back to Sparks. She still had a thing with the boys in Sparks, Nevada. Only now the balance had shifted.

She was wounded. That was painfully clear. There weren't going to be any true relationships in Teresa's future.

III

Jackee thought she knew what she was getting into with Karl. A corporate attorney, Jackee had seen Karl in action when they'd worked together on a couple of public offerings.

She knew he was a bastard. She thought she was tough enough to deal with that.

Karl had something Jackee wanted. A six figure income and prospects for more.

Combine Karl's earning power with hers. Combine Karl's potential with hers. And all of a sudden you were talking about some serious horsepower.

Jackee had plans. She had financial objectives. At the time, a merger with Karl Heulenberg seemed like a good business decision.

Jackee hadn't factored in the prospect that Karl, in his effort to reach his own financial objectives, had been structuring the payouts from his deals for a long-term bonanza. Unfortunately, it was a long-term he'd never see.

Jackee hadn't assigned a high enough risk factor to the possibility that Karl's business would go bust. Jackee hadn't done sufficient due diligence to realize that Karl's business would take Karl ... and her ... down with it. It was a fall from which she still hadn't financially recovered.

IV

Jackee hadn't told Detective Siemens that Karl's three former wives had eventually sought each other out. Nor had she told the Detective that they had formed a 'survivors of Karl Heulenberg' club. Karl's three former wives tried to be good friends to each other, because Karl had damaged their ability to form close friendships with anyone else.

Jackee had told Detective Siemens that she had kicked Karl out when his business failed. And that Karl had blocked her attempts to divorce him and separate her assets from his. Jackee told Sam she had lost everything because of Karl Heulenberg.

Jackee also told Detective Siemens that she was technically still married to Karl. She wasn't about to let that prick off the hook when there was no downside for him.

She told the Detective that she planned to wait until Karl made a comeback. Pricks like him always make a comeback. Jackee told Sam that when Karl had something worth taking, she'd be there to claim her half.

Jackee told Detective Siemens that Karl had called one night, back before the quality of the creditor calls had sunk to such a crude level that Jackee all but stopped answering the telephone at night. She told the Detective that Karl was drunk, and broke, and slobbered on and on about how he'd make it all up to her some day. How he'd make it all up to Helen and Teresa some day too ... he was such a liar. Jackee told Sam that was more than three years ago, and it was the last time she had spoken to Karl.

Jackee told Detective Siemens that she wished she could be more helpful, but that she had no idea where Karl was these days. She told the Detective that Helen and Teresa wouldn't know where Karl was either.

Jackee told Sam that the only place, other than San Francisco, that Karl had ever talked about was Kauai. Karl had it fixed in his mind that Kauai was some kind of paradise and he'd planned to vacation, maybe even retire, there some day. If she had to suggest a place to start looking for Karl Heulenberg, it would be Kauai.

Jackee knew she hadn't been much help. But it was the best she could do. She had been sitting in the sun sipping a wine cooler, out on the small balcony, off the tiny living room of her cramped apartment, when she returned Detective Siemen's call. She was back, sitting in the sun, sipping another wine cooler when she called Helen. She had fixed herself a third wine cooler just before she rang up Teresa.

But, now the sun was setting and it was getting cool out on the balcony. Time to move inside. Time for a glass of cooking wine as she prepared herself another solitary meal.

She hadn't seen or heard from Karl Heulenberg in more than three years, but he could still ruin a day. Why did that Detective have to call?

Maybe she should file divorce papers after all. Maybe she should at least change back to her maiden name. Maybe she should have another glass of wine.

Chapter 19

Kate had developed the lead, but now it was Ski's turn to see where it took them. The next call to Mary Louise should come from a real detective.

"Bonjoir. Musée de Lumière, en quoi pourrais-je vous servir?"

Kate had warned Ski that whoever answered the phone would probably answer in French.

"Mary Louise Richter, please," Ski asked in the most official tone he could manage.

"This is Mary Louise. And you are?"

"Detective Johnson."

"Shit! So Detective Johnson, what can I do for you?" Mary Louise hissed.

"I just want to ask you a few questions."

"Oh, Christ!" Mary Louise exclaimed, "I thought we had gotten all that behind us years ago!"

"Excuse me ma'am?"

"I believe we reached an understanding."

"I'm sorry ma'am, but you've lost me."

"Look young man. Every couple of years some new 'detective' gets handed my file and I have to start this mess all over again. I've been down this road with you vice guys and the yahoos they send in from the IRS enough times.

"I've been out of 'the business' for years. No one's ever found a single law I broke or taxes I didn't pay. And like I told the last kid who came sniffing around, I AM tired of having the past dredged up and I WILL file a harassment suit if you DON'T leave me alone." As she exhaled, Mary Louise added, "Is that CLEAR enough for you?"

"Excuse me ma'am. I'm not from vice." Ski started slowly. "I'm only interested in trying to locate some individuals."

Mary Louise, who had begun to settle down, answered, "If you're looking for artists, collectors, or investors, I might be able to help. If you're poking around in that other life, probably not."

Ski indicated that he just wanted to read Mary Louise a list of names and have her indicate if she recognized anyone on the list. Mary Louise agreed to cooperate. She didn't need to get hauled in for questioning again, and the threat of a harassment suit was hollow. She couldn't afford the negative press now that she'd started her new life.

As Ski was reading through the list of the thirty-three bombing victims, Mary Louise mentioned it was funny that Ski was the second person that day to ask about John Baxter. She went on to acknowledge that she had in fact known John Baxter, as well as Paul Hunt, and Farley Yount.

In Ski's mind, Mary Louise had so far passed the honesty test. The three individuals she admitted knowing were the three East Coast victims who had had the mysterious appointments with 'MR' or 'MLR.'

"Do you know how we can reach any of these three individuals?" Ski asked.

"No," Mary Louise responded. "Those are all names from my past life."

"Past life?"

"You really don't know who you're talking to, do you?" Mary Louise chuckled.

"Ma'am?" Ski said not knowing how to respond.

"Son, some people used to think I was a prostitute. I dated a lot of rich and influential men. Sometimes they'd give me gifts," Mary Louise's voice trailed off. But before Ski could speak, she continued, "I never solicited a date. I never set a price for an evening. I declared all my gifts as income. I paid taxes on everything I received.

"Like I said, I've been investigated up one side and down the other, but I've never been prosecuted. That's what I mean by my past life. But I've moved on from that life. Now do you understand?"

"Yes ma'am. I think I understand," Ski stammered. "Would you mind telling me what you do for a living now?"

"I'm an art dealer now," Mary Louise exclaimed with pride in her voice. "I pulled together some things from my old life, begged and borrowed. Now I own two galleries, the Musée de Lumière, and the American Art Investors Gallery."

Mary Louise glanced about, taking in the bold pen and ink drawings, delicate pencil sketches, and subtle watercolors that adorned the walls, tabletops and easels spread throughout the gallery. The natural light that streamed in through the massive storefront and clerestory windows breathed life into the gallery and the treasures it held. "The Musée de Lumière is my love. I import works from young French artists I consider promising. So far no one else in New York seems to agree that there's value in these pieces. But they'll come around.

"And, I could really care less if any of these works ever sell. I love my collection and would be perfectly content to keep it all here in my gallery just for my own selfish enjoyment.

"That's where the American Art Investors Gallery comes in. Rich collectors with no personal taste just love things 'American' and anything they think has 'investment' value. So I carry works by all the hot young American pop artists at that gallery. It's all such crap that I can't stand to even go in there anymore.

"But that crap sells well. If art values continue to rise, everyone's happy. If they fall ... well, I've been screwed by enough rich men in the past that it wouldn't hurt my feelings to see the tables turned. In the meantime, the American Art Investors Gallery pays the bills, and I'm free to spend my days in my museum of light."

Ski was speechless.

"Are we through here, young man?" Mary Louise asked as she was about to hang up the phone.

"Ma'am, did you know that John Baxter was dead?" Ski asked before Mary Louise could end the conversation.

"Yes. I know John died," Mary Louise answered.

"Why didn't you say so?"

"Well, you didn't really ask."

"Did you know he'd been murdered?" Ski asked with an edge to his voice.

Mary Louise stated flatly, "Yeah, I read about it in the *Times*."

"Do you know anything about the murder?"

"Nothing more than what I read in the paper."

"Did you know that Paul Hunt was dead?"

"Christ no!" exclaimed Mary Louise, "I only dated Paul a few times, and when he quit calling,

I thought he'd either stopped traveling to New York, or he'd found someone else he preferred."

"Farley Yount is also dead. Know anything about that?"

Mary Louise dropped the receiver and slumped in her chair. She could hear Ski's voice, but she couldn't respond. She couldn't think. She couldn't move.

After awhile the phone went dead. "If you'd like to make a call," the irritating voice from the receiver instructed, "please hang up and try again."

Mary Louise reached over, picked up the receiver, and set it back on the phone, which immediately began to ring.

It was Ski, "Are you all right?"

"Yes, I think so," Mary Louise whispered. "Farley was more of a friend than a date. I've known Farley for years. It hurt us both when I got out of the business. He still wanted to be friends. Still wanted to date."

After she had paused for a moment, Mary Louise continued, "But I needed a complete break with my old life. I just couldn't go on seeing Farley."

"So you were out of ... the business ... when Farley Yount died?" Ski stumbled as he searched for the right words.

"Farley was very much alive the last time I saw him," Mary Louise sighed. "I had no idea he had died."

Ski knew he had to ask, "Mary Louise, did you know Baxter, Hunt, and Yount were <u>all</u> murdered?"

"Murdered?" She nearly dropped the phone a second time.

"You're going to have to excuse me now; I need to go lie down," and with that Mary Louise Richter gently hung up the phone.

Ski paced around Kate's kitchen for quite some time before he was able to respond to her questions. "She's our 'MLR' that's for sure, but I don't think she knows anything about the murders." Ski thought Mary Louise Richter had been surprisingly honest about her past and was honestly shocked to learn that Hunt and Yount had been killed.

Kate thought Ski was too gullible and that Mary Louise Richter could have led him to any conclusion she wanted. Maybe she was hiding something. Maybe she was a great liar. Maybe she had tricked Ski into thinking she didn't know anything about Hunt's or Yount's murders. Maybe. Maybe. Maybe.

The one thing Ski and Kate could agree on was that they didn't know what to do next and needed to discuss all this with Sam.

Chapter 20

Hatred, for most White Wings of Vengeance disciples, was a beacon that illuminated everything that caught their glare as they panned the social landscape. Every type of individual, organization, institution created a shadow of suspicion. No one ... nothing ... was to be trusted.

Hatred, for Slip, was a laser. The infrared beam generated by a sniper's scope. His targets were clear. The rest was a distraction. Noise. He joined to find a tool, not to be converted.

Even though Slip was still just a kid, he became a leader by default. He did not choose to lead. He did not covet his position. He did not demand the power one could claim by being a leader ... a leader of the White Wings of Vengeance.

But Slip had a presence. He had a purpose. He had a passion. And within the context of the Wings of Vengeance organization, nothing Slip or anyone else could do would deny him a position of prominence.

Without conscious intent, Slip sold his flock what they wanted to buy. He fed their fears. He bolstered their confidence. He gave them a sense of belonging. A sense of being understood.

Mostly, Slip searched his followers for the chosen. The tools. The implements of his obsession.

There had been others before, but Arnie ... Arnie was a real find.

II

Like many identical twins, Chipper and Solomon Hanover had a unique bond. An ever-present connection. They complemented ... they completed ... each other.

Chipper and Solomon. Chipper, because his mother wanted one of the twins to be light-hearted and see all the beauty and possibilities in the world she dreamed of. Solomon, because his father wanted one of the twins to be grounded and to bring a balance of wisdom and caution to the world.

From the moment they were carried home from the hospital, it was clear that their sum was greater than the parts. They brought a full spectrum of light into any room they entered. And when the two were alone, they shared a completely separate world.

The Hanovers lived a modest existence. But there was never a shortage of love, of comfort, of security. The boys grew strong and balanced.

Among family and friends, Solomon was nicknamed Sol, Chipper shortened to Chip. But in their private world, they were both Slip, the front and back of the same coin. One could not exist without the other.

III

Slip squatted on the side of the road. There was action all around him. He could see the officers running. See their mouths moving. See their arms waving. But all was silent.

Slip surveyed the quiet chaos. His ears rang. His legs ached.

Suddenly there was an atomic blast of noise. The blaze. The officers yelling. The emergency sirens blaring. Slip passed out.

When he regained consciousness, Slip was in the hospital. His pelvis and both of his legs were broken.

For the rest of his life, Slip would walk with a slight limp. He had pain in his hips that would never leave. He would grow to covet the pain. To wish there was more. But Slip didn't realize all that now. He was only eight. And he was alone in the hospital.

As Slip began to recover, he began to catch glimpses of the accident. A flash here. An image there.

He was standing in the back seat of the family van to reach for another comic book. Later, a fireman said "He's it," as he was being loaded into the back of the ambulance.

But the crash ... the crash came first ... he felt the crash ... heard the crash ... just as he stood up. Then the fire ... he could see the blaze.

As he was recovering, they told him that he must have slid out of his seat belt an instant before the accident. His family always wore their seat belts. Standing up probably saved his life.

He saw the flames again and again. Sometimes he could see the wheels of the family van spinning in the air. Spinning in the flames. Why was the van upside down? Why was it burning? Why was he outside watching?

Slip had been thrown from the van upon impact. He was saved. How could they do that to him?

There were people running all about. Firemen, policemen, TV reporters, the guy in the black suit and chauffeur hat. But it was all in slow motion. Silent, slow motion.

Slip carried two images with him for the rest of his life. The family van ... upside down ... in flames, with his mother, father, and twin brother still inside. And the jet-black limousine that had caused the accident. The limousine with the businessman sitting in the back ... reading a news-paper ... as his family burned.

Slip lived with the physical and mental pain of the crash. He had enough to share. Pain to share. Pain all around. Wherever his laser focused.

Chapter 21

When Sam, Ski, and Kate met that evening at Ted's, they added new meaning to the phrase, 'low energy.' In the past, one of them had always been able to find some hopeful sign in the work they had just completed, or been able to suggest a new tack to follow. Tonight they were sapped.

Sam had been unable to either clear Jules Jewel or place him in the vicinity of either of the car bombings. Heulenberg's trail was stone cold. Professor English was having a rough go at extracting much in the way of patterns from the data Ski and Kate had provided on the 714 homicides. And Ski was pretty sure that Mary Louise Richter wasn't a murderer.

"I really thought we'd be on to something concrete by now," Sam offered flatly, trying to start a conversation. "But we're no closer to solving either Watson's homicide or your Grandfather's than when we started."

Kate still shuddered every time Jonathan's murder was mentioned.

"The most concrete thing we have to go on is thirty-three car bombings. But they may, or may not, be related. On the one hand they look like too much coincidence. On the other hand, not enough.

"To be honest with you, I'm not sure where to go from here. Believe me, that Jules creep has the capacity for these types of crimes, but I'm not sure he's capable of getting more than half-a-dozen blocks from his trailer, much less across town, to pull off a car bombing. He lacks the means, or as far as I can tell, the motivation."

Ski and Kate both searched for something to contribute to the conversation. But finding nothing worth saying, they just sat silently, staring down at their drinks.

Hating the silence, Sam continued, "Following the money ... usually takes you where you need to go ... maybe we're on to something with that prick investment banker. But he's pulled a disappearing act."

"I still think Mary Louise has something to do with all this," Kate interjected.

"All we've found so far is a bunch of worka-holics," Ski observed to himself. "Bunch of guys who busted their butts for a payoff they never got to see."

Looking over at Kate and Ski seated next to him at the bar, Sam added in an almost apologetic tone, "There just isn't a money trail. I thought we'd find someone who profited from some of these deaths. But as far as I can tell, everyone came out a loser. These guys were underinsured, if anything. They were key men in their organizations, and everyone we talked to was sure their companies would fall on hard times without their leadership. No one profited. Everyone lost."

"Man, I'd love to have gone short on them," came a voice behind Sam.

Turning towards the voice, Sam asked, "Come again?"

Without looking up from his drink, the slightly overweight man in the slightly rumpled suit mumbled, "Sorry to interrupt."

Now completely turned, Sam asked again, "Wait a minute here, what'd you say?"

The voice responded without turning to face Sam, "Hey, no offense, I didn't mean anything. I said I was sorry I interrupted."

"No, I'm interested in what you said!" Sam stated in a voice he hoped conveyed that he wasn't pissed off this guy had been eavesdropping on their conversation.

The suit looked up from his drink, turned to Sam and said, "Listen, I didn't mean to say anything, it just came out. I'm sittin' here minding my business, just trying to unwind, and you guys start talking about people getting blown up. How could I not listen in?"

"Like I said pal," Sam reiterated with the calmness in his voice devolving into a more agitated tone, "I don't give a shit about why you said anything, I'm interested in what you said!"

"I just said that I'd love to have gone short on one of those guys," the suit offered reluctantly as he turned away from Sam. "Just gone short, that's all I said, no offense meant," the suit concluded.

Sam waved to catch the bartender's attention. "Todd, my man," Sam declared in a voice that was louder and sweeter than necessary, "Another round here, and another for our friend."

When the round of drinks was served, Sam leaned toward the suit and asked him to join them. Sam then suggested they all move to a booth where they could talk in private.

The suit turned out to be Donny Rausch, a stockbroker who worked at one of the local boutique brokerage houses. After being introduced to Sam, Kate, and Ski, Donny explained what he had said. "Short-selling is a type of stock transaction. Basically you sell a stock you don't own with the obligation to replace it some time in the future."

"Wait a minute," Sam chimed in, "you lost me here. You sell a stock you don't own?"

"Yeah, that's the way it works," answered Donny.

Still confused, Sam shook his head and volunteered, "I don't get it. You sell a stock you don't own."

"Yeah, that's sort of how it works," Donny offered warming up to his new friends. "But selling a stock you don't already own is just the first part. The second part is that you have to replace that stock in the future."

"Man, you've lost me too," Ski stated. "What's the point?"

Given the opening he had hoped for, Donny leaned toward the center of the table separating him from Kate and Ski. Sam, seated next to Donny, also leaned in.

Lowering his voice to a conspiratorial level, Donny continued, "The point is, with a short sale you try to pick a stock you think is headed down. Most everyone thinks that you have to pick stocks that are headed up to make money in the stock market. Not so. You can make just as much money on a stock that goes down as one that goes up."

Sam dropped his head to the table, "Now you've really lost me."

"Let me give you an example," continued Donny. "In a normal transaction, let's say you buy one hundred shares of General Motors stock for $50 per share. Your investment is $5,000, $50 times 100. Now the stock goes up to $60 per share and you sell. You gross $6,000 on the sale, $60 per share times your one hundred shares. Your profit is $1,000, your $6,000 gross less your $5,000 cost. That's a normal stock sale. Follow me so far?"

After receiving acknowledging nods, Donny continued his dissertation on the workings of the stock market. "So that's a normal stock market transaction. You buy a stock. Then you sell the stock. If the price has gone up, you make a profit."

Taking a deep breath, Donny plunged on. "With a short sale, everything's backwards. The first thing you do is sell the stock.

"So let's say General Motors stock is at $60 and you think that's too high. So you sell one hundred shares of GM stock short at $60. You'd get $6,000 for selling the stock."

"Stock you don't really own," offered Kate, starting to see how all this works.

"Yeah, you get $6,000 for selling stock you don't own," added Donny. Now it was back to Sam, "Wait a minute, you'll give me $6,000 for stock I don't own? That sounds like easy money."

"We're not done yet," Donny continued, leaning back and raising his voice to a more normal level. "Now that you've sold one hundred shares of General Motors stock you don't own, you're obligated to replace the stock in the future."

"You're losin' me again here Donny," announced Sam. "You're losin' me."

"Just let me finish," responded Donny. "Back to our example. You went short on General Motors stock because you thought that $60 per share was too high. Let's say you were right and the stock falls to $50 per share. Now you can <u>buy</u> one hundred shares of GM stock for $5,000 and replace the hundred shares called for in your short sale agreement."

Sam started to interrupt but Donny raised one of his hands to indicate he was not finished. "Just let me finish. You sold one hundred shares short at $60 and received $6,000. Now you've replaced those shares with one hundred shares you bought for $5,000. Just like in the regular sale, your gross was $6,000, your cost was $5,000, and your profit was the same $1,000."

"I get it," exclaimed Ski. "What I can't figure out is, who in the world is going to give me $6,000 for selling a stock I don't own? I mean that sounds like the easiest scam in the world."

Picking up on Ski's observation, Sam added, "Yeah, why sell one hundred shares of GM stock you don't own? Why not a million shares? I mean, why not just pocket $60 million bucks and take off?"

Sensing he was on a roll, Sam continued, "Why would anyone work in this country if Wall Street will let you sell stock you don't have to own?"

"Two things to remember about Wall Street," Donny responded. The Street will always find new ways for investors to place bets. And, the Street never allows an investor to place a bet, lose that bet, and leave the turd on the Street.

"Short sales work," Donny continued, through slightly clenched teeth, "because not just anyone can make a short sale. You've got to have an established relationship with the brokerage house. They have to know who you are and feel confident that you'll live up to the second half of the transaction and replace the stock you've sold short within the contractual time frame.

"And, most importantly, the brokerage house has to be holding more than enough other collateral in your account to cover your short sale, just in case you turn into a flake. So if you want to sell $60 million of GM stock short, you better have $70 or $80, or maybe $100 million in your brokerage account. Now, does all that make sense?"

After receiving nods of acknowledgment from around the table, Donny wrapped things up, "Back to my original comment. A lot of companies out there are a 'One-Man Show.' Take the key man out of the equation, and the stock of that type of company will fall like a ton of bricks.

"When I overheard you talking about a bunch of entrepreneurs, in the primes of their lives, getting blown up for no apparent reason, my first thought was, 'God I wish I'd gone short.' I know that's cold. I guess seeing every situation you encounter in life as a chance to get an edge on the market is just an occupational hazard."

After a minute or two of silence, Sam cleared his throat and asked, "So someone could have made a killing off these deaths?"

"Shit, yes," replied Donny. "If any of these guys ran companies that were publicly traded, especially if the stock was thinly traded, you could have made a fortune going short before they were … before they were … relieved of their management responsibilities."

Sam ordered another round of drinks. Then it was Donny's turn. Then Kate's. And finally, even Ski kicked in a round. All in all, the four had a great time over the course of the evening, in the booth, in Ted's bar, downing drinks, and discussing the finer points of stock manipulation … and its incentive for murder!

Chapter 22

After weeks of trading e-mails, Ski finally arranged a phone call with Dr. English. This was just too important of a conversation to have over the Internet.

"I'm not used to looking at this kind of data," Professor English began. "Usually we deal with scientific observations gathered under controlled conditions, not a large number of unsolved murders. There's more consistency to the data, more uniformity in the nomenclature, more conformity in the format.

"So it took some time to come up with a set of rules for converting your data into a standardized format that could be analyzed. Based on the quality of data you provided, I can see why you were unable to come up with any patterns."

"So you made up some rules for taking our database and changing it into something you could analyze?"

"Well, I had to. Otherwise, any analysis would continue to see nothing but randomness."

"What would happen if one of your rules didn't match reality?"

"Well then my analysis would be faulty."

"So you've really created a new database, and your analysis could be faulty?"

"Well, I guess you could look at it that way, but I seriously doubt if my analysis is faulty. I do have some standing in this arena."

"But do you have any experience interpreting police records?"

"Well, no. But I've always been a big fan of NYPD Blue."

Ski's enthusiasm waned as Professor English went on to describe some of the rules he had developed. His interest returned as Dr. English began to summarize his results.

Professor English concluded that the vast majority of the 714 unsolved homicide cases were, in fact, unrelated random acts. But he did detect what he considered three possible patterns. He labeled these "Clones," "Clusters," and "Crimes with Commonality."

Ski feared that the good Professor had spent too much time making up rules and labels and not enough time analyzing the data.

Clones were groupings of crimes that had some common characteristic, even though they occurred in various locations, with various types of victims, and spanned some period of time. "Strangulation using a rope or article of clothing, for example, or crimes committed in vacant buildings, or bodies dumped in shallow graves."

Clusters were crimes that occurred in a specific area within a specific time frame. "Knifings, shootings, and car bombings. Could be anything, but they all had to take place in the same metropolitan area within a thirty-day period of time."

Crimes with Commonality involved similar victims. "Women, children, prostitutes, transients, and so forth, no matter where or when the crimes occurred."

After describing his categories, Professor English went on to explain how he then used the categories as the basis for sorting through all of the 714 homicides. Any crime that didn't have a possible fit with one of these criteria was deemed to be a random act and excluded from further analysis.

Dr. English then reanalyzed the remaining homicides for additional points of similarity. He also cross analyzed the remaining database using selected factors from other seemingly unrelated databases he had at his disposal.

By analyzing Clusters in combination with the unrelated databases, Professor English found that the homicides in the Clusters statistically had more in common with weather patterns such as heat waves, monthly pay periods, welfare check receipts, and sunspot activity than they did with each other. Based on this result it became clear that Clusters were probably random acts or copycat crimes.

But, within Clones and Crimes with Commonality, Dr. English was able to detect some possible patterns.

The connections were just on the borderline of statistical validity. And they were very much dependent on the translation rules Professor English had created for standardizing the database.

"It is possible," Dr. English concluded, "that there is one or more serial killers involved in these homicides. There are subtle patterns in the data, but it's impossible to say for sure whether the patterns are a result of a common killer or just the fact that there are only so many types of potential victims, only so many types of murder weapons, only so many ways to dispose of a body."

"I guess it's not surprising that a serial killer profile didn't jump out of the data, Doc," Ski offered. "There is a regional task force that does nothing but work cases that may be tied to the serial killers we know are out there. Any case that could be connected with their investigations had already been excluded from the database you analyzed. So, if you've come up with some new patterns, they would be different than anything the task force is already looking at."

"Well, I hate to be equivocal on this, but I honestly can't say for a fact whether or not there are patterns here."

"If you had to offer a hypothesis, not a statement of fact, but just a hypothesis, what would you say is going on here?"

"Just as a hypothesis, I guess I would say that there are at least two possible patterns in the data."

"Be more specific, Doc."

"Well, if I had to state a hypothesis, and it'd be just a hypothesis?"

"Yes, Doc. Just a hypothesis."

"Well, just as a hypothesis, I'd say there is one serial killer out there who is very violent, but very meticulous. He pops up randomly all around the region based on no apparent rhyme or reason. His methods vary, as do his victims. His patterns are very close to being undetectable."

"You said you saw at least two patterns in the data."

"Yes, the other pattern, just as a hypothesis, involves an equally violent individual. But this killer is anything but meticulous. This killer's victims tend to be younger boys and older men, which would suggest that we're dealing with either a homosexual or a female, though the level of violence in the crimes would push the scales more toward a male homosexual if I had to guess. This killer appears to circle up and down the Coast.

"The patterns are a little stronger here. In fact, I'm kind of surprised some of these cases haven't already been pulled out and sent to the task force you mentioned because I'd be pretty confident in saying someone's been involved in several homicides on the West Coast over the span of the past ten years."

"Have either of these hypothetical serial killers been involved with a car bombing?"

"No, I don't remember there being any car bombings in the database."

"That's right! We had already pulled all of those cases because we looked at them separately when we were first analyzing the data."

"So, there's some data I didn't have available?"

"Yeah, we found a pattern of car bombings that covered thirty-five cases, of which thirty-three seemed to involve victims with similar profiles. We pulled those cases out of the database before I ever contacted you about the seemingly random killings."

"I certainly would like to look at that data. Integrate it into my analysis and see if it matches in some way."

"Sure, Doc. I'll e-mail you a file right away. But just based on what you have already, did either one of your hypothetical serial killers ever use explosives?"

"No, I don't think so."

"Do you think they'd be capable of using explosives?"

"I don't see why not."

"Thanks, Doc. I'll get that other data to you right away."

Chapter 23

Fletcher's head snapped back and then his whole body lurched forward. The impact of the steering wheel on his chin was like the short right hook Ali used on Liston. Just like Sonny, Fletch was down for the count.

Up until 1994, Fletcher had managed to operate freely, but now this freak accident put him squarely on the police radar.

Several blocks away, in the alley where he was sleeping, Arnie was oblivious to the sirens that were racing to Fletcher Pound's rescue. As was usual after a Wings of Vengeance meeting, Arnie was oblivious to everything.

Arnie had finally stumbled onto another meeting. These were unfamiliar faces. But they had sandwiches. And while Arnie had to ask, a second bag of potato chips was provided, along with a full beer he didn't even have to share.

They said they had been expecting him. They must hear the voices.

They said their 'associates' in San Francisco had said Arnie was headed their way. They said that Arnie was supposed to have been on a bus. That they went to pick him up at the bus depot, but he wasn't there.

Arnie saw a glimpse of a beach. There was a bus. The voices said he should have stayed on the bus. No, the voices told him to get off of the bus. He couldn't remember. He didn't know where he was. He didn't know how he'd gotten there.

Arnie was hungry and they gave him a second sandwich, another bag of potato chips, and another beer. Thank God he'd found the meeting. Thank God the voices had helped him find the meeting. Thank God the voices would help him remember what he had to do next.

II

What was supposed to have been a ten-hour bus ride from San Francisco to Los Angeles had turned into a three-and-a-half-week trek. The voices were asleep when the Greyhound pulled into the station.

As far as Arnie was concerned, there was no reason for him to be on the bus, no reason not to get off the bus, and certainly no reason to get back on the bus. So, Arnie had gotten off in San Luis Obispo.

When the voices woke up, Arnie was lost. They told him to start walking. And he did.

The voices told him to walk with the sun on his right and then keep walking in the same direction when the sun went down. Arnie would walk until the early hours of the morning and sleep past noon.

The voices kept directing him south. On the few occasions he rose before noon, by keeping the sun on his right, Arnie'd back-track until the sun passed overhead but then he'd resume his southward trek.

Arnie was constantly amazed during his walk-about. He'd get hungry, reach in his pocket, and find the wad of money. He didn't know whose money it was. He didn't know where it came from. He didn't know how much there was.

All he knew was that when he'd get hungry, he'd reach in his pocket and find some money. He'd buy a burger or a sandwich, pick up a bag of potato chips, get one of those 64-ounce monster soda pops, and start walking.

Arnie got picked up by the cops several times. They'd invariably snatch him off the side of the freeway before he made it into town. Haul him to the station where they'd determine he wasn't drunk but certainly wasn't someone they wanted loitering about their town. So they'd drive Arnie to the southern boundary of their jurisdiction where they'd deposit him with a stern warning to keep heading south.

These were voices Arnie knew he needed to pay attention to, so he'd resume his southern march. Without the cops' transportation, Arnie's journey would have taken several days longer.

Arnie's last 'lift' took him all the way from Malibu to the edge of Santa Monica. From there Arnie wandered down to Venice. That's where the voices told him to stop, where the voices helped him find the Wings of Vengeance meeting, where the voices directed him to do what he needed to do and then find the alley and get some sleep.

And, that's where Arnie Nugent was apprehended just as the emergency vehicles were converging on the scene where Fletcher Pound lay unconscious.

Chapter 24

Even though he was still slightly hung over from the night at Ted's listening to Donny and his 'short sale' theory, Ski was so excited that he had to get to work. He arrived at his cubicle hours before the start of his shift.

Sam was already there. Sam never did go home. And now, he was asleep at his desk in a position he'd pay for when he woke up.

Sam had scattered files all around their office space. He had scrawled lengthy notes on a yellow pad, but Ski still couldn't decipher Sam's handwriting, so he had no idea if Sam had made any progress.

Not wanting to be associated with the pain that Sam would encounter when he unfolded from his awkward repose, Ski tried to be as quiet as possible as he fired up his computer. Sam stirred at the booting-up sound. Fortunately, he drifted back to sleep before the computer issued a series of chimes indicating Ski had e-mail.

Apparently neither Kate nor Donny had been particularly successful at avoiding Mr. Insomnia. There were seven e-mails from Kate, and four from Donny.

Kate started with a list of questions Ski and Sam should look into on all the cases. She quickly moved to information she had tracked down on-line, which she was forwarding to Ski. And then she indicated that she planned a crack-of-dawn visit to the stockbroker who handled her trust funds.

Donny's e-mails, in various forms, all offered his assistance in tracking down trading patterns. He needed more information on the companies involved, which he asked Ski to provide.

After retrieving his online mail, Ski moved on to his main task. Retrieving one file at a time from the disaster that was Sam's workspace, Ski quietly assembled a brief synopsis of the information he had on each of the companies managed by the bomb-blast victims. As he worked, he noticed for the first time that each of the victims was repeatedly referred to by employees, customers, friends and relatives as the "Key Man" in their particular organizations. He wondered why he'd never noticed that common thread before.

As he neared the end of his summaries, Ski began to make more noise as he moved about the cubicle. He didn't want to startle Sam awake, but he knew he couldn't send either Kate or Donny the information he had gathered without his partner's OK.

Beginning to purposefully cough as he fussed about the work area, Ski finally managed to break through the fog in Sam's head. It didn't take long for Sam's bloodshot eyes to fix on Ski as the probable source of the pounding in his temples.

Gathering himself, as he searched for the proper invective, Sam stumbled on fresh brain tracks laid down the night before and remembered that his current state was self-inflicted.

"Coffee," Sam uttered softly with his face still hovering about two inches over his desktop. "Please sir, may I have some coffee," Sam politely continued, realizing a comrade could be useful to him at that particular moment in time.

"Sure, Sam," answered Ski softly. "Your normal cream and sugar or would black be better today?" Ski took Sam's grunt, while he unkinked his neck, as an indication that black coffee would be in order.

Ski had always appreciated the fact that Sam never asked him to fetch coffee. As the senior member of the team, Sam could have invoked that privilege and Ski would have obliged. But, either Sam realized that particular request would have been hurtful to Ski, or he just didn't mind getting his own coffee.

Given the current situation, Ski was more than happy to round up coffee – black coffee – for Sam. He wanted Sam as alert as possible, as quickly as possible, so he could show him the information he had compiled and get Sam's blessing to forward it on to Kate and Donny. He also wanted to see if Sam had ever noticed the repeated "Key Man" reference they had overlooked.

Sam gave the go-ahead for Ski to provide Kate with the information he had organized on each of the businesses run by the bombing victims. He figured it was best to see what Kate's investment advisor could come up with before involving Donny, another civilian, in their investigation.

They had been pacing their cubicle for a couple of hours when Sam hung up the phone, declared "This is bull shit," and told Ski to call Donny and ask for help.

Apparently Kate's advisor, Simon Bream, had just arrived at his office. It was only 8:45 in the morning, still reasonably early by most people's standards, but to Sam, Ski, and Kate it seemed like mid-afternoon.

Simon had been just as gracious as humanly possible to Kate, but informed her that his talent was in managing the "client" side of the business and that all research was handled out of his firm's New York office. Simon would fax off Kate's list of companies to New York, and if the firm had any research reports or investment recommendations already available, he could have them back in a couple of days. If actual research was required, it could take a little longer, maybe a couple of weeks.

"Typically," Simon explained to Kate, "the New York boys come up with their recommendations and we, out here on the front lines" — like there were battle lines separating Westwood from Beverly Hills — "we provide that information to our clients, or in the case of trust funds like yours where we have portfolio responsibility, we take action. Our clients expect us to decide which companies are worth analyzing. We're not really used to having a client ask us to look into this company or that company."

Vowing to have her trust fund yanked from that "condescending asshole" as soon as possible, Kate passed on the news to Sam that her broker wasn't going to be any help.

Ski was surprised when the receptionist at Donny's firm informed him that Donny was ill and that he could talk to one of Donny's associates or leave a message. Given that they had been trading rounds at Ted's the night before, Ski could envision Donny being a little under the weather. But he had received e-mails from Donny already that morning and assumed he was at work.

Ski decided to return the last of Donny's e-mails and see if he was OK. Ski got an almost instantaneous response from Donny. "I'm really at the office. Told Sally to hold my calls

— tell people am sick — so I'm clear to help you guys. Sally was supposed to put you through, but sometimes she forgets. Call me on my back line, 677-4426."

Donny grabbed the receiver on the first ring. "Got some good stuff already," announced Donny without even saying hello or checking to make sure it was Ski on the line. Donny had remembered a couple of the victims and a couple of the company names that had been tossed about the night before. Using that information, he was already "on the case."

Ski jotted down Donny's fax number and told Donny he would fax him the summary information he had compiled. Donny said that he'd work on it right away and suggested that everyone meet at Ted's that evening to go over his findings. Donny then reiterated, "But I gotta tell ya, I got some good stuff already. Yeah, really good stuff ... OK, see you tonight about 6:30."

At 3:20, Ski received a breathless call from Donny. Donny had plowed through the information supplied by Ski, and while there were a few loose ends he needed to tie up, he thought they should get together as soon as possible.

Sam and Ski had already arranged a 3:30 meeting with an important, reluctant, witness in one of their other homicide investigations. They did, after all, have another dozen or so open cases at the time. So Ski couldn't promise Donny they could get away much before 6:00.

At 4:05, Sam declared their witness an official no-show. He handed the file off to Sizemore and asked him to interview the witness if she wandered in later that afternoon. Then he put in a call to Kate.

Kate had dropped out of school when she found she couldn't concentrate on anything but her grandfather's murder. She planned to return to the MBA program next term, but right now she was free to meet Sam, Ski, and Donny whenever and wherever they chose.

Even though his office was several blocks further away from Ted's than the precinct house, Donny had already staked out their booth and ordered a round of beers by the time Sam and Ski arrived. It usually took Kate about 15 minutes to drive from her condo to Ted's, but she arrived before Donny had finished telling Sam and Ski how he went about pulling information on Ski's list of companies.

Donny had started with a general check of corporate records and SEC filings. He then researched his firm's database of corporate analyses and stock recommendations. Finally, he ran the first cut of a report on market activity for each company's stock.

He hadn't finished the complete analysis of regular and short sales trading volume for each company's stock; that would take most of the night. But he had enough.

As Kate slipped into the booth, Donny took a deep breath and launched into a description of what he had already uncovered. The previous evening – as Sam, Ski, and Kate listened to Stock Manipulations 101 – the general feeling was that, even though these cases spanned both Coasts, if they could tie a couple of the unsolved cases together through short sales activity, they would have a whole new way of looking at them. Now the three sat in rapt silence and listened as Donny revealed that there had been unusual market activity in the stock of all thirty-three companies just before, and then again after, the Key Men in those companies had met their untimely demise.

They were all speechless as Donny went on to say that, in every case, the companies involved had similar profiles. They were all up-and-comers. They had all created a profitable niche for their particular product or service and had grown beyond the initial entrepreneurial/venture capital phase.

In addition, all of the companies had gone through IPO's and had publicly traded stock. But they were also thinly capitalized, with either the founder, a venture capitalist, or an investment banker still holding most of the outstanding stock. Public shares of thinly traded stock, Donny explained, could swing more wildly than public shares of stock in a company with a large number of shares outstanding and diverse shareholders.

None of the companies had yet reached market dominance or the mature phase of growth in which there is depth of management. Each and every company was still very much dependent on the vision, will, and energy of its founder. Its "Key Man." Take the Key Man out of the picture and the stocks would drop, as Donny had said, "like a ton of bricks." Which is exactly what had happened.

"Like I said," continued Donny, "All I know so far is that there was heavy trading in all of the stocks both before, and after, each Key Man was removed from the picture. So far, I can't tell if any of that activity involved short sales. I still have a lot of work to do tonight in order to piece that part of the puzzle together. But I'll bet a dollar to a doughnut that short sales are what I'm going to find!"

Donny folded his arms across his chest and sat back with a satisfied smile on his face. Sam was the first to break the silence, "Jesus, Donny! Great work! We're gonna have to get you some kind of a 'citizen detective of the month' award or somethin'."

Ski just shook his head. Kate, looking like she might cry, slowly reached across the table to shake Donny's hand ... the proudest moment to date in Donny's otherwise uneventful life.

II

The four met at the House of Pancakes for breakfast the next morning. No one had been sure what time Ted's opened and, in any event, breakfast at Ted's had sounded like a really bad idea. So it was breakfast at the IHOP... where everything, especially at 6:30 in the morning, was a little too plastic, a little too bright, and a little too cheerful.

Donny was the last to roll in. He looked like Sam did the previous morning.

Donny suffered from a middle-aged reaction to pulling an all-nighter, just as Sam had the previous day. Plowing through daily trading activity records for these small (in a Wall Street sense) companies had taken its toll, and it took Donny two cups of IHOP coffee to become coherent.

"I'm sorry," Donny started, with his eyes focused on his second cup of coffee. Sam, Ski, and Kate felt like they were simultaneously kicked in the solar plexus.

Now everyone stared at their coffee as Donny, after a minute, continued, "I'm really sorry ... I thought I'd get through everything by this morning ... but it's just going too slow ... I'm sorry ... I just couldn't get it all done."

"That's it?" exhaled Sam. "You're sorry 'cause you didn't get done?"

"Yeah, I'm really sorry. I thought I could do it. I hope you guys aren't too disappointed." Donny mumbled flatly still staring at his coffee.

"Jeez, Donny," Sam continued, "There's no timetable here. Homicide investigations don't come with an expiration date. Sounded to me like you had a ton of paper to sift through. We – at least I – didn't expect you to finish everything last night."

Sensing that Donny's nerves were a bit frayed, Ski chimed in with his cheeriest voice, "Yeah, Donny, you can only do what you can only do."

Kate, who was seated across from Donny in the too plastic, too bright, IHOP booth, just reached over and patted him on the shoulder.

After allowing for what he considered an adequate moment of silence, Sam ventured the question Ski and Kate were also waiting to ask. "So Donny ... did you find anything?"

"Oh, tons," replied Donny still staring at his coffee. "Yeah, tons of good stuff. But I didn't get done."

"Forget getting done. Just let that go, will you Donny?" Sam blurted, his voice starting to rise. "We could give a shit whether or not you got done. We just want to know what you found!"

"Oh ... I found tons of stuff," replied Donny.

At that point it was clear to everyone that this was going to be a four- or five-cup-of-coffee morning for Donny. And that they'd need to be patient if they were going to get Donny beyond the mumbling phase.

After placing their orders with the way-too-cheery waitress, the conversation drifted to previous all-nighters. Sam, Ski and Kate took turns recounting stories of drunken bashes, last-minute term papers, and Vegas road trips. Donny just stared at the cup of coffee he held in both hands as though it were his most prized possession. And that morning it probably was.

The sausage, egg, and pancake breakfast Donny inhaled did more for him than the five cups of coffee he had ingested. As he finished, Donny remembered that, not only had he not slept in more than twenty-four hours, but all he'd had to eat since his bowl of cereal the previous morning was half a jelly sandwich, a banana, several Pepsis, and a couple of beers.

Sam was the first to decide that Donny had sufficiently recovered and that it was time to get back to business. "So Donny, you said you'd found tons of good stuff last night."

"Yeah," chimed in Donny, with some life in his voice. "Yeah, tons of good stuff." As Donny continued, "Like I said, I didn't get finished," the others held their breath waiting to see if Donny slid back into his funk. "But, I found tons of good stuff," Donny concluded.

While he had made some progress in rejoining the living, Donny still wasn't volunteering any information on his own. Not that he was playing coy or anything; his brain just wasn't fully engaged yet.

Kate took the lead, "So Donny, tell us, what kind of good information did you find?"

"Oh, tons of stuff. There was heavy short selling in every company I looked at," Donny stated, offering a little bit of new information.

"Every company?" asked Kate, realizing she was now in twenty questions mode.

"Yeah, every company," replied Donny.

"And how many companies did you look at Donny?"

"Not all of them. Guys, I'm sorry ... I didn't get finished," mumbled Donny.

"We know you didn't get finished Donny. We said we don't care about that. What we care about, Donny, is exactly how many companies did you look at?" Sam asked, having resumed his accommodating tone.

"Oh, jees ... I didn't really count," Donny replied as he started to stand up as if to rush back to his office to get a tally for Kate.

"Sit down, Donny," Kate said gently as she motioned for Donny to take his seat next to Ski. "We don't need an exact count. Just a ballpark. What da-ya think, Donny, ballpark, how many companies did you look at?"

"I guess about twenty, maybe twenty-five of the thirty-three," Donny offered flatly.

"Jesus Christ!" exclaimed Sam. "You've already looked at twenty to twenty-five of these companies, and there was short selling in every case just before the Key Man was terminated?"

"Yeah," replied Donny. "Every case."

"Jesus," Sam uttered shaking his head. "Well, we knew the what and the where. And now we know the why. All we need to do now is find Heulenberg, and prove he is the who."

At that point, Ski, also shaking his head observed, "You were right all along Sam. Follow the money. Money's the motive. It just took awhile to find the <u>right</u> money trail."

Kate raised her coffee cup, "Here's to Donny showing us how to make money through someone else's misfortune."

"Here's to Donny," Sam and Ski added, raising their coffee cup to join Kate's toast.

"Here's to short sales," Donny replied, clinking coffee cups with the others.

Raising his cup above the rest, Sam concluded, "Here's to catching the bastard."

"To catching the bastard," was the final toast, offered in unison.

III

The table was quiet for several minutes as each member of the foursome slid into their own private thoughts. Ski finally broke the silence, "So, Donny. Any idea how much of a motive we have here? Any guess as to how much money our bad guy could have made off the short sales?"

Donny emerged from his fog for a moment to do some mental calculations. "Kind of hard to tell exactly. I'll need detailed trading records.

Need to look at trading in the companies I didn't get to last night. Don't know if I'll be able to tell exactly who sold what, when they sold, and when they covered the short sales ..." Donny trailed off, losing his exact train of thought.

"Just a ballpark Donny," offered Sam. "Just a ballpark number."

Donny slouched slightly forward, closed his eyes, and began rubbing his temples between the thumb and index finger of his right hand. No one was sure whether he was thinking or falling asleep.

Looking up after a silent moment or two, Donny concluded, "I'd guess that if our bad guy went short anywhere near the peak of the market for each company's stock ... and then covered the sale when the shares hit bottom after the news of the murders got out ... I'd have to guess that the take was somewhere between $50 and $75 million."

"Jesus!" exclaimed Sam. "$50 to $75 million!"

"Yeah," answered Donny, "It's just a guess at this point. But I'd guess $50 to $75 million. Maybe a little less. Probably more."

"I don't know if we need more!" Sam exclaimed, again shaking his head. "$50 to $75 million is plenty of motive where I come from."

IV

Kate drove Donny home after the IHOP breakfast. No one wanted to turn him loose on LA's unsuspecting traffic.

It took a lot of convincing to get Donny to agree to go home and go to bed. Donny was sure that it was his civic duty to go back to his office and finish looking into the companies he hadn't gotten to the night before.

Donny had indicated that while he could obtain information on general trading activity, getting their hands on the detailed trading records showing who was initiating the 'short sales' would require subpoenas. Brokerage houses fought tooth and nail to keep clients' records confidential.

Sam's description of the slow subpoena process didn't appear to dissuade Donny from wanting to immediately complete his task. It was only Kate's gentle smile and her offer to drive him home that made Donny agree to catch a couple of hours of shut eye before resuming his research.

Donny's multiple cups of IHOP coffee appeared to finally kick in as Kate negotiated the freeway traffic. Then he started to get revved up over the "bastard" that had bumped off all these "good men."

Kate was afraid Donny'd never be able to get to sleep. But, once he was home and in sight of his bed, Donny was like a drowning man who had just spotted a life raft. Without changing clothes, he climbed into bed, pulled up his covers, and wrapped his arms around his pillow like a lover.

Kate lingered outside his bedroom to make sure he stayed in bed. Within less than a minute, she heard the heavy breathing that signaled

Donny was out. Kate let herself out of Donny's apartment and realized, when she reached her car, she really had no place to go.

Sam had made it clear that it would take a couple of days to get all the paperwork together and approved before they'd have any chance of obtaining subpoenas for the detailed trading records Donny needed. Sam and Ski still hadn't had any success in tracking down Karl Heulenberg, and they had other investigations they needed to attend to. They had plenty to do while waiting for the subpoenas.

With Donny down for the count, and Sam and Ski busy, Kate suddenly felt very much alone. It was then that Kate had an urge she hadn't experienced for some time. The urge to shop ... The urge to shop for shoes.

So, Kate shopped for shoes. Katherine decided on a pair of emerald green heels that she was sure would go with something in her wardrobe. Kate bought a pair of practical black flats that reminded her of several other pairs of practical black flats she already had in her closet. Kat picked up some socks and a new pair of running shoes.

Kate headed straight for the ocean and took a long stroll along the shoreline. New shoes in the car, sun on her face, a slight breeze at her back, and the sound of surf in the background. For the first time in months, Kate relaxed.

Chapter 25

Legend has it that the Island of Kauai was first inhabited by the *menehune*, the Polynesian equivalent of leprechauns. It seems reasonable that this little island <u>would</u> be home to little people.

Only 33 miles long and 25 miles wide, Kauai packs incredible diversity into an area less than half the size of Yellowstone National Park. The eastern beaches feature the hotel and condominium developments that have come to define Hawaii's tourist destinations. The western Na Pali coast is an impassable stretch of jagged, thousand-foot ridges rising straight out of the sea, a mysterious land that time forgot. The southern reaches sport the Waimea Canyon, a gash so dramatic it's often compared to the Grand Canyon, as well as beaches so arid they can go years between rainfalls. Then there's the northern coast, the Princeville coast, with its lush hills and valleys that lie in the shadow of Waialeale, the mountain at the heart of the island that accepts over 500 inches of rain each year.

500 inches of rain! The LA Laker's starting lineup, plus the sixth man in their rotation, laid out, head-to-toe, don't measure 500 inches.

When Tommy Chou first joined the Kauai police force, the island hadn't yet become a tourist destination. And while the terrain was diverse, the population was quite homogeneous. Tommy felt like he knew every plantation owner, every agricultural worker, and all their families.

But that was nearly forty years ago. Now with over half a million tourists invading the island each year, the explosion of maids, busboys, and bartenders working at the resorts, and the influx of new businesses to serve both the tourists and those who serve the tourists, Tommy felt like he hardly knew anyone.

The island had changed and so had Tommy. Long gone were the days when Tommy Chou was one of Lihue's most eligible bachelors. Gravity had redistributed Tommy's once powerful chest, shoulders, and upper arms to his midriff, and added insult by curving his once erect spine and eroding the cartilage in both his knees. With his thinning gray hair, hunched posture, and hobbled gait, Tommy looked more like a kindly great grandfather, which he was, than a police chief, which he also was.

Over the years, the job had changed even more than Tommy. Gone were the days when the Kauai Police Department's greatest concern was breaking up a Friday night tavern brawl. The seventies brought drugs to the island, and prostitutes followed the tourists.

Tommy tried to keep up, but here he was, a sixty-two year old man who still called himself Tommy. That's how flexible he was.

The world, at least his world, had changed far faster than Tommy Chou could adapt. He hardly recognized the beaches anymore, with new resorts and tourist facilities constantly changing the landscape. How was he supposed to recognize the names or faces of a constantly changing population?

"I'm sorry Detective Siemen. We just don't have any information on a Karl Heulenberg," Tommy reiterated for the fourth time. "If he did in fact move to Kauai, he never ran afoul of our department. We just don't have any record on him, at all."

"Can you just poke around a little for me?" Sam pleaded. "We think he moved to Hawaii about four years ago, and he was possibly headed for Kauai. Can I fax you over what information we have on Heulenberg, along with some background on the homicides we think he might have had a hand in?"

"Sure," replied Tommy, thinking that this Detective Siemen must think he's had nothing better to do over the past several years than to sit at the Lihue airport and personally greet every arriving passenger. Bet Siemen doesn't have a dossier on everybody who passes through LAX. "I'll see what I can find," Tommy concluded as he hung up the phone.

Just what was he supposed to do? Send his men out on a door-to-door search? Put this Heulenberg guy's picture on milk cartons? Didn't he have enough of his own problems to worry about?

He'd liked to have brushed the whole thing aside, but unfortunately Tommy was somewhat 'old school.' He'd never been able to completely adopt the aloha attitude toward work that kept most of Kauai's new crop of employees from worrying much about doing today what could possibly be put off until next week. God only knows where this small dose of Protestant work ethic came from, but there it was and Tommy couldn't just round-file Sam's request the way his brain said he should.

He'd poke around a little. He'd do that much for a fellow cop. But it'd be on <u>his</u> schedule.

He couldn't ask any of his men to waste their time on this wild goose chase. No, he could waste his time, but not theirs. This would be Tommy Chou's own little project.

II

After he'd received the faxed material on Karl Heulenberg from Sam, Tommy did check around. He still had contacts at the phone company, the power company, and the banks.

But like Tommy, his contacts had moved through the ranks and were now upper management. Like Tommy, his contacts wanted to help. Like Tommy, his contacts wouldn't even think of asking staff to spend their time on this matter. Like Tommy, his contacts followed their own time schedules.

All the good intentions got mixed up in inefficiency, so what little information that was compiled on Karl Heulenberg was compiled slowly. It was a couple of weeks before Tommy was ready to report back to Sam.

"Well, he was on the island for about a year," Tommy explained. "But that was over three years ago.

"He apparently just showed up one day. Rented a room in kind of a flop house. Worked selling timeshares at one of the resorts. Didn't do very well at it, according to their records.

"Then one day, about a year later, he just disappeared."

Sam, who was desperately hoping for more concrete information on his prime suspect, asked "What do you mean, just disappeared?"

"Just that! Just disappeared."

There was stunned silence on Sam's end of the phone line, so Tommy continued, "One day he was at work. The next day he wasn't. Looks like he left in a hurry. Left some clothes and other personal stuff in his room. Left a little money in a bank account that he never withdrew, which was eventually used to pay off some of the bills he also left behind."

"Any idea where he went?" Sam exhaled, closing his eyes and literally crossing the fingers on his right hand.

"Not a clue," Tommy offered. "This Heulenberg guy just showed up on the island one day. Scratched out a meager living. According to his landlord, never had any visitors. Never made any friends.

"Then he just vanished. Didn't leave a trace. I wish we could get some of our tourist friends to have as little impact on our fair island as your Mr. Heulenberg had, during the time he was here."

Trying to muster some enthusiasm in his voice, Sam offered, "Hey, thanks for trying. I knew the trail was pretty cold."

"Sorry I couldn't be more help," responded Tommy. "I know how these open cases can gnaw at you."

"Yeah, this one's really under my saddle," Sam concluded, realizing that what he had just said didn't make a lot of sense. "Listen, let me know if you run across anything else. And, thanks again for trying."

Almost as an afterthought, Sam added, "Hey, I may be headed your way for a vacation someday. If I ever make it to Kauai, maybe you'll let me buy you a beer."

"You got it, brudder," Tommy answered. "But only if you let me buy every other round."

Cops are all the same, Tommy thought to himself. Always planning an exotic vacation they'll never take. Always willing to buy another cop a beer. Thank God some things never change.

Chapter 26

B ased on Donny's theory — and his estimate that the potential profit from the short sales could exceed $50 million — the foursome's investigation took on new dimensions.

Sam was more convinced than ever that Karl Heulenberg was their man. Heulenberg knew how vulnerable some of the 'short sale' victims' companies were. He was himself financially desperate. And, he had disappeared.

Sam didn't need any more evidence than that. What he needed was some evidence as to Karl's whereabouts. "Find Karl and we find our killer."

Ski wasn't so sure. He was working on his own theories.

He'd already spent a lot of time and effort looking into fringe groups. Maybe some wacko or cult of wackos wanted to kill off entrepreneurs as a political statement or as part of a bizarre scheme for creating what, in their twisted view, would be a more perfect world. Ski wasn't ready to give up on that theory just yet.

Ski's new favorite theory was that the car bombings were, in fact, tied to the short sales, but involved organized crime. With or without Karl Heulenberg's involvement.

"Why are you so sure there's no organized crime involvement?" Ski asked Sam. "I mean there's sure enough 'motivation' to get their attention."

"It's called organized crime for a reason," Sam answered. "'Cause they're organized." Sam added for emphasis.

"Some of 'em may be bozos. But if they ever figured out a scheme like this that could net them millions, they'd never, ever, car bomb all thirty-three victims. There'd be so many different ways these guys would have been taken out that we'd never be able to tie them together."

"So, what if Heulenberg put out hits on these guys? Had the mob do his dirty work."

"Two problems with that," Sam responded. "Most professional hits don't involve a method, just a result. You might be able to put out a contract that specified the means one time, but it'd be difficult to do that a second time, much less thirty-three times, because a professional killer would certainly see repeated car bombings as significantly increasing the odds of getting caught. And these guys just don't get caught."

"What if Heulenberg really wanted car bombings, so he hired different killers for each job? They wouldn't necessarily know he was asking them to use a method that had been used before."

"That leads right to the second reason Karl couldn't have arranged all these as hits. He wouldn't know how."

"Well, it can't be that hard," Ski replied.

"You think not? You're a cop. How would you arrange a hit?" Sam asked.

Turning his attention to Kate, "You're a civilian. How would you go about contacting someone in the underworld to take out a contract on someone you wanted dead?"

Kate was speechless.

"There's got to be some way to make a connection," Ski offered.

"Maybe," Sam answered. "If you had years. Were willing to start at the bottom of the organization with a small drug deal or something. Work your way up through a series of connections to where they trusted you, which would mean you'd have had to engage in all kinds of illegal activities.

"Then, maybe, you'd be able to get to someone who could get to someone who could put you in touch with someone who could place a contract. But if this kind of connection was easy, law enforcement agencies would have more success at setting contract killers up, so that they could take them down."

"For as long as I've been a cop, I've only came in contact with one individual I was pretty sure was a contract killer, and that was by sheer coincidence."

"Is this another one of those stories you haven't bothered to tell me yet?" asked Ski. Ski had been teamed with Sam for nearly a year now, but was constantly learning new details regarding his partner's past. Ski, who still didn't know that Sam had been married, and divorced ... three times ... and had a daughter who was a successful city desk reporter for the Miami Herald, picked up most of the bits and pieces he had learned about Sam from the off-handed, often snide, comments made about him from the other 'old timers' in the department. Now he saw a chance to get some good stuff directly from the source.

"Come on Sam, you can't toss something out there like that and not come through with the story."

"I was just trying to say it's not likely a cop – much less a civilian – is going to know a hired gun."

"Come on Sam, the story!"

"It really wasn't that big of a deal. Just a set of circumstances. I'm working what we thought was a homicide investigation when ..."

"You 'thought' it was a homicide investigation?" Ski interrupted.

"Let me tell the story, OK? And no interruptions from you either," turning his attention to Kate.

"No interruptions," Kate pledged.

"OK, where was I?"

Not a peep from Ski or Kate.

"I was on this homicide investigation back in 1994. We got a call on a bum sleeping in an alley, covered in blood. We pick the guy up, but there's something wrong with the picture. This guy's coat is literally soaked in blood. His hands and arms are covered with blood. But his pants, his shoes, they're clean. Well not clean, by any stretch of the imagination, but no traces of blood.

"Anyway, we find this guy, half soaked in blood. We roust and cuff him and it's clear right away that the guy's not really with it. He's moaning, almost talking in tongues, snickering, but making no sense at all. He's got no identification, but there's a couple of hundred dollars stuffed in one of his pockets.

"The only other thing we find is some hate literature from one of those white supremacist organizations. There's scribbles all over the margins, some of which make some sense, some of which don't.

"Anyway, we haul this bum in and lock him up while we look for a victim. That's where it gets strange.

"We never did find a victim. Held on to this guy as long as we could and then managed to get him committed, because he never did make any sense, and if he hadn't committed a crime, he'd sure been close to one.

"Lost track of this guy. The last I heard he just wandered off from the facility."

"And that was your contract killer?" Ski asked hesitantly.

"No. He was just one of the reasons I was down at County when I did meet our hit man. The other reason was Ian Proctor. But that's another story.

"The hit man's name was Bruce Boswick, but his street name was Fletcher Pound. I still can't figure out how these guys settle on names. Fletcher Pound, go figure.

"Anyway, Bruce had had an unlucky day. Otherwise we'd never have had him in custody.

"Bruce is stopped at a red light at Sepulveda and Venice Boulevard when this kid rear ends him. Kid's out crusin' in the new Range Rover his parents bought him for his 16th birthday. Had his license for, like, a week. Kid's heading up Sepulveda when he decides he needs a new tape, leans over to check out his collection, and wham, his Range Rover is up close and personal with the rear end of Bruce's car.

"Bruce takes a knock on the forehead and is out like a light. The area's just crawling with cell phones and 911 is flooded with calls.

"The emergency crews are on the scene in just a couple of minutes. Bruce is still out cold and the kid's pretty freaked.

"The impact from the Range Rover sprung Bruce's trunk lid, and inside, the emergency crew sees all sorts of weapons. They call in the cops, who now have probable cause to haul Bruce in as soon as he regains consciousness.

"If Bruce hadn't been knocked out, or if the trunk lid hadn't popped, we'd never have gotten him into the system. But there it was, a trunk filled with enough guns, knives, ammunition, and explosives to resupply the Fighting Seabees.

"So Bruce is in the slammer on weapons charges at the same time we've got this vagrant locked up while we're looking for a body.

"I still wouldn't have come across Bruce if it wasn't for Ian Proctor. Ian had just been sentenced for this unbelievable crime spree. Now he's claiming responsibility for a bunch more crimes we know he didn't commit. And trying to claim that others were responsible for, or at least involved in, crimes we knew were Ian's.

"At first it looked like Ian was trying to add an insanity defense for an appeal. Or maybe just draw attention to himself. What didn't make sense was that it looked like he was building up a lot of ill-will with people he was going to be incarcerated with.

"Ian claims that Bruce committed two murders that were clearly Ian's work. This was a vicious crime involving a nurse and her elderly stepmother.

"I wouldn't have bothered interviewing Bruce, but I was already going to be down at County, and when he drew a Smithee for a prosecutor it was clear he wouldn't be around for long. So I went to see him about Ian's statements."

"Smithee?" asked Kate. "What's a Smithee?"

"You don't know what a Smithee is?" answered Sam. "Like in Hollywood?"

"No."

"In Hollywood, they've had Smithees for years. For example, you're the producer of a movie and things aren't going well. The director quits and you need to bring in someone to finish the film. The new guy agrees to work on the project, but things are already so screwed up, he doesn't want his name associated with it, so he uses an alias.

"It's supposed to be an inside joke. When the credits roll, the director is listed as Allen Smithee. If a Smithee produces or directs a Hollywood movie, you know someone wanted the paycheck but not the blame.

"In law enforcement, we've got the same thing. Every D.A.'s office, every public defender's office has at least one incompetent attorney. These guys usually get all the shit cases no one else wants.

"But every once in awhile they get assigned to a high profile case. You just know some political pressure had been brought to bear on the D.A.'s office, or some judge has pre-determined this case needs to be lost. When that happens we say the attorney is a Smithee, from the firm of Smithee & Smithee.

"Now, we've got a Smithee prosecuting Bruce. And even though it's an open and shut case, you just know that somehow he'll walk.

"So I interview Bruce. Turns out to be a pretty nice guy. He seems genuinely offended that Ian would try to implicate him. He kept saying, 'What was the point?' And, 'What kind of message did he want to send killing a nurse and that poor old lady, for Christ sakes?'"

"Anyway, I visit Bruce a couple more times. You know, being in his profession, I'm guessing he's not going to get a lot of visitors.

"Next thing I know, Ian's taken care of, all the evidence against Bruce disappears, and the nut case that started all this has been transferred out for psychiatric evaluation.

"And?" implored Ski when it was clear that Sam had finished his story.

"And nothing," Sam responded. "The point of the story is this. If that spoiled kid hadn't rammed into the back end of Bruce's car. And if Bruce hadn't been knocked unconscious and the trunk lid sprung. And if I hadn't been down at County working another case and overheard that Proctor was making wild claims, I'd never have meet Bruce Boswick, my one and only suspected contract killer.

"And you think Karl Heulenberg was able to find thirty-three Bruce Boswicks, who don't know each other, or at least know of each other's work, and hire them to carry out his car bombing scheme?"

"You make it sound pretty unlikely," offered Ski.

"Unlikely," responded Sam. "That reminds me of a third reason Heulenberg wouldn't hire out hits.

"You contract for a hit and you introduce a wild card into the mix. If we're really looking at the number of murders we think are related and the kind of money Donny thinks is involved, don't you think Karl would be a little worried about being double-crossed, or paranoid that someone would mouth off at the wrong time?

"No, Karl's in this on his own."

Chapter 27

The team's routines had returned to normal by the time the detailed stock trading records they'd subpoenaed finally arrived. The pattern in the short sales transactions was there; it just came with a little twist they hadn't anticipated.

They had hoped for a paper trail that led straight to Karl Heulenberg. What they found was a series of trades involving half a dozen different brokerage houses, which executed the short sale transactions on behalf of thirty-three different corporations.

"This guy is smart," observed Ski.

"Well, it makes sense, if you're trying to hide a paper trail," added Sam. "We've got to get this bastard!" flashed Kat.

"We've got to," Kate reiterated, softening her tone, but not the anger in her eyes.

"Sam, I've gotta ask," started Ski. "Isn't it time we lay all this out for the lieutenant? Have him put together an interagency task force or something. I mean, this is now a pretty big case for just two homicide cops."

"And two assistants!" Donny added.

"Task force?" Sam replied. "Do you want to get to the bottom of this case or not?"

"Well, sure I do, but," Ski had started, when he was cut off by a wave of Sam's hand.

"Let me tell you what we get from a task force. We get at least a year of arguing over who's going to be in charge.

"We get another year of fighting over who'll get all the credit and who'll get all the blame. That'll take a year, even though I can tell you the outcome right now. The FBI will get the praise if the case is ever solved, and we'll get the blame if it's not.

"On a task force, we'd pull in the SEC and the IRS and then kiss good-bye any possibility of cooperation from them. On a task force, everyone pledges to share information, but they actually begin hoarding it, hoping you're dumb enough to share your information with them so they can scoop the case and look like heroes.

"Should I go on?"

II

Donny went to work, further analyzing the new data. As best as he could tell, the total take from the short sale maneuvers was in the neighborhood of $123,000,000 ... give or take $5,000,000.

With specific instructions from Donny on how and where to search for corporate records on the thirty-three mystery corporations, Sam and Ski headed off to track down ownership. Their investigation quickly turned into a game of hide and seek. The 'short sale' killer, in planning this caper, had been far more paranoid about being traced than they had anticipated. He had created dozens of corporate entities that traded ownership back and forth and amongst themselves as if they were playing Monopoly. Ski finally resorted to laying out the maze of corporate ownerships using a flow chart on his computer, just so he could keep things straight.

Anyone looking at just one or two pieces of the 'short sale plot' in isolation would have gotten completely lost. But Sam and Ski had the big picture ... all thirty-three events. When it was all said and done, everything led back to CE Ltd., a Maldavian corporation. In one form or another, CE Ltd. controlled the maze of interlocking corporations that eventually initiated the 'short sale' transactions.

But the ownership trail stopped at CE Ltd. And unfortunately, the Maldives was one of those banking secrecy, money laundering, tax evading havens that provided absolute privacy for anyone who wanted to hide behind a corporate cloak of secrecy and was willing to pay the Maldives' exorbitant registration fees.

The trail ended. They knew there was a bad guy or maybe bad guys out there. They knew there was a 'short sale plot' that had resulted in thirty three deaths and over $100 million in profits.

They knew all that, but the trail was dead. There was no way to go further. They'd reached the end of the line, and it looked like the bad guy had won.

Ski was so depressed that he couldn't even talk when the four met at Ted's. It fell on Sam to pass the grim news to Kate and Donny.

"Just petered out," Sam started. "When we got offshore and ended up in the Maldives ... our contacts at the State Department tell me there's no way we'll ever get our hands on any confidential corporate records from over there. Corporate secrecy's 'Big Business' there. We could be investigating World War III and they'd still tell us to buzz off."

Not much else was said that evening. After one round of beers, the group said their "goodbyes" and drifted off.

III

Three days later, Kate called for a meeting at Ted's. It was her show, so after everyone had said how dull things had been without their drink-and-discuss meetings, Kate took center stage and laid out her idea.

Kate's plan was actually pretty straight forward. "It came to me when I started thinking more about my grandfather again and less about all the other victims. I started rehashing in my mind all the bits and pieces of what we knew about grandpa's murder and it came to me." Kate held everyone's interest as she continued, "The explosive devices involved in all of the bombings, including Jonathan's, used a simple detonator that required the murderer to have a straight line of sight from his position to the victim's automobile."

"If we can't track him down," Kat flashed, "maybe we can catch him in the act."

"Catch him in the act?" Sam exhaled. "And just how do you propose we do that?"

"Anticipate who his next victim will be and tail that guy 'til we catch our killer," Kate answered.

"And just which of the 250 million people in this country do you propose we tail, Kate?" Sam inquired sarcastically.

"Anyone who fits the profile!" Kate responded.

Donny saw the possibilities immediately, "Yeah, we look for other 'Key Men' in companies with closely traded stocks."

"And then what?" queried Sam, still not quite grasping the concept. "Trail a bunch of CEOs around for the rest of their lives, waiting for one of them to get bumped off? I don't think the

Lieutenant would consider that a good deployment of the homicide squad's resources."

"No, don't you see?" continued Donny. "We figure out who could be a potential target. Then I set up a kind of early warning system on my firm's computer. You know, track the stocks in companies we identify as being at risk. Then if there is any unusual trading activity in any of the stocks, we'll know who we need to watch."

"Yeah," Ski interjected, "No one's at risk until there's a big short sale."

"So I'll see if there are any more companies out there that fit the profile, start tracking their stocks, and if there's any short sale, you guys swoop in and nail the bad guy."

"Easy as that," Sam uttered as almost, but not quite, a question.

"Easy as that!" stated Donny unequivocally.

Chapter 28

After he'd finished his research, Donny was ready to reconvene everyone at Ted's. Kate was the first to arrive and immediately sensed a problem. A strange couple was already seated in their booth.

Ted's attracted a late-arriving crowd, if you could call the sparse clique of regular patrons and assorted lost souls a crowd. There had never been a problem with the availability of their designated booth in the past.

Kate, trying on an unaccustomed, flexible outlook, scanned the bar for an acceptable alternate booth. Finding none, she became the rich bitch who knew that what she wanted, and what she deserved, and what she would get, were all one and the same thing.

So Kate walked straight up to the couple in the booth, announced that she was meeting her fiancée and his two best friends in a few moments, that this was the 'special booth' where her 'Beau' proposed, and that she'd like to buy the couple a drink if they would move to another booth.

Jake and Anne — especially Anne, whose eyes twinkled at the request — didn't think anything could be cuter than having a 'special booth.' Jake and Anne already had a 'special song' but would now be on the lookout for a 'special booth.' They were happy to move, and equally happy to accept Kate's offer of a free drink.

Sam, Ski, and Donny all laughed when Kate whispered her story of the conquered booth.

"It just wouldn't have seemed right meeting anywhere else," said Ski. Sam agreed, but added that he would've just flashed his badge, told the two they were interfering with "official police business," and saved the cost of the two drinks. The group cracked up over the image of Sam, doing his best Bogart, rousting poor Jake and Anne for "official business." Then they all agreed that it really was "official police business," and if they needed that particular booth, in that particular bar, for conducting their "official police business," well, so be it.

Jake and Anne sipped their gratis drinks, watched the giggling foursome, and tried to guess whether the gorgeous girl who had interrupted their discussion on how to best invest 401k retirement funds, was engaged to the tall skinny black kid, the dumpy middle-aged white guy or the short, balding older fellow who deserved to be arrested by the hair police.

They concluded that it had to be the black kid. He was the best-looking, although Anne sensed he was painfully shy. There seemed to be a real chemistry between the two younger members of the foursome. Jake and Anne agreed that the others were clearly losers.

Donny launched into his findings as soon as they finished laughing over Kate's territorial imperative. "Two hundred and sixty-four more companies out there fit the profile."

"Two hundred and sixty-four," mused Sam. "I don't know whether I expected more or less. I guess our job would be easier if there was only one. But then again there could have been thousands, for all I know about business."

"I'm supposed to know about this kind of stuff," stated Donny. "I had no idea what I'd find. But two hundred and sixty-four's the number, at least as best as I can tell."

"These guys ought to be listed as an endangered species," Ski observed. "Only two hundred and sixty-four remaining."

"We've got to stop him," Kate mused, "before he wipes out an entire class of entrepreneur."

Donny went on to describe the system he had rigged up on his computer. He'd had some help from one of his clients, a geek now worth millions, who was thrilled to trade some programming time for a chance to snatch up a couple thousand extra shares of stock in the next IPO from Donny's firm.

With the new programming, Donny's computer automatically tracked trading volume in the stocks of the two hundred and sixty-four thinly traded companies he'd identified. If there was any unusual activity, the computer would flash a warning on Donny's terminal. If Donny didn't acknowledge the warning within thirty seconds, the computer would deliver an audio alarm. If Donny didn't acknowledge the audio alarm within 30 seconds, the computer would call him on his cell phone and issue a prerecorded verbal warning.

Sam and Ski were so impressed that they insisted Donny set his computer so it would call them on their cell phones too, as soon as any unusual stock activity was detected. Kate wanted Donny to leave her a phone message, as the idea of an automatic computer warning, well, that was just too creepy for her.

Donny handed Sam three large envelopes containing information on the two hundred and sixty-four companies he had targeted. Sam immediately handed the envelopes to Ski. Rank had some privileges.

At Sam's direction, Ski agreed to sift through the material and develop a standardized profile on each company and its "Key Man." Sam wanted a one-pager that gave him names, addresses, phone numbers, all the vital information they would need to warn the potential victims if Donny's system detected any unusual trading activity.

The companies that Donny had identified were scattered across the country. Sam wanted to contact the homicide squad chiefs everywhere there was a possible target so he'd have hands and feet on the ground if there was an alarm, but he realized that this effort would involve weeks of non-stop phone calls. He decided that the first thing he should do was compile a list of contacts in major cities and gather site maps for the possible targets located in LA.

Kate volunteered to help Ski organize the mountain of information he generated on the two hundred plus companies. It was the only thing Kate could think of to do, and she wanted desperately to help.

II

Three weeks later to the day, at 9:15 in the morning, Donny's alarm sounded. Donny was on the phone with a client and hadn't noticed the warning on his terminal. When he looked up at his computer screen, he felt as if someone had kicked him in the stomach.

Donny gasped and blurted to his client, "Something horrible has happened." Donny could only extract himself from the phone call by assuring his client that the "something horrible" had nothing to do with the stock market and that his client's investments weren't in jeopardy.

Sam and Ski were in the middle of a staff meeting when both their cell phones rang. They answered the calls in unison, and in unison, received the message from Donny's computer. Hastily excusing themselves from the meeting, Sam and Ski ran back to their cubicle to call Donny and see what was up.

Donny's direct line was busy the first time Sam dialed. Sam decided that Donny was probably trying to call them and that they should keep their line clear for a minute or two. Sam told Ski that if they didn't hear from Donny in the next couple of minutes, he wanted Ski to track down the nearest patrol car and have it diverted to Donny's office to "find him."

As Sam was delivering his instructions, the phone rang. It was Donny on the line.

There had been an unusual amount of activity in Zebron Industries' stock that morning. 40,000 shares had already changed hands.

Following the protocol they had previously established, as soon as Donny gave them the name of the possible target, he hung up and started looking into the trading activity to see if he could determine if it involved any short sales.

Sam started to pace. Ski nervously flipped to the back of the black three-ring binder he had set up containing all the one-pagers he'd compiled for Sam.

Zebron Industries. They were lucky.

Zebron Industries was located in Long Beach. They could cover this one themselves. Not have to rely on someone else's, eyes, ears, and instincts.

Ron Zebbrouski, founder of Zebron Industries and the potential victim, fit their risk profile to a tee. Zeb, a 44-year-old, former national spring-board diving champion, had developed a line of simple wooden toys that were now quite the rage with yuppie parents who wanted to inject something "real" into the spoiling of their precious, pampered, only children.

Sales of Zebron toys on the West Coast had grown exponentially over the past three years and the company was poised to launch a national product rollout. National distribution of Zebron toys would really put the company on the map.

Zeb was the company's chief designer as well as its centerfold, and the talking head that the regional business press loved to interview. He had been working on a new line of plush, yet down-to-earth, stuffed barnyard animals that would double the company's product line.

The buzz on the street was that, between the new product introduction planned for later in the year and the company's aspirations for national expansion, Zebron would experience triple-digit growth in both sales and profits for the foreseeable future. That was great news for the thousand or so investors who owned the 20% of the company Ron had sold off though a locally underwritten, Initial Public Offering from a few years earlier.

Ron had used the IPO proceeds to ramp up his production capacity in order to keep up with the demand for his wooden fire trucks, tractors, and delivery vans. He knew he'd have to sell off more of the company at some point to finance his expansion plans. But he was holding off as long as possible, since the price of Zebron's thinly traded stock kept soaring.

There was even talk on the street that one of the giant toy companies had its eye on Zebron. If that turned out to be the case, Ron Zebbrouski and his stockholders stood to make a killing from any buyout.

There hadn't been a lot of activity in Zebron Industries' stock because there were never many sellers. Most stockholders were zealous in their belief that Zebron was a long-term gold-mine worth holding. Typically, only a few thousand shares of stock changed hands in a week.

Donny's system was triggered when a 40,000 block of Zebron stock was traded. That sale was followed by the execution of another 30,000-share sale.

Preceding these two large stock transactions, a rumor had hit the Street that the investment bank that had underwritten Zebron's IPO was about to sell some of the stock they had acquired during the initial offering. Terms of the IPO had restricted the underwriter from selling any stock until now, and it made sense that they would want to take their profit in a stock that had already more than tripled in value. Besides, the smaller investors were glad to see some stock hit the street so they could increase their holdings.

The 70,000 shares cleared the market without any negative impact on Zebron's stock price. In fact, the "ask" price for Zebron Industries actually increased after the dust from the two big trades had settled.

No one realized, but Donny soon discovered, that these were not straight sales. While the large blocks of Zebron stock were in fact coming out of the underwriter's portfolio, the sales actually involved two short-sale arrangements that the underwriter had entered into with two corporate clients.

As soon as Donny confirmed that the two large transactions involved short sales, he placed an emergency call to Sam and Ski. Sam had been pacing around the small cubicle since Donny's first call, even though there were other cases he should have been working. Ski flipped through files, but his mind was on Zebron.

While he was still on the phone with Donny, Sam motioned to Ski, using the international sign for 'dial the phone.' Sam wanted Ski to use his cell phone to call Zebbrouski and warn him his life was in danger.

On his first try, Ski reached Zebron's automated telephone system. "*Thank you for calling Zebron industries. You have reached our automated receptionist. If you have a touch tone phone, enter 1 now. If you have a rotary phone, please stay on the line and an operator will help you.*" Ski hit 1.

"*Please choose from the following four options: If you are calling to place an order, please enter 1 now. If you are calling for customer service, please enter 2 now. If you are calling to verify employment or to check on employment opportunities at Zebron Industries, please enter 3 now. If you know the name of the party you wish to contact, please enter 4 for our automated directory.*" Ski hit 4.

"*You have entered Zebron's automated directory. Please enter the last four letters of the last name of the person you wish to contact.*" *Ski hit Z, E, B, R.*

"*You have made an incorrect entry. To try again, please enter 4. To speak to an operator, please press zero.*" As Ski scanned his write-up to check the proper spelling of Zebbrouski's last name, the line disconnected.

Ski immediately re-dialed Zebron's phone number. "*Thank you for calling Zebron Industries. You have …*" Ski hit 1.

"*You have reached Zebron Industries' automated …*" Ski hit 4.

"*You have entered Zebron's automated …*" Ski hit Z,E,B,B.

"Your call is being transferred."

"You have reached the office of Ron Zebbrouski. Ron is either on another call or away from his desk. Your call is important to Ron, so please leave your name, number and a short message and he'll get back with you as soon as possible. That is, unless Ron is designing a new toy, in which case it might be some time before he is able to return your call. But hey, no one wants to interrupt a toy genius at work. At the tone, please leave your message."

Ski hated all phone messages, but he especially hated messages that tried to be cute. Ski left a brief message identifying himself, leaving both his regular and cell phone numbers, and stating that this was an urgent matter that required immediate attention.

Sam had finished talking to Donny by the time Ski started dialing Zebron for the third time. "What's the problem?" asked Sam.

"Fucking voice mail!" Ski fumed.

With his third call, Ski just held on the line, waiting for a live operator. "Zebron Industries, may I help you?"

"Mr. Zebbrouski," Ski exhaled.

"Please hold ... Mr. Zebbrouski's line is busy. Would you care for his voice mail?"

"No, No!" Ski shouted into the receiver, "This is extremely urgent! Does Mr. Zebbrouski have a secretary or assistant I can talk to?"

"Ms. Fields is Mr. Zebbrouski's assistant, but she's on vacation this week," replied the phone receptionist. Trying to be helpful, she added, "Would you like Ms. Fields' voice mail?"

"No," continued Ski lowering his voice so as not to sound like a disgruntled customer. "I need to talk to someone who can get Mr. Zebbrouski on the line. This is urgent police business," he added, almost as an afterthought.

"I'll put you through to Sally McGreggor. She's Mr. Lawrence's secretary, but she's trying to help out while Jeanne is in Hawaii."

Receiving far more information than he needed, Ski asked politely, "Could you please just put me through to Ms. McGreggor?"

"Certainly," replied the voice on the phone, adding, as she'd been trained, "And thank you for calling Zebron Industries."

Sally McGreggor was already at her wit's end just trying to keep up with her own workaholic boss. Covering for Jeanne was pushing her over the edge. Every time Sally imagined Jeanne relaxing on a white sand beach, sharing a Mai Tai with some good looking, eligible bachelor from Kansas, she got even more upset.

She was in no mood to take some crank call from some jerk pretending to be a policeman, just to get a call through to Mr. Zebbrouski. "No, I'm sorry Mr. Zebbrouski isn't available. Would you like his voice mail?" she started politely. "No, I'm afraid that I can't interrupt Mr. Zebbrouski ... I'm sure it is urgent police business, but it'll have to wait until Mr. Zebbrouski finishes his conference call ... No, I don't know when he'll be finished. Sometimes these calls go on for hours ... I certainly will tell Mr. Zebbrouski that you called ... Yes, I have the number right here ... Yes, I'll certainly tell Mr. Zebbrouski not to leave the building without calling you first ... Yes, I understand that this is very important ... a matter of life and death ... Yes, Mr. Johnson, I've got all that ... Yes, Mr. Johnson I understand ... Yes, Mr. Johnson. And thank you for calling Zebron Industries," Sally concluded wearily.

Some bozo that one, thought Sally to herself. Thinks Ron's about to drop everything and take his call. Probably one of those cold-calling stock pushers who ring up every time Ron gets his name in the paper. Not today sucker. Not today.

And with that, Sally went back to filing and being pissed at Jeanne. For Sally, this week just couldn't get over fast enough.

III

Sam had gathered up his maps and site plans and, as soon as Ski ended his conversation, they headed out to grab a squad car. Sam told Ski exactly where he wanted to be dropped so that he could see anyone who might be aiming a triggering device into Zebron Industries' parking lot.

Armed with a badge and not just his voice, Ski would find Zebbrouski and escort his butt out the back of the building. They had radioed ahead and a patrol car was going to meet them at Zebron's rear exit, to whisk Zebbrouski back to headquarters. Ski would then join Sam as they waited for the killer to make a move.

Ron Zebbrouski really was on a conference call when Ski had been talking to Sally McGreggor. Even if he hadn't been, she would have used the same excuse.

For some reason, Sally had learned that no one ever insisted on being "put through" when one of the executives was on a conference call. Bankers, lawyers, and the buyers from major chains would usually insist on "holding" or having a meeting interrupted when they wanted to talk to one of her bosses. But, for some reason they always yielded to a conference call. So, when Sally was answering the phones in the executive offices at Zebron, there were lots and lots of "conference calls" in process.

Ron had wrapped up this particular call pretty quickly. It had been clear from the "get go" that the guys in New Jersey weren't ready to talk seriously about providing shelf space for Zebron toys in their stores. So after a five-minute conversation that wasn't going anywhere, Ron indicated that he thought the distributor, who wanted to carry Zebron's line of toys, and the boys in Jersey, who had the stores, should continue to work on a deal, but that he didn't have anything to add at the time. Ron excused himself from the call and moved on to a more rewarding use of his time.

Sally was down at the copier when Ron emerged from his office to head out for his regular Wednesday racquetball match with the one friend he still had from high school. It was unlikely that Sally would have given him Ski's message even if she <u>had</u> been at her desk since Ron hurried to catch the elevator that was about to leave without him. Sally still thought Ski's call was a crank.

Half-a-second sooner and Ron would have reached the elevator before the doors met. Having missed his ride, Ron, without the slightest hesitation, continued down the hall and headed into the stairwell. Already anticipating a satisfying victory, he bounded down two steps at a time.

After weaving in and out of freeway traffic for a couple of miles, Ski opted to crank up the siren and clear his path. Five more minutes and they'd be heading into Long Beach. He'd still be able to use the emergency strobe lights until they were within a few blocks of Zebron, but once they hit the city limits, he'd need to cut the siren. For the moment, the auditory commotion from his vehicle cleared the fast lane, and Sam and Ski were topping 85 m.p.h.

As he emerged from the stairwell, Ron caught a glimpse of Sandy Gains in the lobby waiting for an elevator. Sandy was a salesman's salesman. He always had a good story, and if he spotted Ron, it would be fifteen minutes in the telling.

Ski was perspiring as if he'd just run five miles. Sam was shuffling papers but unable to concentrate on any of the information he had in his lap. The freeway traffic congealed the instant Ski killed the siren. They were back to bobbing and weaving.

For an instant, Ron felt a twinge of guilt as he slipped back into the stairwell. Sandy was a good guy, and normally Ron enjoyed their little chats. But this was racquetball day. Sandy's story would have to wait.

Ski turned the squad car off the Long Beach Freeway and onto the Seaside Freeway heading toward the industrial area just east of San Pedro. Looming ahead was a towering pillar of black smoke.

Zebbrouski's car was still ablaze as they pulled into the Zebron Industries' parking lot.

Chapter 29

It was a somber gathering at Ted's that evening. Sam staked out their booth while Ski paced up and down the sidewalk in front of the bar until first Donny, then Kate arrived.

Ski was highly agitated and could hardly sit still. "We've gotta warn these guys Sam," Ski started, about to shake his index finger at Sam for emphasis. This was the first time Ski had ever raised his voice to Sam, and he quickly decided that adding finger pointing wasn't in order.

"Can't," answered Sam in a steely voice that sent a shiver up Ski's back. "What da ya mean, can't?" Ski flashed.

"Can't," Sam continued, "at least not yet."

"For Christ sakes, why not?" Ski sputtered.

"Word gets out that we're on to this guy and we'll never catch him," Sam stated matter-of-factly.

"Christ, Sam, these guys' lives are at stake ... we didn't do such a great job of catching the bastard today, and he was right in our back yard!" Ski uttered through clenched teeth. "I don't want to ever, ever, again drive up to some guy's business, or to his home, for Christ sake, and find he's just gotten toasted."

"Look, I know you're upset," Sam offered after a minute of silence. "We're all upset. But we can't rush out and tip our hand and let this guy know we're on to him. That's all I'm sayin'."

There was a prolonged silence in the booth. Finally, Ski looked directly into Sam's eyes and said, "Sam, these guys' lives are at risk. We have to tell them."

Sam started to speak but was cut off. "If we just sit here and do nothing, and let another one of these guys get blown to bits ... if that happened, if we weren't legally considered accessories to the murder, I'd consider us morally responsible."

"I'm not saying we just let these guys go about their daily routines as unsuspecting sitting ducks while we wait for this prick to strike again. All I'm saying is let's not fly off and blow this thing because we're upset. We've got some time before we have to put everyone on notice," Sam offered in his best calming voice.

"I'm not following you," said Kate, joining the conversation.

"Look," started Sam, "He doesn't strike every other day. He lets things cool down. That's what I mean by time."

Ski observed, "He's picking up steam. There's less and less time between attacks. And now he's hit three times in a row in the same metropolitan area, and he's never done that before."

"And?" asked Sam.

"And! What I'm saying is, he's changing his pattern," answered Ski.

Donny, feeling the need to participate in the discussion observed, "Maybe he's getting over-confident. Maybe he'll make a mistake."

Ski just shook his head and said, "Maybe he knows we're on to him, or maybe he just sees the end in sight and wants to wrap things up in a hurry."

Wanting to end this discussion, Sam jumped back in, "I'm not saying we don't tell the guys they're at risk. I'm not saying we don't tell them soon. All I'm sayin' is that we've got a little time. Let's take just a little time. Regroup. Come up with a new strategy. Then we can notify everyone who needs to know what's going on."

It was agreed that they'd take a couple of days to see if they could come up with any new ideas. They also agreed that more drinks were in order.

II

Kate ended up driving Ski home that evening. It was the first time anyone had seen Ski get really hammered. But after the day he'd had, Ski had made a conscious effort to get really hammered.

Kate would have stayed with Ski that evening. She would have held him tightly to let him know that what had happened that day wasn't his fault. Let him know things would be OK.

Kat was up for a sleepover as well. Ski's sensitivity had gotten to Kate. Kat was interested in other things.

But Katherine had watched Ski work his way from beer to rum-and-cokes and finally on to tequila shooters. Katherine knew that such a lethal mixture had a second life and would revisit Ski sometime, probably sooner rather than later, that night. Katherine wasn't about to clean up what was sure to be a serious mess.

Sam didn't even wait to hear from Ski the next day before reporting Ski'd be out sick. Ski, who'd spent most of the night crawling between his couch and the toilet, took refuge in his bedroom, where the extra blanket he had thrown over the small window kept the sunlight at bay.

Kate, can of chicken noodle soup in hand, dropped by around 1:00 pm just to make sure Ski was still with the living. Ski saw Kate's visit as some form of divine intervention and couldn't stop confessing his sins, vowing repeatedly he'd never drink again.

Based on Kat's prior experience, Kate realized Ski had yet to completely metabolize all the alcohol he had consumed. So she just gently patted him on the head and forgave him his sins. Kate's quiet reassurances and the chicken soup combined to put his mind at rest. And Ski finally relaxed into the first real peace he'd enjoyed since realizing they'd arrived too late to save Zebbrouski.

Kate started to tidy up Ski's apartment when she remembered what she'd likely find in the bathroom. Mother Teresa she wasn't, so after a superficial sweep of the living room, Kate whispered good-by and headed for the beach. She had her own thinking to do, and the sound of rolling surf always cleared her head.

Chapter 30

Most of the new money, the huge chunks of new money being churned out by a booming economy, was going into extremely conspicuous consumption, investments in venture capital funds, or back into the adolescent businesses that were creating all the new wealth. The little charitable giving coming from the new rich was directed mostly at the liberal causes of the moment. And those causes were valued in direct proportion to the "star" quality of the Hollywood celebrity, or the sports hero, or the fashion icon, who was passionately pushing the message.

Philanthropy was still part of the "old money" circle. But old money was stagnant. And therefore so were the charities and institutions that relied on its kindness.

Consequently, Terrance Newberry's generous donations to the organizations, foundations, and charitable trusts that offered him a seat on their Boards were seen as a breath of fresh air, a chance to add some new blood, rather than as an effort to buy his way into society. Besides, Terrance always offered sound investment advice. And, while he was generally viewed as dour and unsophisticated, he certainly looked the part of "old money."

After fading to black back East, Terrance Newberry emerged on the Southern California social scene, the product of extremely successful personal investing.

While the previous Terrance had fit in with the Young Turk crowd, the reinvented Terrance was definitely "old school." Everything from his Beverly Hills mansion, complete with English butler and assorted other Central Casting staff, to the satin smoking jacket he wore even though he didn't smoke, to the polo horses he didn't ride, all shouted "old money."

Cocaine and scotch had been replaced by the occasional brandy. Sleeping around, or not sleeping at all, had been replaced by a monogamistic relationship featuring dates at the country club, appearances at the opera, and evenings at the theater.

A Bentley was his car of choice, even though any normal male his age, and with his money, would have driven a Ferrari. Dinner at Terrance's would likely feature Chateaubriand, Welshire pudding, and a heavy, old Bordeaux instead of the California cuisine and fresh Chardonnay his chef preferred.

But no matter what trappings Terrance draped about his persona, society knew his place. Old money is old money. New money is new money.

Terrance could try as hard as he wanted. But the bottom line was that it would take a few generations before Terrance's lineage would be accepted as "old money." Until then, Terrance would be tolerated, appreciated for what he'd accomplished financially, and accepted as a source of fresh cash.

But a member of society? No, not that. Terrance might be a financial equal, but not a peer.

Not now. Not ever.

II

It was Kate who first raised Terrance as a suspect in the car bombings. Serendipity played a huge role.

After Donny developed his list of individuals who fit the 'short sale' target profile, Kate started helping Ski organize his files on the potential targets. In her spare time, she began researching the private and social lives of some of the higher profile executives who were at risk. As she combed the society pages, she would occasionally come across an article that mentioned her grandfather. Kate started collecting the excerpts, thinking that one day she'd compile them into a scrapbook to help keep her grandfather's memory alive.

Every time the investigation hit a dead end, Kate's sense of loss associated with her grandfather's death would peak. She hadn't yet forced herself to take the existential step of organizing the clips she had collected on Jonathan and committing them to the cold, fixed format of a scrapbook. But whenever Kate was really down, she would flip through the various newspaper and magazine articles, looking for pictures of her grandfather that would give her comfort.

It was during one of these sessions, after Ron Zebbrouski's murder, that Kate realized there was one picture in her collection she always avoided. She finally forced herself to confront it.

III

"It was there all along," Kate explained to Sam and Ski in as animated a delivery as she had mustered in some time. Standing in Sam and Ski's cubicle, Kate wildly waved the picture she clutched in her right hand. "It was right there under my nose, but I couldn't bear to look at it," she continued.

Sam took control: "OK, we're all ears. But you got to slow down so we can follow you. OK, deep breath. One point at a time. Start at the beginning."

Kate followed Sam's advice, took a deep breath, gathered her thoughts, and started. "I've been collecting these articles that mention my grandfather. You know, to make a scrapbook or something." She stopped for a moment, took another deep breath and continued, "Anyway, there was this one picture I couldn't ever bear to look at." Another deep breath, "because ... well, because ... it showed my grandfather the way most people will remember him," Kate paused.

Feeling more like a psychologist than a detective, Ski inquired, "And just how is it that most other people will remember your grandfather?"

"As a bitter, intolerant, old man!" Kate exclaimed. "As a bitter, old man," she exhaled, slumping over in her chair.

After a moment, Kate straightened her back and continued, "but he really wasn't like that. That was just the face he put on in public. I think he really thought that it was his right ... in fact I think he thought it was almost his responsibility ... to act rude in public."

Kate could tell from the blank expressions on both Sam's and Ski's faces that they'd missed the point and she'd need to explain further. "It may seem hard to comprehend from the outside, but the really rich have this, like, unwritten code of conduct."

"Very rich kids are supposed to be insufferable. Very rich boys are expected to be irresponsible. Very rich girls are taught to be proper and, above all else, unattainable. Very rich parents are expected to be unhappy and overburdened by the demands of being rich. Very rich matrons finally get a chance to be generous and are understanding of everyone else's faults. But very rich old men are supposed to realize that everyone is just waiting for them to die. So they are mean, and cranky, and self-fulfilling. They make everyone <u>want</u> them to just die, so that everyone else can move up a notch in the very rich scheme of things."

Sam and Ski were speechless, so Kate continued, "Grandpa acted like he was supposed to act in public. He was short-tempered, mean, and condescending. It was his role, and he fulfilled his obligation to play that role."

"But in private," Kate explained. "In private, he was just a sweet, frightened, generous, little old man."

"I want to remember the loving grandfather I knew. Not the mean and demanding patriarch Jonathan Newberry was to the rest of the world."

Kate handed the picture she had been clutching to Ski and added, "So I couldn't bear to look at this picture of grandpa that was taken a couple of years ago, because it's the worst of the "public" Jonathan. The Jonathan I don't want to remember."

The newspaper photo was of Jonathan Newberry, in full tuxedo, lashing out at a younger man, also dressed for a night at the opera. Jonathan had clearly just ripped his left arm from the younger man's grip and looked like he might be about to raise the cane he held in his right hand. Jonathan's eyes flashed. And while the younger man had started to cower, his expression was clearly that of intense hatred.

The caption under the photo stated, "Head of Newberry clan puts black sheep in his place."

Ski read the caption out loud. He started to read the article but Kate snatched it back before he could finish the first sentence.

"You don't need to read it all. I'll tell you what went on. At least what came down through the family rumor mill," Kate continued, settling back in her chair.

"Terrance Newberry, at least that's what he calls himself, is the other man in the photo. He and his relatives have been an embarrassment to the family for years. Actually, generations."

After catching her breath, Kate continued, "One of the original Newberry Brothers — the brothers who started amassing the Newberry fortune by cornering the market on South American rubber — had two sons. One of the sons was clearly cut from the Newberry cloth and grew up to make the family proud. The other son was not very bright, good looking, or energetic and became an alcoholic ne'er-do-well who was a family embarrassment.

This second son had a wife and children, but like most of the Newberry men of the time, had a mistress on the side. Well, the mistress, like many other mistresses, got pregnant, but unlike other mistresses, didn't have the problem taken care of.

She disappeared, had the child, and then returned expecting to be embraced by the Newberry family. Well, that just wasn't going to happen. She took the money the Newberrys offered to get her and her son out of town, and everyone thought that was the end of it."

Kate stood up and started to pace around the tiny cubicle. "And, while they did disappear, that wasn't the end of it."

"Apparently this bastardized offshoot of the Newberry lineage moved up-state and began to fester in the shadow of the Newberry's growing fame and fortune. They developed their own family folklore that was passed down from generation to generation.

"Over time, the folklore on our side of the family tree transformed us from being the descendants of common merchants who had profited from political connections and slave labor in a far off land into aristocratic members of high society. The folklore on the bastard side of the family transformed them into the victims of an epic social wrong, instead of the descendants of a common sexual indiscretion."

Still pacing, Kate continued, "All of this simmered until it was time for Terrance's mother to fit him with the family's ball and chain. Terrance's mother accepted that burden with a vengeance.

"She relentlessly pursued her claim to a share of the wealth and status the Newberrys by this time enjoyed. She went so far as to actually sue the family.

"Well, she won the right to use the family name. But the court denied her any monetary damages. And she certainly wasn't added to the guest list for family outings."

Kate took her seat and reached for the picture she'd set down on Ski's desk. "I guess she passed on this insane obsession of being a 'Newberry' to Terrance. All of a sudden, Terrance bursts onto the social scene, making noises that he belongs. He's showing up everywhere, creating these uncomfortable situations for the family."

"One night he tried to corner Jonathan as he was leaving the opera, demanding that Jonathan stop blocking his attempt to reconcile with the rest of the family. Well, Grandpa put him in his place. Told him that at best he's the bad seed from some distant memory of a syphilitic old drunk who didn't deserve to call himself a Newberry.

"I guess Terrance started going on about all the money he's got and his rightful place in society, and Jonathan cut him down to size, telling him, and everyone else leaving the opera, that his money, no matter where it came from or how much of it he had, didn't count for shit. Jonathan went on that it was an embarrassment for Terrance to be using the family name, just 'cause some hack judge said he could.' And that, in Jonathan's opinion, 'which still counted for something in this town,' Terrance Newberry, or 'whatever his real name was,' wasn't fit to curb a Newberry dog."

"Jesus," Ski offered, "laid into him pretty good!"

"Apparently that wasn't the worst of it," Kate continued looking down at the newspaper article. "Through his public outburst, Jonathan put the rest of the local society crowd on notice that Terrance Newberry was persona-non-grata.

"Terrance had apparently been buying his way into the social scene through generous donations to a multitude of causes. And while the museums, galleries and charities continued to accept his cash and invite him to their public functions, the invitations to sit on Boards, attend private receptions, and be seen at the right places, at the right times, and with the right people, all those trappings of social standing ceased.

"Jonathan, with one wave of his hand, had not only banished Terrance from the family but from the social position he had been bred to covet. He must have been crushed," Kate added as her voice drifted off.

Sam wheeled his chair over to where Kate was sitting and took both of her hands in his. "Kate ... dear ... I can see why this Terrance guy would have a thing for your grandfather, and we'll certainly look into any connection he might have with your grandfather's murder. But Kate, honey, this doesn't have anything to do with the 'short sale' murders."

Kate started to speak, but Sam continued, "Remember, we determined from the get-go that Jonathan's murder didn't have anything in common with the others.

"Kate, Heulenberg is our man. We just need to find him."

"We determined," Kate responded, "that grandpa didn't have the 'short sale' victims' profile. We never concluded that there wasn't anything else in common. The bombs were similar. There's nothing that says the 'short sale' killer and grandpa's assassin couldn't be the same person, but just have a different motive when it came to Jonathan."

"I guess that's a possibility," Ski observed.

"That's my point!" exclaimed Kate. "Terrance had a clear motive for wanting to kill Jonathan. And a different, but very real motive, for killing the others also."

"And that motive is?" queried Sam sarcastically before he really thought about his question.

"Follow the money, Sam," Kate answered. "Follow the money."

IV

Kate went on to explain that, as far as she could tell, no one knew where all of Terrance's money came from. He had just popped up on the social scene one day, spreading large sums of cash around like it was coming from a bottomless pit.

Kate observed there was a money trail here that Sam just might want to follow if he wanted to find a motive linking Terrance to the 'short sale' bombings. Sam had to agree.

The three also agreed on assignments aimed at uncovering a money trail, or any connections Terrance might have to any of the 'short sale' victims or the companies that had been ruined by the 'Key Men' murders.

Sam would hit the police records to see what kind of information, if any, there was on Terrance Newberry. Ski was already working on getting copies of Karl Heulenberg's tax returns, so he would expand his effort to include Terrance's tax records to see if they revealed the source of his wealth. Donny would go back through the information he had collected to see if Terrance's name popped up anywhere. And, Kate would make inquires to see if anyone who had come into social contact with Terrance had any clues regarding his finances.

Chapter 31

For awhile, Arnie appreciated being in the State of California's care. He got three meals a day. The staff was generally nice to him. And, they made him take the medication that quieted the voices down to a whisper.

As Arnie's head cleared, he began listening to other voices ... those of other inmates.

Those voices talked about how the nurses mixed poison in with the medicine. About how the orderlies put powder in the food that made your dick stay limp. About how the doctors drilled into your skull to see what was going on inside your head.

Arnie didn't like what those voices were saying. He didn't want to be poisoned. He didn't want a limp dick. He didn't want some doc looking inside his head.

So Arnie started palming his medicine. He stopped eating, and he wouldn't allow himself to go to sleep.

It wasn't long before the old voices returned. The familiar voices. The voices that told Arnie it was time to move on.

Arnie just walked out of the facility. It shouldn't have been that easy. But it was.

Following the directions in his head, Arnie kept the sun on his right, and headed south.

Arnie, who had been lost inside the mental health system, was now lost outside. One would think someone who'd been diagnosed as an extreme schizophrenic and who had either been a part of — or at least witness to — a vicious crime would be under closer watch. But he wasn't.

The reports of Arnie's disappearance got caught up in the politics and the bureaucracy of the State's mental health operations. Once the asses got covered, Arnie's 'situation' got papered over. From that point on, he couldn't have been a freer man had he been declared cured and escorted out the front door by the Chief Clinician.

II

Arnie wasn't getting very far. The stay at the mental facility had compromised his circadian rhythms, and he was now rising at dawn and bedding down for the evening shortly after dusk. Arnie's hospitalization had been effective in one sense. It put him on a sleep cycle that would be considered 'normal.'

Keeping the sun on his right meant Arnie would strike out on a northern course in the morning, reverse direction some time between noon and one o'clock, and end up in the evening in the general vicinity of where he started.

Depending on the cloud cover, his energy level, and the vagaries of the day, Arnie might move a little farther north, a little farther south, closer to, or further inland from the coastline.

For awhile, he slept on the beach, which was near to where he'd been picked up in the alley, half-covered in blood. The voices told him to stay away from that alley.

One day at the beach, he saw a young woman in the parking lot putting on a new pair of shoes. She was alone and the beach was deserted.

The voices started telling him what he should do to this woman. The voices were arguing in Arnie's head. They said so many things, shouted so many directions, screamed so many obscenities that Arnie got confused.

His head pounded. His heart pounded. His prick pounded.

He had to sit down. He had to sort out all the instructions and get some clear directions.

Suddenly, the voices were in unison. The decision was unanimous and Arnie knew what he had to do. He was set to act.

But she was gone. She was just a speck on the horizon. He'd never catch up to her.

The voices told Arnie to be patient. They told him to wait. She'd return. He'd be ready this time.

Then the voices got bored. They changed their mind. The voices wanted potato chips. One of those little bags of potato chips.

Arnie would have to start panhandling. Unless he could find the place where they held the Wings of Vengeance meetings.

Arnie wandered off. Sun on his right. Heading south.

Chapter 32

Kate was again the first to develop a positive lead on Terrance Newberry.

Sam had determined that Terrance was free of any criminal record. Terrance was so clean he didn't even have any moving violations. If it weren't for the mandatory LA parking tickets, Terrance Newberry didn't exist as far as the police were concerned.

Donny hadn't fared any better in his search of company records. He couldn't find a single entry, reference, or footnote that tied Terrance to any of the companies that had been devastated by the 'short sale' tragedies, or the interlocking group of investment firms that initiated the short sales transactions. But then again, he'd never been able to directly link Heulenberg to the transactions, either.

Ski also struck out in his effort at obtaining Karl's and Terrance's tax records. The IRS had tightened its rules on the release of information, even to the police, after news of agents nosing around in celebrities' tax returns had hit the press. Ski needed a subpoena before the agency would release anything. While that was in process, Ski had nothing to report to the group when they gathered at Ted's to hear Kate's news.

In her search of the society columns, Kate hadn't found any information on the source of Terrance's wealth. Terrance had been understandably coy when it came to his finances. "Investments," was his standard response to questions from Trustees or reporters about his business interests.

But Kate had learned from the family rumor mill that Terrance had attended an L.A. university after being spurned by Stanford. "Typical," thought Kate, and then went about combing yearbooks and graduation records.

Kate quickly identified Terrance as a USC graduate with a degree in finance. Through alumni records, she traced him to his job at the New York brokerage firm.

When Kate entertained the rest of the group with the tale of how she impersonated a loan processor in order to get information on Terrance's past from the brokerage company, the group was reduced to tears.

She had pretended to be new on the job and had invented a story that she just needed some basic information to complete a loan file so Terrance could close on a house he was buying. She went on and on as to how she'd screwed up by not getting the information sooner and added that she could lose her job, which, as a single mom, she couldn't afford to lose if she didn't get the loan closed, NOW!

Kate had cleverly called the brokerage house at 12:30 East Coast time, guessing that the person with the least seniority would be covering the phones during lunch. Her timing couldn't have been better.

The entire human resources department was in the hands of a clerk when Kate's call came through. The clerk knew she wasn't supposed to give out any information over the phone but, as a single mom herself, she couldn't ignore Kate's alleged plight. Besides, just that morning, she'd been shown how to access the computerized personnel records, records that weren't considered as sensitive as the employee files kept under lock and key in the boss' office.

So, the clerk rationalized that she could help out another traveler in the slow lane of single-momdom and practice her data retrieval skills all at the same time. What could be wrong with that?

Kate learned that Terrance had been a research analyst with the firm. He'd only worked there two and a half years when he resigned for reasons not listed on the computer. His annual base salary at the time he left the firm was $86,900 per year. The previous year he earned $82,500 in base salary and was paid a $12,000 bonus at year end. When he left the firm, he was paid a $4,500 bonus, which would have been greater had he stayed through the full year.

The clerk couldn't give out any personal information. "That's not allowed." But she could tell Kate, off the record, that there was a question mark behind the "eligible for re-hire" entry on Terrance Newberry's computerized employment record.

Terrance Newberry had walked away from what, in New York terms, would be considered a subsistence wage job. His stake consisted of a $4,500 bonus. Less than nine years later, he resurfaced in LA social circles as a multi-millionaire.

"Follow the money," concluded Kate. "Looks like it leads a path to Terrance Newberry's door."

II

After their meeting at Ted's, the group took on additional assignments. Armed with the new information, Ski would renew his efforts to obtain the subpoena he needed for the tax records. Donny planned to contact Terrance's former employer and, posing as a potential employer, see what additional information he could develop. Kate would dig further into Terrance's social life to see if she could find any more links to his past.

After they had gathered whatever additional information they could find, Sam and Ski planned to interview Terrance. Had Martin and Sizemore dug a little deeper in their investigation of Jonathan Newberry's car bombing, they would have uncovered the public incident that resulted in Terrance's social blackballing and they would have certainly talked to Terrance about the matter. But they hadn't.

So it wouldn't be unusual for two detectives who had taken over the investigation, Sam and Ski, to now contact Terrance ... Terrance who had had a public fight with a murder victim ... under the guise of wrapping up loose ends in what was otherwise a dead-end investigation.

Frustrated with his inability to track down Karl Heulenberg, Sam was thrilled to have someone to interview. There was some risk in contacting Terrance but they planned to limit their questions to the 'opera incident.' They hoped Terrance wouldn't realize that he was a possible suspect in Jonathan's death, much less in all the 'short sale' murders.

"He may have already made one mistake," Sam stated. "We have to give him a chance to make more."

"What mistake?" asked Donny.

"Well, if he's our killer," Sam started.

"He killed my grandfather out of hate," Kate finished.

Ski added, "He broke his pattern."

"If he's our guy, he's figured out a horrible, but ingenious way to get rich," offered Sam. "If he'd stuck with his original plan, no one would have ever caught on."

"But," Kat flashed, "if he hated my grandfather, my family, at such a primal level that he had to lash out ... if he made that mistake ... we'll nail him."

III

Ski finally obtained a subpoena for Karl's and Terrance's tax records covering the past several years. He'd contacted the IRS and hoped to have the records in hand within a couple of days. Then he and Kate, based on her business school background, would see if they could trace either Karl's or Terrance's income. If not, maybe they could at least build a case for tax fraud. That would give them a way to get a possible killer off the streets while they continued their 'short sale' investigation.

Donny managed a chat with Terrance's former boss at the brokerage house. His brief interview didn't yield any new information.

"Terrance was a hard worker. He was kind of a loner, but didn't have any problems working with the other analysts or brokers."

Nothing specific. Nothing that could lead to a lawsuit. The kind of lawsuits that come about when someone doesn't get hired because of something a former employer said. Or the kind that can even result from someone hiring a former employee, based on a glowing recommendation, and the new employer sues when the employee doesn't work out.

Every time Donny tried to probe for useful information, the reply was, "You'll have to ask Terrance about that." Or, "I don't really remember; Terrance can probably fill you in on that."

Donny tried to find someone else in the firm who would be more helpful. But there had been a one hundred percent staff turnover in the analysis department in the past nine years, so none of the analysts Donny contacted knew Terrance. As he probed around the organization looking for someone who had, the receptionists began to recognize Donny's voice, and stopped putting his calls through.

Kate managed to pick up bits and pieces of information here and there, but nothing substantial. She learned some inside dirt on Terrance's steady girl. Plenty of money of her own, but new money, just like Terrance's. No real social standing.

A vacation home somewhere back East, probably Martha's Vineyard. Talk of a place in the Caymans.

No one was sure of much of anything. No one really knew much about Terrance other than he just showed up, all of a sudden, and wanted to be one of 'them.'

He had the money. He was better than those nouveau computer geeks who didn't care about culture or social standing.

But Terrance Newberry was someone who no one ever took the time, or made the effort, to know. He was OK. He was tolerable.

At least until that 'thing' with the real Newberrys. Then he was invisible.

From Wall Street to Beverly Hills, Terrance Newberry was a memorable figure nobody could remember. Kate found it impossible to dig up details on a person's life who was no longer considered significant.

There weren't going to be any revelations. No smoking guns. No more mistakes.

It was time to confront Terrance. Time to throw a little doubt, a little fear in his direction. Time to push him and see if he'd make a mistake.

Chapter 33

When Slip first heard about Arnie through the White Wings' network, he knew he needed to arrange for Arnie to be transferred to his unit. There were only so many implements like Arnie around, and Slip liked to keep his toolbox full.

Arnie was a Stradivarius, a Steinway. Alone ... an inanimate object. But in the hands of a master ... an instrument of God.

Slip would make his music through Arnie like he had through those he had mastered before. He'd play Arnie and draw out God's sweet music. God's sweet ... vengeful ... horrible ... apocalyptic music.

But Arnie hadn't been on the bus when it arrived. He hadn't been heard from for days. When he did surface he was immediately grabbed by the cops. Slip would have to wait. Or he'd have to find another tool.

Slip could wait, or he could tune a new instrument. Either way, he was fine. He had his targets. He had time. They weren't going anywhere and neither was he.

II

While Slip's Wings of Vengeance brethren were drawn to the intense flame of his very public hatred, it would have been interesting to see how they would have felt about his secret hidden life. Some would have felt betrayed. Some would have been amused. All would have been confused.

While there was always more than enough hatred to go around, Slip was the magnifying glass through which the venom of the White Wings of Vengeance's was focused on business leaders, capitalist superstars, the corporate elite who were sucking the life out of the working class. The bastards who controlled everything. The worthless dogs who were more interested in reading the financial pages than in helping some poor family who could be dying in the street, right before their eyes.

None the less, he was one of them. Well, not really a member of the financial elite. But the settlement from the automobile accident set up a trust fund he still lived off of ... a trust fund that was substantial enough to elevate Slip several rungs above the working class he claimed to champion.

III

"The Lizster," as he called her, was the only investment advisor Slip had used after gaining control of the trust fund. He liked her.

She never commented negatively on his shaved head or singular black leather attire. She never asked what Slip did with the funds he withdrew or the wire transfers he made from his account. And best of all, she made solid investments. So much so that, no matter how much he spent, every quarterly statement delivered to Slip's secret P.O. box yielded a balance greater than the previous.

Had Slip ever contemplated his life after he completed his mission, life after the White Wings of Vengeance, the trust fund might have been a quandary. But the infrared focus of his hatred so consumed his consciousness that he never thought about a future beyond doing what he knew he had to do.

For Slip there was no future. There was only now. There was only loneliness. There was only doing what he had to do for his twin.

Solomon's death created a void that was impossible to fill. Without parents or his twin,

Slip struggled. Between his guilt over surviving the crash and the emptiness of his life, Slip and thoughts of suicide were constant companions. But he didn't take his own life. He had the images seared in his brain that told him he needed to live. He needed to get even.

For now, the trust fund was another tool. Another implement for carrying out his mission.

Chapter 34

Behind the massive wrought iron gate and ivy-covered stone wall was the meandering drive to the main house. The stately oaks, acres of manicured lawn, and formal gardens belied the fact that Terrance's estate was actually in the heart of Los Angeles.

At the end of the cobblestone drive was Terrance Newberry's home. A structure of such substance that it created an instant and lasting impression of gravity.

Built in the 30's by one of the first real stars of talking pictures, the three-story mansion looked like it belonged on a Scottish moor, rather than in California. More a manor than a home, the property had originally been designed with extensive guest lists in mind, and parties that ran for days, not hours.

The main house could easily accommodate thirty couples. The guest cottages, another twenty.

To say that Terrance, his butler, chef, two house cleaners, and three full-time gardeners rattled around the estate was an understatement. The top floor of the main home was never used. Besides the master suite, no one even ventured up to the second floor, except to clean. No more than a quarter of the main floor was ever in use. The guest cottages were maintained, but for no real purpose.

Terrance had been planning a party, an extravaganza befitting his home, when his fall from social grace rendered his 'coming out' moot. So, except in the memories of the few guests who had been to intimate dinner parties, the trustees and foundation directors who had made personal solicitations, and his one steady girlfriend, Elizabeth, the house, the gardens, the majestic setting, everything behind the massive ivy-covered walls didn't exist to the outside world.

Terrance was in his study when Sam and Ski arrived. Their visit wasn't unexpected as they had called ahead for an appointment.

Oscar, Terrance's very English butler, seated the two detectives in the foyer before leaving to inform Mr. Newberry that his appointment had arrived. The opulence of the entry rotunda, the ante-bellum stairway that swept up to the

second and then the third floors, the gilded por-
traits of someone's ancestors, all left Sam and Ski
speechless.

The rich aren't immune from killing off a
spouse now and again, so prior investigations had
exposed Sam to some pretty snazzy houses. The
Malibu homes with their ultra-modern decor and
ocean views to-die-for had impressed him the
most. But this palace, well, it took the cake.

Ski had led an architecturally sheltered life
and had never seen anything like Terrance's home
in real life. After being overwhelmed by the size
and scale of everything in his line of sight, Ski
was struck by how weird it must be to live alone
in a museum.

Ski would have preferred something more
spacious than the closet-for-an-apartment he
lived in. But he liked the idea that an empty pizza
box blended nicely with his decor. You could wear
dirty sneakers in a place like his.

Overwhelmed by the coldness of the structure, Ski began to fidget. He found it increasingly
harder to breath normally. So he was glad when
Oscar returned. "Mr. Newberry is just finishing
up a call," the butler announced. "He'll be able to
see you shortly. Can I offer you gentlemen some
coffee, or possibly some iced tea?"

Sam asked for coffee. Ski indicated that he
would appreciate a glass of water.

"Cream or sugar with your coffee?"

"A little of both, please."

"Ice and a little lemon with your water?"

"Some ice would be nice."

"I'll fetch your beverages and then see if Mr. Newberry has completed his conversation."

II

Oscar escorted Sam and Ski down a long hall, past the ballroom, the music room, and the game room, and finally to Terrance's study.

The massive study would have been quite overbearing if it hadn't been for the floor-to-ceiling windows and French doors that opened onto a terrace overlooking one of the manicured formal gardens. A second set of open, interior French doors connected the study with the library.

The library caught Ski's eye, with its mahogany, floor-to-fifteen-foot-ceiling bookshelves, leather bound editions, deep maroon soft leather couches, and marble fireplace. For an instant, he could imagine lounging on one of the couches, fire in the fireplace, cup of hot chocolate in one hand and a good page-turner in the other. In the same instant, he realized his humble collection of paperbacks looked more at home on his plank and cinder-block shelves than they would in some small corner of that Monticello-ish setting.

Ski was snapped back into the moment as introductions were exchanged.

Sam explained that they were wrapping up a few loose ends on the Jonathan Newberry tragedy.

"Are you aware of Jonathan Newberry's untimely death?" Sam asked Terrance.

"Certainly," Terrance responded without the slightest flinch. "Tragic."

"Mr. Newberry," started Sam.

"Please call me Terrance."

"Terrance," Sam continued. "We're talking to all of Jonathan's relatives to see if anyone can shed any light on this case. We would have talked to you sooner but, frankly, your name didn't come up when we initially checked with the next-of-kin and we just recently became aware of your connection to the family.

"To tell you the truth, we haven't come up with much to go on. We're just hoping to pick up some kind of a lead that could develop into something. Can you think of anything that might help us with this case?"

Terrance, who was seated behind a massive walnut desk, leaned forward, rested both his elbows on the desk, and stated very matter-of-factly, "I'm afraid I can't be of much help to you detectives. I wasn't at all close to Jonathan."

Pretty cool character thought Sam. "Is that right?"

"Listen," Terrance continued, "if you haven't heard it already, there was no love lost between us. In fact, I had a pretty big blow-up with Jonathan the last time I saw him."

"Is that right?" Sam stated flatly, his eyes focused on the note he was making in his pad.

"I'm embarrassed about it now, but yes, we had an unfortunate incident."

"What was that all about?" asked Sam, now studying Terrance's face for some sign of guilt.

"It's really a personal matter," Terrance stated, and then added, "Jonathan, and his side of the family, refused to acknowledge that my side of the family even existed. I wanted to be accepted by the other Newberrys and Jonathan stood in the way."

"And so you fought with him?"

"Well, you don't really fight with an old man, you know. I mean, I raised my voice to him on one occasion. It was a foolish thing to do. As I said, I'm embarrassed the whole thing even happened. But if Jonathan didn't want me as a part of the clan, so be it. It wasn't that big of a deal to me." After finishing his little speech, Terrance smiled at Ski and settled back into his high-backed leather chair.

"And that was the end of it?" Sam asked, exercising a great deal of restraint.

"That was that."

Sam leaned forward in his chair and asked, "Can you think of anything that might help us wrap up this investigation?"

"No, I really can't." As he rose from his chair, Terrance stated coolly, "Now, if you gentlemen don't have any other questions, I do need to make some travel arrangements."

Oscar stepped through the door to the study as if on cue. Terrance had obviously completed his part of the interview and was about to leave when Sam asked offhandedly, "So you didn't have any part in Jonathan's murder?"

"For Christ sakes, no!" exclaimed Terrance. "I told you, we had a quarrel. I'm sure lots of people quarreled with Jonathan. He was a disagreeable, stubborn old fool. But just because we quarreled doesn't mean I wished him dead. I'm sure there were lots of people who profited from Jonathan's death. I certainly wasn't one of them. I'd suggest you check out the relatives who were in his will."

Shaking his head as he strolled from the study, Terrance concluded, "Oscar, could you please show these gentlemen out?"

III

Easing the squad car down the cobbled drive, past the manicured lawns and the stately oaks, Sam was the first to speak, "Cool customer that one."

"Creepy cool," Ski mumbled.

As they passed through the massive wrought iron gates, Sam observed, "He knew we knew about his fight with Jonathan. Or at least he figured that we'd hear about it sooner or later. So he gets it right out there. Tells us just enough so that we think he's bein' straight. Then passes the whole thing off as a little family tiff. Nothing of any consequence."

Taking in mental images of the neighborhood as if it was a foreign country, Ski stated absentmindedly, "Voice never cracked, didn't break a sweat ... to sit there and chat with two cops ... well, if he is involved in this, that was quite a performance."

"I'm just afraid all we did today was tip him off," Ski added, closing his eyes and leaning his head back against the headrest.

"We at least accomplished something."

"That being?" Ski inquired, his eyes still closed.

"Well, while you and our buddy Terrance were pretending neither of you knew the other knew about Terrance's fight with Jonathan, I was checking out Terrance's trash."

"That's weird, Sam."

"It may be weird, but you never know what you'll discover if you keep your eyes open and don't just look, but really see." Sam continued, "In this case, what I saw was an envelope from one of those brokerage houses Donny identified as a source of the 'short sale' trades."

Ski's eyes shot open and he sat up straight, "No shit?"

"No shit," Sam answered. "Couldn't make out any of the writing, but I'd swear the logo on the envelope that was sitting there in Terrance's waste basket was the same as the logo on one of the reports Donny dredged up."

"Christ, Sam, that's great!" Ski exclaimed, then added, "But what's it mean?"

Sam was quick to answer, "Doesn't mean anything yet. But it could be a way to link Terrance to the 'short sales,' and link the 'short sale' profits to Terrance's newfound wealth. I don't know what it means yet. But at least it's a place to start."

IV

Sam decided to stake out Terrance's mansion. It was a difficult assignment because they couldn't very well just park across the street without being pretty obvious.

In the city, where everything's in clear view, nothing is noticed. There's always an empty office, apartment or parking space where the private work of a stakeout can proceed in public.

However, a neighborhood of fine homes, carefully planned privacy, and little traffic isn't conducive to innocuous snooping. So Sam and Ski took turns cruising the tree-lined lane that ran in front of Terrance's property. They took turns casually strolling the neighborhood. They were clearly out of place.

They spent so much time on the move that they couldn't really keep an eye on Terrance's property. And, it was obvious they wouldn't go unnoticed for long in a neighborhood where everyone's place and pattern were as established as the stately oaks that lined the streets.

Sam was frustrated. He had been setting up stakeouts for years and had never encountered a situation where he couldn't blend into the surroundings. But here, everything was just too perfect.

Unburdened by the baggage of years of experience, Ski quickly saw an easy alternative to Sam's traditional stakeout strategy. They weren't looking for a pattern to Terrance's comings and goings. They weren't looking for shady characters slipping into or out of the estate under the cover of darkness.

They weren't looking for any unusual activity. All they wanted to know was when Terrance's mail was delivered and when his trash was set out for pickup, since Sam's plan was to rifle Terrance's mail and pick through his trash.

Sam knew that even if they found some incriminating evidence, it wouldn't stand up in court. He needed something concrete, something tangible, something other than speculation if they were going to be able to continue on with their investigation.

So Ski, in his very best 'white' voice, the 'white' voice he'd used to deliver certain punch lines when telling certain jokes to his black friends back at JC, called up the local post office and sanitation company. Posing as a soon-to-be new homeowner in Terrance's neighborhood, it took Ski all of ten minutes to determine the schedules Sam wanted.

Sam was genuinely pleased that Ski had an easy solution to a problem that had stumped him. Like any good partnership, one needs to see what the other can't. There was hope for this one.

Armed with Ski's time schedule, the detectives were able to plan a jog past Terrance's property just as the mail was being delivered.

For four days in a row, the mailman passed by the mailbox built into the gate at the entrance to Terrance's drive without leaving a single piece of mail. Not a bill. Not a letter. Not a catalog. Not even a credit card solicitation.

During his original stakeout, Sam had observed Oscar leaving the estate at 9:30 and returning about 10 minutes later. Now he realized that Oscar's morning trip was to a post office box, where all of Terrance's mail was collected.

There'd be no illegal search of Terrance's mail. No way to quietly intercept some correspondence from one or more of the trading companies that had executed the 'short sales.'

In a sense they were luckier with Terrance's garbage. Oscar didn't take the trash directly to a landfill.

And while the trash they spirited away one morning contained the roast duck carcass, empty caviar tin, and empty cognac bottle you might expect to find in a rich person's garbage, it didn't contain a single unshredded piece of paper.

Any paper product that had passed through Terrance's possession had been shredded to a consistency that was so fine it wouldn't have made decent confetti. Whatever entered Terrance's possession as a paper document exited as a fine powder.

More frustrated than ever, Sam and Ski talked about seeking a court order for a phone tap but then concluded that, if Terrance was this careful with his trash, it wasn't likely a tap would turn up anything.

Chapter 35

After scaling a mountain of unproductive phone contacts and generating an avalanche of unreturned voice mail messages, Donny finally succeeded in tracking down someone on Wall Street who was willing to talk about Terrance Newberry. Donny must have caught Philip shortly after an old fashioned three martini lunch. Now a bond trader with Gould Capital, Philip was more than happy to talk.

In fact, Donny would later tell the group that it was as though Philip had this story bottled up inside and was just waiting for a chance to spew it out. Once he got started, it was all Donny could do to get a word in edgewise.

"Yeah, we worked together ... Terrance and me ... I had a couple years' jump on him in the department but, once he got over his rookie jitters, he came on like gangbusters. Bet you didn't even know we were roommates for a while."

"No I didn't. Like I said, I don't really know a lot about Terrance. That's why I called ... for information on his background."

"Uh huh. Well, just why are you so interested in Terrance, anyway?"

"Ah ... because ... because ... I'm a reporter for the LA Daily News, and I'm doing a story on Terrance. USC graduate makes good ... you know, that sort of thing. And ... Terrance is pretty shy. Doesn't like to talk much about himself ... so I'm piecing together a little historical perspective to flesh out ... you know ... my column."

"So, Terrance has made something of himself? You know, he was on the fast track back here 'til he hit a couple of speed bumps. Then he just wandered off."

"Oh, Terrance is doing quite well. Personal investing, he says. But as I explained, he doesn't like to talk about his past much."

"Not surprising he's done well. Damn good analyst. Made the rest of us look pretty bad at times.

"Terrance was thorough. Never made any silly mistakes. Didn't miss the details that came back to haunt some of the other analysts."

"Is that what made him special?"

"In part, but he really had an eye for companies on the rise and he worked hard at developing a network of inside sources. The brokers loved him because he uncovered a series of winners. It wasn't long before the top traders started claiming 'exclusives' on his reports ... reports they only shared with their most profitable clients.

"Terrance was definitely on track for a promotion to trading or maybe even mergers and acquisitions. He'd have been rolling in the big bucks if he'd hung in a little longer."

"You said you and Terrance were roommates?"

"Yeah. We were both making good money back then. Close to a hundred grand a year each, which wasn't bad for the late eighties. But those were Manhattan dollars, so you had to partner up on rent if you wanted to live within walking distance of the Street ... and enjoy, you know, some of the pleasures of the city."

"So Terrance wasn't all work and no play?"

"Not after a while, he wasn't. I mean in a sense, Terrance was the ideal employee, at least in Wall Street terms. Didn't have a family. No social life, at first, to interfere with his job."

"But that changed?"

"Well, yes and no. I mean he certainly developed a social life ... but ... he never let it interfere with his work.

"You have to understand something about the Street. It's a fishbowl. Everyone knows what's going on. Everyone knows who's hot. And everyone wants a piece of the action.

"It didn't take long before Terrance was in play. The brokers wanted a piece of him ... the women wanted a piece of him. He did an admirable job of servicing both. The boy had some serious stamina."

"He was able to balance all that action?"

"Balance? Shit yes. He loved it. Loved to push himself. And then there was his time management system."

"Time management system? Was he one of those guys that was married to his day-planner?"

"Not that type of time management."

"Well then what type?"

"Hey, I don't want to sully Terrance's reputation. Especially if he's some big shot out in LA now."

"I'm just trying to get a sense of what makes him tick. Off the record, what was his secret system?"

"No big secret. Just a little coke to keep him alert when he was bedding some starry-eyed clerk. Two or three scotches so he could catch a couple of hours of sleep, that's all he seemed to ever need. Then a pot of coffee to clear his head before he did it all over again. Anyone else might have called it substance abuse, but Terrance called it 'time management.'

"That's off the record, though. Quote me and I'll sue your ass."

"Strictly off the record. Sounds like Terrance was having a pretty good time."

"Yeah, I guess so. Couldn't ever really tell with Terrance. He didn't open up much. The few times he did talk about his family ... mostly his mother ... it sounded pretty grim.

"Funny thing was, it sounded like he came from this ... really negative upbringing ... but his work was always so positive. He went out of his way to find companies with really bright prospects. Until things went sideways for him."

"Sideways?"

"Yeah, run of bad luck."

"His time management system start to catch up with him?"

"Naw, he could always handle that stuff. It was the things beyond his control."

"Like what?"

"Well, if I remember it right, it started with RealTran. Terrance got a tip that this little company, RealTran, was about to announce a new process for scheduling, routing, and tracking bulk container shipments. Sounded like pretty boring stuff except it promised to cut as much as 8% off the typical transportation bill. Making that kind of dent in shipping costs ..."

"Sounds like that would have been a huge breakthrough."

"Would have been. And getting a position in RealTran's stock before word got out would have been very, very profitable."

"So what happened?"

"Terrance did his homework ... issued his report ... brokers sold the shit out of the stock ... then it tanked."

"Tanked, why?"

"Well, RealTran's system was the brainchild of the company's founder. I think his name was Geoffrey Bellows. Geoffrey was the resident genius. But all his work was recorded in a personal shorthand only he understood.

"Geoffrey went off on a ski holiday while our brokers were busy pushing RealTrans stock. He was apparently a better systems designer than a skier, because he missed a turn, smacked head-first into a tree, and died instantly."

"Jesus!"

"Yeah, so the stock tanked. Terrance had no way of knowing this guy was a shitty skier and, when people found out what really happened, the whole mess got blamed on the unpredictability of the 'stock gods.' But it really upset Terrance.

"Then ... it couldn't have been two months later ... Patsy Wells, the CEO of Well Springs Cosmetics, died of a drug overdose."

"I remember that. She was a big-time celebrity for a while. The more of a 'bad girl' she was, the more PR she got, and the more cosmetics she sold."

"That was Patsy. Terrance kept hearing about Patsy from his bed-mates, so he looked into the stock. Looked like a winner and Terrance put out a glowing recommendation.

"Unfortunately, Patsy had a congenital heart problem and once she started putting more powder up her nose than on her cheeks, she took a dive, and so did Well Springs stock.

"So now, that's two strikes on Terrance. And the big brass start saying that Terrance was developing a 'bad aura.' You have no idea how superstitious it gets on the Street.

"From then on, Terrance became pretty negative. I mean, he still did good work ... but he concentrated on companies on the decline. He stopped recommending buys

... went strictly for the sell.

"In fact, he pulled a big coup with one of his 'short sale recommendations' ... but nobody noticed."

"Tell me about that."

"The company was called Focal Point Lighting, and they were all the rage on the Street. Focal Point was developing a proprietary lighting system that produced an even bath of focused light without casting any heat on the subject. The buzz was that their system was going to be huge with commercial photographers and videographers.

"Terrance went against the tide. His analysis went something like, 'hard to patent product' ... vague talk of 'competing systems in the works' ... 'reluctance of old school photographers to invest in new equipment.' It just went on and on. I accused

Terrance of substituting sheer volume for any real analysis. But he was right."

"Focal Point's system didn't pan out?"

"Actually it did. But the CEO was murdered ... ugly scene ... and there weren't any succession plans in place. The company was in chaos. They got bought out shortly after that for a fraction of their real value."

"So Terrance was back in favor?"

"By then he'd already been marginalized as a burnout. You've got to be upbeat to sell stocks for a living and no one much liked all the negative stuff he was churning out.

"There was a little talk about Terrance maybe losing his 'bad aura' but mostly he was still on the outs. Not long after that, he cashed in his 401k, turned in his resignation, and took off. That was the last I heard of him.

"So you say he's doing well. What's he up to these days?"

"You should ask him that yourself. But, hey, I'm racing against a deadline. Gotta go."

Chapter 36

On Wednesday, Sam and Ski had run into a dead end on their trash search. On Thursday, Donny had filled in the missing pieces of Terrance's Wall Street puzzle. That Friday, Sam didn't show up for work.

Out of ideas, Sam had vowed to confront Terrance again, turning up the heat and directly accusing him of having a hand in Jonathan's death. Sam felt their only hope was that Terrance might slip up if he knew he was a murder suspect.

"Newberry residence," Oscar answered in his polished British accent. "No, I'm sorry, Mr. Newberry is out of town ... I'm sorry, I can't tell you where he is or when he'll be back ... Mr. Newberry never informs me of his plans; that way I can't disclose his whereabouts ... No, I don't see anything unusual in that. How else is he supposed to get away for a little rest? ... No, I'm sorry, I can't schedule an appointment for you as soon as he returns. As I said, I don't know when he plans to return, so you see it would be quite impossible for me to schedule an appointment without that knowledge ... Certainly, Detective Siemens, I'll be sure to give Mr. Newberry your message ... Yes, Detective Siemens, I understand it is urgent ... I'll give Mr. Newberry your message as soon as he returns. I'm quite sure that given the gravity of your message, Mr. Newberry will contact you as soon as he's able ... I'm quite certain Mr. Newberry still has your card, but please give me your phone number so that it will be possible for Mr. Newberry to call you directly upon his return ... Very good Detective Siemens, I'll be sure Mr. Newberry gets your message ... Oh, and sir, please do have a good day."

Sam spent his lunch hour that Thursday huddled at his desk making phone call after phone call. Ski hadn't been Sam's partner all that long, but he knew enough to leave Sam alone when he got into one of his obsessive moods.

So Sam made his calls and Ski started to clean up some of the files on other cases they had, frankly, been neglecting. It was a quiet, and, at least for Ski, a productive afternoon. A nice mindless break from the intense strain the 'short sale' bombings had put on the two detectives.

In his younger days, Detective Samuel Siemen had been known for going AWOL on occasion. But it had been years since anyone could remember him disappearing while he had a case in process. So it was unusual, though not wholly without precedent, when Sam didn't show up for his shift that Friday.

Ski was concerned because he couldn't reach Sam at home. But he knew how the dead-ends on Newberry and Heulenberg were getting to Sam. So he assumed Sam was either drunk at home, or drunk somewhere else, and that expecting to reach him by phone was a futile exercise.

Kate promised to look in on Sam at noon. Can of Campbell's Chicken Noodle soup in hand, she wasn't any more successful at raising Sam in person than Ski had been on the phone.

Well, Sam was a big boy. He'd sleep it off and turn up sooner or later.

In the meantime, the break gave Ski a chance to attack even more paperwork. Ski accomplished so much on Friday that he put in some time on Saturday and again on Sunday.

By Sunday evening he was about caught up. He hadn't heard word-one from Sam, so he figured he'd gone on a multi-day bender.

Imagining the sorry shape Sam would be in on Monday, Ski knew Sam'd appreciate the clean files and completed reports. Nothing worse, first thing on a hangover-Monday, than to have to take a ration of crap from the lieutenant for being behind on reports.

II

Ski wasn't shocked that Sam called him at home early Monday morning. He'd half expected the call, guessing that Sam would not want to stroll into the office without knowing what had been going on and to gauge the lieutenant's blood pressure over his disappearing act on Friday.

What surprised Ski was Sam's animated delivery. Ski expected the flat, thick-tongued, unfocused, monosyllabic, stream of unconsciousness he associated with a weekend of liquid self-abuse. Instead, here was Sam, sounding as perky as if he'd just hit a $5,000 winner in the 'Jacks are Wild' lotto, telling Ski to meet him and the rest of the team at the IHOP.

Trying to keep up with Wall Street meant Donny was always at work early, so Donny's car was already there when Ski rolled into the half-full parking lot. Their IHOP meetings had been so infrequent that they hadn't yet designated a 'favorite booth,' so it took a minute of scanning the premises before Ski spotted Sam and Donny.

Sam was holding court when Ski slid his stretch frame into the booth. Disheveled and reaching for a cup of coffee before even saying 'good morning,' Ski looked more like the binger than Sam.

It was a good three rounds of coffees before Kate completed the foursome in the IHOP booth. There was nothing in Kate's world that took precedence over a decent morning shower. There could be a 7.6 Richter-Scale earthquake crumbling the building around her and she still wouldn't go outside without first showering and putting on her makeup.

Sam had carried the conversation and hinted that he had some news on the 'short sale' murders, but he wouldn't go into any details until Kate arrived. "We'd be nowhere on this case without Kate. She deserves to be in on everything that happens. Firsthand. It's only fair."

So they'd waited for Kate. As soon as she sat down, Sam launched into his narrative.

"I'd gotten so worked up over that fuck Newberry. Oh, sorry Kate, I guess I'm still worked up over that smug little prick."

"That's OK Sam," Kat interjected, "He is a fuck."

"Anyway," Sam continued. "I'm hot that this guy's covered his tracks so well, so I decide to pay him another visit. Maybe shake him up a little. Maybe he's not so cool if we turn the heat up on him.

"So I'm set to go and do a full court press on him with the news that we like him for more than just being an innocent bystander in Jonathan's murder. I call ahead to make sure the prick's available, and bam, he's out of town.

"Now I'm really pissed. I'm about ready to explode and the prick's on vacation." Sam delivered the last three words in a high pitched sing-song, throwing his hands up in the air in disgust.

After a moment, Sam gathered himself and plunged on. "I'm about fit-to-be-tied. So I decide I got to find this prick, vacation or not.

"Terrance's butler won't tell me where he's gone so, taking a clue from my partner," Sam breaks for a nod of his head toward Ski, who almost blushed at the recognition. "Taking a clue from Ski here, I decide to do the obvious and get on the phone and track him down."

"It was a hell of a lot easier than I thought it would be. I just started calling airlines. At first, I was straight and identified myself as a cop, but that always got me transferred to some worthless supervisor instead of getting any information. So, I started identifying myself as a close relative who needed to get information about a medical emergency to Mr. Newberry, who had left town without letting anyone know his destination.

"Kate was right; call during lunch and you get the low man on the totem pole who hasn't yet learned to be unhelpful."

The group sat in silence as Sam took a sip from his fourth cup of coffee. "It takes a while, because I started with international carriers, thinking this rich fuck's going to Paris or Tahiti or some exotic place if he's on vacation. But finally, I find out that Newberry flew to Boston and picked up a commuter to New Bedford."

"Now I'm thinkin', this guy can go to London or Rome and he goes to New Bedford. What's with that?"

"I made a quick stop at the library to look up New Bedford on an atlas. There it is, Martha's Vineyard. As soon as I saw it on the map, I remembered Kate mentioning that Newberry had a second home back East, probably on Martha's Vineyard."

Sam stopped his oratory, now more interested in getting the waitress' attention because his coffee cup was empty.

"And?" Kate pleaded, creating a gently pulling motion with her two hands as if to physically extract more information from Sam.

"And," Sam continued, once his cup had been refilled. "And so I went to visit Terrance on Martha's Vineyard!"

"What?" the trio exclaimed in unison.

"I went to visit Terrance at his second home on Martha's Vineyard," Sam offered smugly. "Always wanted to weekend on Martha's Vineyard, and here was my chance."

"Are you nuts, Sam?" Ski exclaimed, half-standing, unable to contain himself. "That's completely out of our jurisdiction, and ..." But Sam cut him off with a sharp wave of his right hand before Ski could continue on with the list of laws, administrative guidelines, and departmental procedures Sam violated.

"I know. I know. I'm on this plane to Boston and I start thinking of all the rules I would be breaking. Then it dawns on me. Swear to God," Sam offers, raising his right hand in a Boy Scoutish pledge, "It dawns on me ... I've got no plan.

"Here I am on a plane to Boston, just used up ten years of frequent flyer miles, got a ticket in my pocket to New Bedford, and I have no idea what I'm going to do when I get there. Swear to God! No clue."

After allowing a moment for this admission to sink in, Sam rolled on. "So, I figure, I got the whole flight to come up with a plan. Not to worry. Have a drink. Have another. Something will come to me. Right?

"But I'm like, blank. Decide that maybe I'll just confront Newberry out at his place. Maybe me being out of my jurisdiction and him thinking no one is going to disturb him, maybe I can shake him up. Then I realize that wouldn't likely accomplish anything other than getting me yanked off the case and probably placed on administrative leave.

"But, I gotta do something, I don't know what. I decide something will come to me when I hit the ground, so I took a nap."

Donny starts to say something, but thinks better of it and just shakes his head.

Draining his coffee cup, Sam charges on. "Get to Martha's Vineyard and put in a call to the local constable to get directions to Terrance's place. As the phone starts ringing, I realize that I'm going to have a lot of explaining to do, and whoever I talk to is going to want to tag along since I'm in his back yard. So after the call's answered I hear my voice saying, 'Hi, my name's Jesse Fish. I'm a friend of Terrance Newberry and I'm supposed to meet him up at his place in about an hour. I just got to town and realized I hadn't packed the directions. Could you please help me out?' And bigger than shit, this guy's my newest best friend. Can't be any more helpful without personally escorting me out to Terrance's house. Swear to God, if I'd have asked, I bet he would have driven me there.

"I'd probably have done the same thing. I guess as cops, we really want to be helpful. It just doesn't occur to us that some bad guy might call us for information. But at the time it stunned me how easy it was to find out where someone lived. Especially someone who wasn't anxious to be disturbed.

So, I find his place, but still don't have a plan. I'm cruisin' the neighborhood. Nice places. I can see why rich folks go there to relax. Anyway, I'm cruisin' the neighborhood and come across this absolutely perfect spot for a stakeout.

"Now, I got no plan. I got nowhere else to be. So I set up a stakeout. I watch his place for the better part of the day. Nothin'.

"One lady, looks like maybe a cook, shows up about 6:00 pm and leaves at 7:30 pm. As best as I can tell, after 7:30, there's no one in the house but Newberry.

"I'm starting to think about going in and rousting Newberry when a little after 8:00 pm he strolls out onto his well-lit deck and reads for about an hour. Then it's back into the house where he rustles around for a while. Looks like maybe he's getting ready to call it an early night. Then we get our break."

With that, Sam smugly crossed his arms over his chest as he sat back in the IHOP booth.

"And?" blurted Kate.

"Come on Sam," pleaded Donny. "I gotta pee, but I gotta find out what happened."

"Go ahead and pee," Sam offered relishing the moment as he gestured toward the restrooms.

"It can wait," Donny exclaimed with more than a little pain in his voice. "Just get on with it."

"OK," Sam resumed. "Just for you, Donny boy. Ah, where was I?"

"Terrance is getting ready for bed," shouted Kate, drawing unwanted attention from the neighboring booths.

"Oh, yes. Terrance looks like he's about ready to call it a night when he starts going from room to room in the house turning on a light, then turning it off, then moving on to the next room. Apparently Terrance really roughs it when he's on vacation because, it turned out he was gathering up his own trash."

Sam continued on, "After he made a sweep of the whole house, he brings two garbage bags of trash out to the garage and then conveniently wheels his trash container down to the curb. Sometimes you get lucky, and apparently the next day was trash day.

"So, Terrance hand-delivers his trash, heads back up to his house, and retires for the night. I wait about an hour to make sure he's not some kind of fitful sleeper, and then hit the garbage. Couldn't have been any better if it'd been gift wrapped. One of the trash bags contained kitchen scraps and, you know, real trash. The other one was all shredded paper."

"Shredded paper!" exclaimed Ski.

"Yeah, shredded paper again. But this time with a difference. This time, Newberry's using a cheap shredder. This time, we got nice wide spaghetti strips of paper, pretty much stacked in convenient piles.

"So I grab the trash bag and head home. This time we might have something to work with."

Sam relaxed, smiled, and again leaned back into the leatherette covered booth. Donny excused himself and made a frantic dash for the restroom. Kate and Ski sat speechless.

Kate was the first to break the reverie. "You went through all that to tell us you brought back some trash?"

"Not just trash," responded Sam with some hint of indignation. "Shredded documents, correspondence, maybe something that will link this prick to these murders," he added under his breath.

"Have you pieced anything together yet?" Ski asked, trying to steer the conversation back in a more positive direction.

"Not yet," answered Sam. "But I can tell from some of the colors, that we should be able to identify a couple of the logos from the offshore trading companies that executed the 'short sales.' With a little luck maybe we'll find more."

III

Donny shared Sam's belief that there was a payoff in trying to piece together Terrance Newberry's trash. Ski and Kate were skeptical from the start. And they bored quickly at the tedious process Sam had devised for reconstructing the clues he was convinced lay amongst the pile of shredded paper piled on his kitchen table.

Ski and Kate caught a break when detective Martin called to tell Ski that the tax records he had subpoenaed had just been delivered. Sam and Donny could continue to work on the 'evidence' masquerading as packing material in Sam's kitchen. Ski and Kate would analyze Heulenberg's and Newberry's tax records.

Neither search bore immediate fruit.

Sam and Donny managed to reconstruct a couple of images. But they looked forced and Sam knew they'd never be admissible in court, even if they looked perfect.

All he'd really wanted was something he could use to scare Terrance. What they ended up with wasn't likely to have that effect.

Ski had obtained the tax returns, but the analysis was all Kate's. It had been awhile since Kate felt like she had contributed to the investigation. Now she was glad that, just to piss off everyone in her family, she had enrolled in the MBA program and had suffered through the mandatory accounting classes.

If you believed Karl Heulenberg's tax returns, he never made a dime in his life. The guy was clearly filing fraudulent returns but his evasion involved a couple of domestic partnerships that would be easy enough to trace. No offshore corporation. No 'short sale' transactions.

Terrance Newberry's returns were another story. Fortunately, Kate wasn't intimidated by the reams of forms and schedules. She plowed through the piles of papers as though she was on a mission which, in fact, she was. Unfortunately, Kate didn't find the smoking gun in Terrance's tax returns that they'd hoped for.

Terrance was declaring, and paying taxes on, gobs of income. An average of over $7 million per year for the five years of records they had obtained. No obvious tax fraud. Sufficient income to justify his lifestyle.

There was nothing in Terrance's tax records that tied him to any of the offshore companies that had handled the 'short sales.' Everyone had assumed that if Terrance was hiding his huge 'short sale' profits they'd be in overseas accounts. But on his tax returns, Terrance had disclaimed any ownership of, or control over, any bank accounts held in a foreign country.

Kate and Ski knew that statement could be false. But they lacked the hard evidence they needed to prove otherwise.

The bulk of Terrance's income was reported on a 1099 Interest and Dividend reporting form that came from the local branch of a major New York brokerage house. The stock-trading profits Terrance reported came from the same brokerage account.

No short sales. Everything looked legitimate.

It appeared they'd reached another dead end.

Chapter 37

Tommy Chou felt badly that he hadn't been able to help Sam track down Karl Heulenberg. He'd felt the hole that unsolved cases left behind.

After his last call to Sam, Tommy decided that his hunt for Heulenberg didn't have to be a complete waste of his time. Just because he didn't have a police record on Kauai didn't mean Karl Heulenberg hadn't committed any crimes there. Now that Tommy knew that a suspected criminal had been on his island, maybe he could clear up a few of his own open cases.

Tommy decided to take a fresh look at all the unsolved files from when Karl lived on the island. Based on the case synopsis he'd received from Sam, Tommy looked for violent crimes and financial fraud.

The only unsolved case Tommy found that might have any connection to Heulenberg involved an unidentified body that had been discovered in a big cane field out by the Hanalei Plantation. That case had been on the books for nearly three years now, and not a single lead had developed.

When a victim doesn't have an identity, and no one comes forward with any information, the case goes into the 'don't waste any more time on this one' file pretty quickly. That's where this case would have remained if Tommy hadn't started poking around, looking for Heulenberg.

"Detective Siemens, Tommy Chou here," Tommy started. "Got a minute?"

"You bet!" exclaimed Sam, thinking Tommy might have come up with a lead on Karl.

"Listen, after we talked about Heulenberg a couple of weeks ago, I went back and took a look at all of our open files," Tommy stated. "Thought I maybe could tie up something or, you know, find a new angle to follow."

"You find anything?"

"Don't know for sure," Tommy continued. "Probably not. I just found one open case that might have some connection to your investigation."

Sam was beside himself in anticipation. "What'd you find? A car bombing?"

"No. Nothing that close to your guy's MO," Tommy offered. "We've got an unidentified victim of what could either be a murder or a suicide."

"Murder or suicide?" Sam almost screamed. "Can't you tell which?"

"Not in this case brudder," Tommy answered. "Here's the story. A little over two years ago a body is discovered in a sugar cane field. Gunshot wound in the right side of the skull. Gun next to the body. Could have been a suicide or an execution."

"Couldn't your forensics guys narrow it down? You do have a forensics staff somewhere in the islands?" Sam exhaled. "Don't you?"

Tommy brushed aside Sam's remark and continued on with his narrative, "Of course we have forensics examiners here. We're not some third world country. But there's more to this story than just a dead body, a gunshot wound, and the weapon.

"Like I said, the body was in a cane field. What I hadn't got to yet was that the body was discovered after the field had been burned."

"Burned!"

"Yeah, burned. Every few years, the cane fields are burned to kill off insects and clean out the old cane so a new crop can be planted.

"The body was found in a very isolated cane field and must have been there before it was burned. Between the fire and nature at work, there wasn't much left when the field hands discovered the body the following spring.

"From the position of the body and where the gun had fallen, it could have been either a murder or a suicide. All prints on the gun had burned off in the fire. No gun powder residue. No other physical evidence.

"No identity on the victim. No fingerprints. No one came forward. No missing person's report. Nothing.

"I'd probably have completely overlooked this case if the coroner hadn't classified it as a homicide. He didn't have any reason to do that except that suicide sometimes invalidates life insurance policies and our coroner hates to see insurance companies weasel out of a claim over a technicality.

"I know the gunshot to the head doesn't match with your car bombings. But I thought that, if your guy has a thing for fire, maybe he found out this particular cane field was scheduled to be torched so he whacked this poor bastard out there knowing he'd be toasted."

It all sounded like quite a stretch to Sam, but he said, "Well that's possible. But you never identified the body?"

"That's the weird part," Tommy answered. "Murder or suicide, no one ever came forward looking for our dead guy."

Sam and Tommy agreed that it was unusual, but not unheard of, to have an anonymous victim. And there were already a lot of unusual things about Sam's investigation.

Now that the case of the unidentified victim had been resurrected, even if the body didn't have anything to do with Sam's investigation, Tommy wanted to see if he could put a name on the dead guy so he could close his file. Tommy didn't have the resources to search missing person's records, so he asked Sam for help.

Tommy had tried to help Sam out in locating Karl on Kauai. So, it was only fair for Sam to agree to help with Tommy's request.

The only thing that Tommy had for Sam to work with was the dental section of the coroner's report. Sam passed the report on to Ski so that Ski could run the dental profile through the national missing person's database.

Ski's search came up empty. Not really surprising since the national database was still fairly crude.

Ski took the additional step of running the dental report through the known felon's database. If this guy was a hit, maybe he'd show up there.

No luck. Strike two.

Sam was about to declare two strikes as an out when the trigger in his brain went off. He grabbed Tommy's file from Ski, rustled through his Heulenberg files. And, there it was!

The gold bridge. Tommy's unidentified victim had a gold bridge. Karl Heulenberg had a gold bridge.

It took a couple of hours to locate Karl Heulenberg's former dentist. It took a couple more hours for the faxed dental records to arrive. It would take a couple of days before the actual records would be delivered so they could make a positive ID but, for all the world, it looked like Tommy's dead guy was Karl himself.

Karl Heulenberg was no longer a suspect in the Watson murder, having been killed, or committed suicide, at least three years before the Watson car bombing. And with that, one of the hottest prospects was crossed off the list.

II

Sam called Jackee Heulenberg with the news that Karl was dead. She deserved to know that much. Sam was surprised by the warm reception his 'bad' news received.

Tommy had told Sam that the landlord of the flophouse where Karl had lived still had a box of personal items that Karl had left behind. He'd been afraid to get rid of most of the crap because he was concerned that Karl might reappear just as suddenly as he'd disappeared, and he didn't need a lawsuit or a right cross to the chin from that jerk. He knew Karl had a temper.

Sam asked Jackee if she wanted Karl's property sent to her as the next of kin. She told him to ask the landlord to give or throw away all of Karl's clothes, toiletries, and such, but to please send her any paperwork and books he left behind. "The books were undoubtedly mine to begin with."

Jackee phoned Sam a couple of weeks after he had informed her of Karl's death. She had just finished going through the box of books and paperwork Karl's former landlord had shipped to her.

Jackee urgently needed to know if the authorities had established a date for Karl's death. Could she get a copy of the death certificate? Had the coroner really put down murder rather than suicide for the cause of death?

Sam called Tommy to get the information for Jackee.

It was Jackee, Teresa, and Helen's turn for the last laugh.

In amongst the books and paperwork Karl left behind were three life insurance policies. One for each of Karl's former wives. Each purchased nearly a year before Karl's death. Each in a face amount of $1 million.

Jackee was an attorney so she knew what to look for. Each policy contained a provision that invalidated coverage in the event the insured committed suicide within one year from the date the policy was put in place.

Tommy's information confirmed Jackee's suspicions.

Maybe Karl Heulenberg had been murdered. But if he had committed suicide, based on the coroner's date of death, he had done it eleven months, give or take two weeks, after he purchased the life insurance policies.

Jackee was now sure Karl's death had been a suicide.

Karl must have planned this from the moment he set foot in paradise. He purchased the three term life policies, setting up each of his former wives to receive a million dollars if he died. He selected policies with a suicide exclusion. He'd then taken his own life to invalidate the policies.

Even in death Karl Heulenberg had tried to screw his former wives. He'd promised to take care of them. He'd stuck a million bucks under their noses. Then, from the grave, he planned to yank it back.

But Karl had miscalculated. He must have anticipated a search party. He hadn't counted on the fact that his sudden absence wouldn't draw much attention.

Karl must not have known the gleaned cane field where he took his life was scheduled to be burned. He couldn't have known that, given the ambiguity of the crime scene, the coroner would list the probable cause of his death as a homicide.

If Karl wasn't so full of fury he might have planned better. But he didn't.

Karl would have been surprised as anyone to learn that each of his three former wives eventually collected on the million-dollar policies he'd left behind. Karl would be as surprised as anyone to know that, in the end, he really <u>had</u> taken care of Jackee, Teresa, and Helen.

Chapter 38

Terrance Newberry's tax records hadn't provided any real details on the source of his dividend income, listing accounts at the brokerage company rather than the actual payor. That type of reporting wasn't unusual but, in Kate's mind, worthy of further investigation.

Ski made the appointment. Sam had learned that, when he wanted to, Ski could sound more 'white' that Sam, and in today's world, Ski's youthful 'white' voice sounded more like 'profit' than Sam's older, less educated, voice.

Ski hadn't indicated why he wanted an appointment with Jud Lockhart, managing director of the local SecureFirst office. All he said was that he was an acquaintance of Terrance Newberry's and wanted to stop by and chat.

Jud's job was to chat with people who were friends of people like Terrance Newberry. Once Jud had turned these friends of friends into clients, he would hand them off to one of his brokers.

Jud would then move on to creating more clients, and his brokers would start making money off these new clients for themselves, the firm, and of course, Jud. So Jud was more than happy to meet with Mr. Johnson, Terrance Newberry's acquaintance.

Sam, Ski, and Kate all showed up for the meeting.

As they took their seats around the small oval table in Jud's tastefully decorated private conference room, Ski wasted no time in getting to the point. He was actually a police detective, as was detective Siemen. Ski mumbled something about Katherine being an associate.

Ski informed Jud that they were in the middle of a very sensitive investigation that involved one of SecureFirst's clients. They needed background information on the client's account in order to trace the source of income to see if it might be the laundered profits from a criminal activity.

This, unfortunately, wasn't the first time one of SecureFirst's clients might have run afoul of the law. In Jud's experience, it had always been drug money that people tried to launder through a brokerage account. Strange times, thought Jud.

With so much money to be made legitimately, why do these guys get mixed up in drugs?

"Gentlemen — and Katherine — it was Katherine wasn't it?" Jud continued, as if he were lecturing to a JC pre-law class. "I want to assure you that I'll do everything I can to cooperate. But we do have privacy laws we need to observe, and we'll need all the proper paperwork before we can release any of our client's personal records."

Trying not to raise his voice, Sam interjected "Look, I know there are rules here. But this is serious business. We just need some information. And we need it NOW. If it leads us where we think it will, then we'll get all the 'proper paperwork' so we can use the information at trial."

"I'd like to be helpful," Jud started, "But my experience with drug laundering ..."

Sam cut him off, "This isn't about drugs. This is a murder investigation. Multiple murders."

"And it could have a stock market connection that would change the way that business is done in the future on Wall Street," interjected Kate.

"Wall Street ... murders," mumbled Jud, slumping slightly in his seat.

"But for a murder investigation," Jud asked, "Can't you get paperwork, you know, subpoenas and things, in a big hurry?"

"We can," offered Sam. "Once we have the framework established. But right now we're missing one critical piece of information that could link our suspect to a string of murders. Once we have that, then everything falls into place."

"Well, I don't know," Jud stumbled. "I'd like to help. I'm not sure what I can do."

By now, Sam was up and pacing the room like a caged animal. "Look, you've got to help. We've got a sick bastard out there blowing people up. We've got to stop him. You've got to help us."

Jud took a deep breath, which he held in for an excruciatingly long time. "I'll see what I can do."

"Great," responded Sam, slowing his pace but still circling the small room.

"What exactly is it you need?" Jud asked, with some depth returning to his voice.

"We need information on the source of Terrance Newberry's dividend income. We need to see if any of it comes from offshore," Kate blurted, instantly realizing that she was speaking out of turn.

Like he'd been kicked in the solar plexus, Jud exhaled, "Terrance Newberry!"

"Yeah, sweet Terrance. He may be a real bad guy." Sam didn't want to give out too much information, but he needed to create enough gravity to the situation to push Jud to give them what they needed.

"Terrance Newberry, I can't believe it." Jud mumbled. "Liz will just be devastated."

"Liz?" asked Ski.

"Liz Rockwell," answered Jud still mumbling. Jud had been swaying from side to side in his seat, but now just slumped forward in his chair and, with both elbows providing support from the conference room table, buried his face in his hands.

Sam wasn't in the mood for any histrionics, so he interrupted Jud's pseudo-prostrate pose by placing a firm hand on his shoulder. "Who's Liz?"

"Liz Rockwell," Jud answered for a second time, but as Sam's grip tightened, he realized more explanation was required. "Liz Rockwell. She's one of our senior vice presidents. She's Mr. Newberry's account manager."

Jud took a deep breath and continued, "As I'm sure you're already aware, Terrance Newberry is ..." Jud paused for a moment, realizing there had been, or at least needed to be, a fundamental shift in his protection of, and feelings toward, Terrance Newberry. "Mr. Newberry has been a very important client."

The grip on his shoulder told him he hadn't broken through to Sam yet. "Ms. Rockwell, Liz, is one of our best brokers. No doubt she is the best. And as such, being our best, you know, she handles our most important clients. Mr. Newberry is one of Liz's accounts, and she'll be just devastated to learn that Terrance might have been involved in some kind of criminal activity."

"I'm sure when she reads about it in the papers, she'll be just devastated," offered Sam sarcastically, finally releasing his grip on Jud.

"Oh, she'll have to hear about Newberry's problems sooner than that," Jud stated with some emphasis in his voice.

Ski asked, "Why's that?"

Jud went on to explain that, as the designated account manager on Terrance Newberry's account, Liz Rockwell maintained all of Terrance's personal records. IRS, SEC, and basic accounting information was duplicated on the firm's computer network. But, for privacy and security reasons, individual client account information was maintained on each account manager's computer, and paperwork files were maintained, under lock and key, in each account manager's office.

Jud described how valuable trading information was and how unscrupulous some brokers had been in the past, when it came to using inside, supposedly confidential information, for personal gain. SecureFirst maintained a strict confidentiality policy and, even as the senior manager of the LA branch, he couldn't access Terrance Newberry's records without going through Liz Rockwell.

"Can't you just call up New York?" asked Ski. "There's got to be some kind of master password for the computer and master key for the files."

"Of course there is," Jud responded. "In case an employee quits, or gets fired, or God forbid, dies. But, I can guarantee you that getting a search warrant, or subpoenas, or whatever it is you get, and using that to get into Terrance's files would be a thousand times easier than trying to get New York to sidestep established procedures and deliver the master keys and codes they send out by certified courier. That's what it would take to get into Newberry's records without going through Ms. Rockwell."

"So you're saying if we want the records now, we'll have to involve Ms. Rockwell," Ski offered, once Jud had finished his rant.

"That's what I'm saying. Liz holds the key, so to speak, to the information you say you need."

Sam again rested his hand on Jud's shoulder, only this time without applying much pressure. "Can she be trusted?" Sam asked in a conspiratorial tone.

"Trusted?" Jud exclaimed.

"Yeah, trusted?" Sam answered as he removed his hand from Jud's shoulder and resumed pacing the room. "We're at a critical point in our investigation," Sam went on, stretching the truth, since they were really nowhere with their investigation. "Can we count on this Ms. Rockwell to be, you know, discreet?"

"For God's sake!" Jud was sitting upright now. "If we are anything, it's discreet. Of course you can count on Liz to be discreet. That's our job. That's what we do. We handle sensitive, valuable, private information all day long. Liz is a pro. Of course you can count on her to be discreet."

"Good," Sam said, as he returned to his seat at the conference table.

II

It took several minutes before Jud was able to reach Liz on the intercom. She had blocked out all calls while she was on the phone with one of the firm's New York analysts, tracking down some supply and demand forecasts for a Hong Kong investor who dabbled in commodities.

Liz hated commodities, too risky.

But this particular client, outside of his small, mad-money, commodity gambling account, maintained a very large, very conservative portfolio of bonds with SecureFirst. So, if Mr. Li wanted to trade copper futures, and if that meant that Liz had to spend an inordinate amount of time gathering information on world copper markets, information she couldn't or wouldn't use with any of her other clients, well, so be it. She just had to think of the large, no-brainer commissions she earned off of Mr. Li's bond fund to reconcile herself to the task at hand.

While they were waiting for Liz to unblock her phone, Jud, the two detectives and their 'associate' engaged in a round of small talk. "Weird weather." "Yeah, unusually muggy." That kind of thing. Ski lent half an ear to the lame conversation, but mostly he day-dreamed about what it must be like to work in a glass and steel high-rise: sitting behind a mammoth rosewood desk, trading large blocks of stocks or bonds for wealthy clients, taking home that six-figure paycheck.

Once Jud got through to Liz, she informed him that she only had a few minutes to spare. Mr. Li was expecting her call in 'about five' and she and Jud both knew she couldn't, and wouldn't, miss placing that call on time. Managing communications across time zones, knowing your client's often bizarre work schedule, and never missing a window of opportunity to talk, these were the keys to success in maintaining an international clientele.

Considering she had rushed over to the unscheduled meeting with Jud and the others, and that she would have to rush back to her office in a couple of minutes to make her call to Mr. Li, Liz was the picture of calm, collected professionalism as she breezed into Jud's conference room. Dressed in a dark charcoal brown, almost black suit, with just the hint of dark brown pin stripes, Liz Rockwell certainly looked the part of a successful stockbroker. The single strand of pearls added a touch of class that balanced the unavoidable librarian look created by her thick glasses ... the byproduct of too many hours staring at a computer screen or pouring over the minuscule print used in Dun & Bradstreet write-ups and the footnotes of annual reports.

Lose the glasses, take some of the severity out of the hair style, soften the makeup just a smidge, and Liz Rockwell would be quite stunning, thought Kate. In fact, Kate had the feeling she might have previously met Liz at some function or another in the past. But, she couldn't quite place where or when.

Not wanting to be recognized herself, Kate rounded her shoulders, dropped her gaze, and avoided all eye contact with Liz as the introductions proceeded around the room. She had to be Kate, the assistant. She couldn't afford to be recognized as Katherine Newberry, uninvited guest.

Sam must have realized her predicament because after he had finished introducing himself and Ski, he introduced Kate as Kather ... Kate New ... Kate Newton.

Liz took immediate control of the meeting as the men, who had risen as she entered the conference room, resumed their seats at the table. She explained that she only had a few minutes but, since Jud had informed her that there was an urgent situation that required her attention, she would do what she could.

Jud started to describe the situation, but Sam cut him off. Sam went on to explain that they were investigating some irregularities that might involve Terrance Newberry's SecureFirst accounts.

Liz asked why the local police would be looking into one of her client's accounts. "Isn't that usually the responsibility of the FBI or IRS or some federal agency?"

Liz started to review the normal procedures for gaining access to otherwise confidential client information when Jud interjected that he had already discussed normal procedures with the detectives. Jud began to explain to Liz why he agreed to circumvent normal procedures when Sam again interrupted.

Sam clearly didn't want to go into any of the details of their investigation with Liz. He just stated firmly that Jud had agreed they should be given the information that they needed on Terrance Newberry's accounts. They'd get into why they needed the information at a later date. Right now, they just wanted to confirm their suspicions. Then they'd return with all the proper paperwork and make everything "legit."

Liz looked at Jud, looked at her watch, and then said, "OK, tell me what you need."

Ski explained that they needed to trace Terrance's dividend income to its source. They knew Terrance had reported substantial income through his brokerage accounts. They knew that most of the funds probably came from offshore. They expected that funds might have flowed through several corporate entities. But they needed to find the real source of Newberry's income.

If Liz Rockwell had been shocked at being called into a meeting where the police were asking for confidential information on one of her biggest accounts, she never let on. If she was curious as to why they were interested in tracing Terrance Newberry's income to its source, she never let on. If she was concerned about violating company procedure for releasing the type of information that had been requested, she never let on.

All Liz Rockwell said was, "I'm afraid you'll have to excuse me. I have to make my call to Hong Kong. What you've asked for will take some time to gather together. I've got two important meetings scheduled for this afternoon that, I'm afraid, I can't possibly reschedule. I'll pull everything together this evening, and if you can come back tomorrow, I'll have it for you first thing in the morning."

With that, Liz rose from her seat, excused herself again, and exited the room with the same grace, mixed with the sense of purpose, she'd displayed upon first entering Jud's conference room.

After he'd closed the conference room door, Sam tried to explain to Jud why he'd kept cutting him off during the short meeting with Liz. Sam wanted as few people as possible to know the details of the case they were building against Terrance.

Sam went on about how he was sure that Liz was a professional who was used to handling confidential information. But, once you start talking about someone being a murder suspect, well, it's just too hard to keep that information bottled up.

Tax evasion, bribes, even drugs, those are the kinds of things Liz would imagine are at the bottom of Newberry's brush with 'The Law.' Somehow those are disconnected crimes. They're the kind of thing that someone can keep secret.

But murder. Well, you've just got to share that with your best friend.

Or, what if Terrance <u>called</u>? If he's a tax cheat, well, you can be cool, be collected, help put him away. But how do you talk to a murderer without letting your voice tip off to the suspect that you know he's evil?

Jud agreed that it was best to keep Liz in the dark and he promised not to tell her anything about Terrance being a murder suspect. After Sam made Jud swear for a second time that he would not repeat any part of their conversation to Liz, or anyone else, the detectives, and Kate, rose, thanked Jud for agreeing to cooperate, excused themselves, and filed out of the conference room.

Ski continued to absorb the surroundings as they moved past the bullpen of suit-and-tie'd brokers sitting or standing in front of computer terminals, talking into telephone headsets. There was money being made, or lost, in his presence and he could feel the adrenaline rush that came from the trading floor. As he passed through the brokerage house's luxurious lobby, down the high-speed elevator, out the bustling main lobby, and onto the street, Ski's mind was a thousand miles away from Terrance Newberry.

His thoughts were focused on money. Money! The excitement. The feeling of power. The sense of purpose that must come with having money. Money! If he wasn't careful, he realized, he could get hooked.

III

At 6:50 the next morning, Sam, Ski, and Kate took their seats in the SecureFirst lobby. After only a minute or two, Jud came out to meet the two detectives and their 'assistant'.

Ski wished that Jud had taken a little longer to emerge from his office because, for the first time in his life, he had picked up a *Wall Street Journal*, and it looked kind of interesting. Ski promised himself that he'd stop by the newsstand on the way out and pick up a copy.

After the obligatory pleasantries, Jud stepped behind the front counter and used the reception-ist's phone to see if Liz was available. There was no answer.

Jud asked the trio to wait in the lobby while he went to find Liz. Ski was pleased to have the opportunity to finish the article he had started on the latest Internet company to go public, making its twenty-something founder an instant multi-millionaire.

Jud returned in less than five minutes. Liz wasn't available. In fact, she wasn't there. In fact, no one had seen or heard from her yet that morning.

Sam asked in hushed tones if that was un-usual. Jud whispered back that it was. Liz was usually one of the first to arrive in the morning, and she never scheduled a meeting outside the office without letting the staff know where she was and when she was expected to be back.

Sam was concerned, but Jud surmised that Liz had probably worked late the prior evening tracking down and organizing all the information Ski had requested and was just running behind. Jud convinced Sam that it was still early by most people's standards, and they should give Liz a little more time.

After Sam agreed to cut Liz some slack, Jud headed back to his office. Ski disappeared again into his new, favorite periodical. And Sam and Kate somehow slid into a discussion of the pros and cons of Western line dancing.

Their mental stopwatches must have gone off at exactly the same moment, because Jud emerged from his office just as Sam was about to ask the receptionist to buzz Jud and see if he could have a word with him. Jud had a concerned look on his face as he huddled with Sam, Ski, and Kate.

This was unlike Liz. He had called her at home. She wasn't there. He had tried her cell phone. She wasn't answering. He assumed she was on her way in, but he had given her more than enough time to make the commute from her condo to the office, even considering heavy traffic, yet she hadn't arrived.

No one had heard from her. No one. That wasn't like Liz. He was concerned for her safety.

Sam tried to quiet Jud down and suggested they head back to Jud's office where they could talk in private. Better yet, they could wait and talk in Liz's office.

Liz's office was nearly as big as Jud's and, as far as Kate was concerned, had a better view. The fact that Liz didn't work out in the bullpen but had such a prime office space spoke volumes about her position within the firm.

Sam and Ski claimed seats on the couch that took up nearly one whole wall and Jud pulled up one of the side chairs. Katherine made herself comfortable in the leather executive chair behind Liz's rosewood desk.

Envisioning herself in a similar set up as soon as she got her MBA, Kate's eyes drifted over to the collage of pictures on Liz's rosewood credenza. As she bounced from portrait to portrait of family and friends, her gaze locked onto a casual picture of Liz at the beach. But it wasn't just any old picture or any old beach.

Kate immediately identified the setting as the gravelly beach, in a small cove on a small Greek island, where she had vacationed a few years earlier. It was a wonderful place that hadn't yet been discovered by the hordes of tourists who had ruined most of the other good beaches scattered throughout the Mediterranean.

And there was Liz. Tanned, relaxed, designer sunglasses replacing the coke-bottle-lenses she'd worn the previous day, hair blowing in the breeze. But it wasn't Liz, at least not the Liz that Kate couldn't quite place.

313

"Oh, Christ!" Kate cried. "Jesus, Christ! Why couldn't I see it yesterday?"

Sam, Ski, and Jud jumped to their feet. Ski was the first to reach Kate.

"Christ, it's her!" Kate exclaimed, pointing to the picture of Liz on the credenza.

"Of course it's her," observed Jud. "This is Liz's office after all. It's OK to have a picture of yourself in your office, especially if it reminds you that you do have a life outside of work."

"No, what I mean is it's NOT her. That's not your Liz. That's Elizabeth Rockwell. I knew I knew her!"

"Liz, Elizabeth, around here she's always been Liz," stated Jud.

"But, don't you see?" Kate continued trying to catch her breath. "That's Elizabeth Rockwell. Terrance Newberry's girlfriend, Elizabeth Rockwell. I recognize her from the society clips I put together on Terrance.

"When you introduced us yesterday I felt like I'd met her somewhere before, but I couldn't place her. We hadn't met; I'd just seen pictures of her with Terrance.

"I couldn't put it together yesterday, the glasses and everything. But this picture. That's her. And she knows we've got something going on Terrance."

"I had no idea," Jud gushed, looking like he might faint on the spot. "Strictly against company policy. No dating clients. No compromising relationships. No conflicts of interest." With that, Jud slid into one of the chairs next to Liz's desk.

"OK," Sam offered as he started to pace. "So Liz, Elizabeth, whoever she is, has undoubtedly told Terrance something's up. I was about to try to corner him with the news that we like him as a suspect in the Newberry murder anyway. Maybe we haven't lost much here. Maybe Liz just alerted Terrance something was up. Maybe we're OK here."

Jud slumped further into the chair and looked like he might be ill any second. "I told her," came out as a whisper.

Sam stopped pacing and lunged at Jud, "You told her what?" Sam screamed through clenched teeth, his face about four inches from Jud's.

"You told her what?" Sam repeated.

"Everything." Jud exhaled. "I told her everything."

"Everything!" snarled Sam.

"Everything," Jud reiterated, cowering further back into the chair. "She was all over me after you guys left. Terrance-was-her-client, this. And, she-had-a-right-to-know, that. She said it wasn't fair to jeopardize her standing in the firm by asking for compromising information on one of her clients without her knowing why. And she was right. She threatened to call the Chairman of the Board at home. Wake him up in the middle of the night and disavow any part in allowing you access to Terrance's records without all the proper paperwork."

After a couple of deep breaths, when it was clear that no one was going to interrupt and that his story wasn't complete, Jud continued, "I thought it was important for you guys to get what you needed today! That's what you said. She calls the Chairman directly, and not only would I lose my job on the spot, but whoever replaced me, probably Liz, would have been instructed to show you the door until you had all your search warrants and subpoenas not only in order, but reviewed and approved by our house counsel."

One more deep breath and Jud finished, "So I told her everything."

"That we liked Terrance for a string of murders?" asked Sam.

"Yeah," answered Jud.

Sam now had his face two inches from Jud's, "That we suspect Terrance is hiding profits associated with those murders in overseas accounts?"

"Yeah," Jud responded meekly. "I told her everything. Once I started, it all came out. At the time, I thought it was the right thing to do." Jud looked like a whipped dog as he finished admitting his sins.

Sam allowed Jud about 15 seconds of self-pity and then informed him that he was now considered guilty of obstruction of justice and could possibly end up as an accessory to murder. If Jud looked shaken before, now he was reduced to jelly.

Sam told Jud that his only hope was to get on their side, in a big way. Help them, and they'd do what they could to help him.

Jud knew he was an innocent bystander. He knew that he'd had nothing to do with Terrance's ill-gotten gains. He knew that telling Liz everything was the right thing to do.

He knew all that, but Kafka-ish things did happen. At least they did on TV, which was the basis of his reality away from the office.

Jud had no interest in testing the system. He'd do anything and everything the detectives asked.

After thinking about the situation for a minute or two, Sam concluded that their mission that morning hadn't really changed. They still needed to trace Terrance's income.

Sam informed his new cohort, Jud, that his first assignment was to sit down at Liz's computer and call up Newberry's accounts. Jud told Sam that he wasn't making things up the previous day. He really couldn't get into Liz's computer or paper files.

Sam reached over the top of the desk, picked up the phone, and handed it to Jud. "Do whatever you need to do. Call whoever you need to call. Get whatever code words, instructions, whatever it takes. We've got to find out what's on this fucking computer."

IV

It took more than three hours for Jud to get through all of the explanations, proper channels, and tech support people before he had the clearance and passwords he needed to get into Liz's computer. Once inside, it took another half hour, and help from one of the younger brokers, to figure out how Liz had organized her customers and their files.

While SecureFirst provided basic computer software and technical support, each broker was free to set up their personal computer files however he or she saw fit. So each broker's computer records were organized differently.

Kate wasn't a computer whiz, but she seemed to follow Liz's logic in organizing her files. However, even though she cracked Liz's filing system, Kate couldn't locate anything on Terrance Newberry.

After a while, it was clear that Kate was having trouble accessing Terrance's file not because she was looking in the wrong place. She was having trouble accessing Terrance's file because it had been deleted.

Letting Jud take the lead, the foursome tore through Liz's office, the general computer room, and even the supply room looking for a back-up. Liz obviously had deleted all of Terrance's computer records, purged the trash files on her hard drive ... but if they could just find a back-up.

Liz was thorough. No trace of a back-up anywhere.

Liz's purging of Terrance's files was so complete that no matter what Ski tried, he wasn't able to recover, reconstruct, or un-delete any records.

Liz knew computers as well as she knew the market.

It was going to take a full day for the courier to arrive with the keys to Liz's fireproof files. Everyone tried to remain optimistic that they'd find something in Liz's hard copy files that would tie Terrance to the 'short sales' transaction. However, she'd been so thorough in cleaning out the computer records, in their hearts they knew there really wasn't much hope they'd find anything even remotely useful once the file cabinets were opened.

Chapter 39

Jules Jewel had been almost honest with Sam when he told him he'd spent every evening for the past two years in his shit-ass trailer, reading his Bible. He'd get an urge every once in awhile he'd need to satisfy, but for the most part Jules filled his empty evenings reading his Bible, looking for meaning in his empty life.

It took Jules nearly a year to read the Bible from cover-to-cover the first time. Jules knew he was slow at catching on to most things, so he spent another year reading the good book a second time. It still didn't make any sense.

Jules expected an instruction manual. He wanted specific directions for redemption. He was left confused.

Jules never saw the light. He never accepted Jesus as his personal savior. He never even appreciated any of the poetry, tall tales, or parables he had forced himself to read.

After two years, it was time to do some catching up.

II

Jules tried to catch up for two years of sitting in his shit-ass trailer, reading that worthless Bible, all in one night. He tried to relive his past. Not in slow motion, like when you're drowning, but fast-forward, like on speed.

Jules started with the motorcycle. An easy target, but he wanted to watch the gas tank explode.

Then he moved on to the deserted gas station. There could be some gas fumes left in the abandoned tanks and flammable materials mixed in with the discarded trash in the old repair bay.

The structure burned like any other vacant building. The underground tanks didn't blow. Jules was disappointed.

Frustrated, Jules moved on to a worthy target. He'd torch one of the oil refinery tanks located just off the I-405. He'd share his triumph with the late-night commuters.

But before he could get within 100 feet of the tank he'd selected, Jules was grabbed by security.

III

"OK, Jules, here's the deal." Ski stated flatly after reentering the interview room. "I've talked to the DA. He's willing to make a deal, just to keep you off his calendar."

"I don't need to make no deal."

"Follow me on this, Jules. We got you trespassing on the refinery grounds. You're carrying incendiary material, heading for the tanks."

"That don't mean nothing."

"Add in that you've got a history of arsons."

"Nothin's ever been proven."

"You've got a history of being a suspect in numerous arsons. AND, we got three eyewitnesses who pulled you out of the lineup as the guy who set a motorcycle on fire the same night.

"So don't tell me you don't need to make a deal. You make a deal, or you piss the DA off. You piss him off, become a smudge on his calendar, and you'll find out why you should have made a deal."

"OK ... just for argument, let's say I want to make a deal. What kind of deal can you offer?"

"We know you're a pyro. We want you in the system. We want you to have a record. But, since this is your first 'official' offense, we're willing to cut you some slack if you cooperate."

"Cooperate? Like how?"

"Draw a straight line from the motorcycle fire to the refinery and it runs right through an abandoned gas station that was torched last night. We know that's your work, but it's going to take a lot of effort to prove it. You can save us all a lot of time by confessing to that one."

"And where's the deal come in?"

"The deal is ... you confess to the motorcycle and the gas station fires and we'll drop the trespassing, malicious mischief, and attempted arson charges related to the refinery. And we'll recommend that, as a cooperative first offender, you be given a suspended sentence for the arsons, so long as you attend mandatory counseling sessions for a year. No time, just counseling that you obviously can use. Kid, it's a hell of a deal."

"Do I have to pay for the counseling? 'Cause I'm barely getting by as it is."

"The State of California will be happy to pay for your counseling."

"What do I have to do?"

"Write up a statement describing how you set the motorcycle and the gas station fires. I get the D.A.'s deal typed up. We trade. And that's about it."

IV

The State of California lived up to its end of the deal with Jules Jewel. Essentially, Jules got a walk on the two arsons.

But, Ski had failed to mention one little detail. A transient's body had been discovered inside the abandoned gas station. He'd apparently been asleep when Jules set the fire, and he died in the blaze.

Jule's confession allowed him to walk from the arsons but not the homicide. He'd already made one deal. Now he had no choice but to make another and plead guilty to manslaughter, with its 25-year sentence.

The transient killed in the gas station was never identified. The arson squad didn't find any identification or personal effects besides a wad of charred cash — more than $700 — and a badly burned, handwritten, marginally coherent manifesto that railed against the evils of modern technology ... satellites, cell phones, and other wireless devices that put messages out on the airwaves, to worm their way into people's heads. Messages that could make people listen to things they didn't want to hear. Messages that could make them do things they didn't want to do.

Chapter 40

Elizabeth Rockwell essentially fell off the face of the earth. She left LA the evening that Sam, Ski, and Kate first visited SecureFirst. Ski was able to trace her as far as Paris. From there Liz had booked train reservations to Marseilles, Stockholm, and Athens.

It was impossible to determine if she actually boarded any of the trains. It didn't really matter, because once off U.S. soil, all she needed was a little determination and a lot of cash to disappear completely. And she had both.

Sam was sure that Terrance had also pulled a disappearing act. They'd already wasted the better part of the day breaking into Liz's computer and tracking her flight from the country. Finding a warm trail for Terrance would be even harder now.

Maximizing the resources he could muster to hunt for Terrance, Sam called in Donny to help him, Ski, and Kate make calls. Sam even recruited Jud to work the phones as a demonstration of Jud's good faith effort to atone for his sins.

Sam believed Terrance, who, as far as he knew, was still vacationing on Martha's Vineyard, would want to catch an international flight as soon as possible. So, Ski was assigned the Dulles airport, Donny and Jud split the New York/New Jersey airports, and Kate took Boston.

Sam took a more direct route this time. Using the 'official police business' approach, he managed to obtain Terrance's unlisted phone number in Martha's Vineyard. "Maybe the bastard hasn't left yet. Maybe he's still busy cleaning out his bank accounts."

No answer at Terrance's vacation home.

Sam rang up the local constable, this time identifying himself and the reason for his call. He asked the duty officer to have a patrol car dispatched to Terrance's home to see if there was any sign of his whereabouts.

Not long after his call, word came back that the Martha's Vineyard house looked to have been closed up for the season. There was nothing at the property that would indicate where Terrance was, where he might have gone, or when he left.

The airport search hadn't fared any better. No trace of Terrance Newberry leaving the country.

They immediately speculated that Terrance must have anticipated the possibility he could, at some point, be linked to any one of thirty-odd murders. So he must have had contingency plans for getting out of the country. They already knew he was smart. There was no reason to think he would not have made arrangements for a quick, quiet, and complete disappearance.

As the dead ends mounted, Sam decided to call Oscar. "That pompous butler has to know Terrance's whereabouts. He'll give me that 'I know nothing' crap. But once I hit him with the possibility of accessory to murder and unlawful flight, I'll bet his memory improves."

Sam rang up the Newberry residence, and on the third ring Oscar answered. "Newberry residence ... Well certainly Detective Siemen, I do remember you. You were here at the residence just last week ... Well, Detective Siemen, I'm not sure exactly what you mean, but let me assure you that I wouldn't, how'd you say, give you any crap, about Mr. Newberry's whereabouts ... Please be assured that if you asked me Mr. Newberry's whereabouts, and if I had that information, I'd be more than happy to share it with you ... Detective Siemen, are you actually interested in Mr. Newberry's location, or are you primarily interested in raising your voice to me?"

Sam was wound pretty tight, so he took a deep breath, apologized to Oscar, and then stated "Yes, I am interested in Mr. Newberry's location, and I'd appreciate any help you could provide in tracing Terrance."

"In that case," Oscar volunteered, "Mr. Newberry's right here. Actually, he's still in bed. Returned home late last night."

Oscar continued on, "I put your request for an appointment right at the top of Mr. Newberry's incoming mail and messages. But, as I said, Mr. Newberry didn't return until very late last night. I'm sure he'll set a time for a meeting once he is up and has an opportunity to see what the rest of his schedule looks like."

Sam was speechless. So Oscar filled the vacuum with, "is there anything else I can do for you at this time, Detective?"

"No, nothing else at this time," Sam stammered weakly. "Just make sure Terrance knows that I need to see him on an important matter, as soon as possible. Oh, and thanks."

Sam just stood there in stunned silence. He couldn't believe that the reason they hadn't been able to find any clue as to how or when Terrance Newberry had fled the country was because he wasn't on the run. He'd left Martha's Vineyard to return to Los Angeles. He wasn't on the lamb. He was home, in bed, sleeping like one.

The two detectives and their three civilian 'assistants' had been working the phones out of one of Jud's mid-sized conference rooms. Jud's offices offered the necessary space and telecommunications equipment so that they could make their calls within earshot of each other. By hosting the bull pen session, Jud saw an opportunity to start working off his debt to society. And the SecureFirst offices were certainly plusher than anything Sam or Ski, or for that matter, even Donny, had to offer.

When Sam regained his bearings, he announced to the group, "Fucker's at home, sleeping like a baby."

Donny was the first to react to Sam's declaration. "Come again?"

"Fucker's home, sleeping like a baby," Sam continued. "We can call off the dogs. Terrance didn't split Martha's Vineyard for parts unknown. He flew back to LA last night and he's up at his big house, as we speak, sleep'n like a fuckin' baby."

"Guy's got some real balls," Kate observed.

Jud was caught off guard by the mildly crude statement emanating from such a prim and proper young lady. Kate's comment didn't even register with the others who knew her better and had heard far worse.

As Sam recounted his conversation with Oscar, the group collectively slid further and further down in their chairs as if the entire conference room was being spun in a gigantic centrifuge. Sam, who was wrapped up in his own thoughts, didn't really notice that the others in the room almost cowered as he matter-of-factly regurgitated Oscar's message.

Evil carries weight. Enormous weight. And to know that this man, who might have killed at least 34 other men that they knew of, could sleep – as any normal man would want to sleep after catching a red-eye – just made Terrance Newberry seem all that more heinous.

That sense of evil bore down on the occupants of Jud's mid-sized conference room. Its gravity made conversation all but impossible and the group sat in silence for quite some time, prisoners of their individual thoughts and fears.

II

Sam knew it was his responsibility to pull the others back to the task at hand, but he was busy trying to control his own rise out of his depressed state without flying immediately into a rage. Sam understood himself well enough to know he'd have to carefully manage his emotions from here on out.

The vast majority of homicides were the result of passion, stupidity, or very, very, bad luck. There were certainly sociopaths out there, and Sam had run into his share. But once you started down the road with a sociopath, it became clear that some part of their psyche was missing and they either couldn't tell right from wrong or were indifferent to the distinction. For some reason Sam could deal with that.

Having investigated his share of sick, cruel, and dangerous characters, Sam had encountered only one individual so sadistic he considered him to be pure and simply evil. And, in that instance, things hadn't turned out too well.

Ian Proctor. The criminal justice system eventually determined that Ian Proctor was criminally insane, but Sam didn't consider him just another sociopath. Ian didn't fit anywhere in Sam's system of beliefs.

Ian wasn't stupid. His crimes weren't the result of bad luck or bad timing. He always knew exactly what he was doing.

Ian methodically committed a series of crimes just for the experience ... for the terrific rush that came with his actions. He wasn't indifferent. He was passionately committed to his 'vocation.' And while he appeared to feel some guilt as a result of what he did, it wasn't enough to keep him from continuing to do very bad, very evil things.

Sam became obsessed with catching Ian Proctor. He obsessed with both the police work and the eventual prosecutions. That obsession helped to finally get Proctor off the streets.

More than once, Sam had a toe over the line while investigating the cases tied to Ian Proctor. No matter whether things went well or things went poorly, he couldn't get Proctor out of his consciousness. For months on end, he couldn't let go.

Once Ian sensed what was going on in Sam's head, he was both flattered and amused. He started playing games, which nearly drove Sam over the edge.

When Sam heard the verdict that would put Ian Proctor in a mental institution rather than a prison, and when it was clear that some judge could, at any time, upon finding that Proctor had regained his sanity, order his release, well, Sam felt he had to act.

Sam, apparently, wasn't the only one unhappy with the verdict because, two weeks after the end of his trial, Ian Proctor was found in the prison washroom with his cut-off-balls stuffed in his mouth and a gaping incision running from his rectum all the way up his chest to his larynx. Ian Proctor had been gutted like a trophy buck.

The Proctor investigation and trial had taken nearly four years out of Sam's life. It took another two years after Ian's execution before Sam seemed to be his old self again. Sam would tell you in all honesty that, even today, he still couldn't get Ian Proctor out of his head.

So Sam Seiman knew evil. And, because of his brush with Ian Proctor, he'd come closer than anyone would have suspected to losing everything.

He made it back and was able to deal with all the other aspects of homicide work. He had just hoped, and even prayed, that he'd never have to face that kind of evil again.

Now that he'd come back, it was clear to Sam that Terrance Newberry, like Ian Proctor before him, could be pure and simple evil. That smug, calculating, cold-hearted bastard had come back. And was at home, sleeping like a baby.

Sam knew that Liz had told Terrance everything she had learned from Jud about their investigation. Sam knew Terrance had the means and the opportunity to disappear forever without missing a beat in his luxurious lifestyle.

But there he was, back in L.A., sleeping, when he should have been in some prison washroom, gutted like a buck. Just like Ian Proctor.

Sam had a death grip on the conference room table to steady himself, even though he was sitting down. So Sam was in no position to draw the others out of the private worlds <u>they</u> had each entered, upon hearing that Terrance hadn't fled the country but had instead returned to LA for a good night's sleep.

III

Jud finally broke the silence. He had the least knowledge of the events that had led up to the moment, so it was easier for him to extract himself from the gravity of it.

Also, at least in his mind, he had the most to gain from Terrance's decision not to flee the country. Jud wanted to make sure this good fortune led to a swift and satisfactory resolution of his current status as an 'accessory.'

"So, what do we do next?" Jud offered, clearing his throat as four pairs of downcast eyes rose to look in his direction. "I mean, isn't it good news Newberry's still in the country? He's right here in Los Angeles. Can't you just go arrest him? Can't you put him behind bars and then track down Liz, or do whatever else it is you need to do?"

"I wish it was that simple," Ski offered.

"You've got to be able to do something. I mean, Christ, one minute you're frantically trying to track down a guy you're sure has fled the country. The next minute you find out he's right here in your own back yard. And now you're bummed out. I don't understand."

Ski started to say something but was cut off by Sam with a wave of his hand. "You've got to understand something, Jud," Sam said as he rose from his chair and began to slowly circle the room. "Terrance has to know we're on to him. You and our friend Ms. Rockwell took care of that. If he's still in the country, he has to be confident that Liz cleaned up any trace of evidence we might have uncovered that could have tied his income back to the short sales transactions."

Sam paused for a moment and Jud was about to speak when Sam picked up his thought and carried on. "He's got to be convinced that we don't have anything that can link him to the car bombings. And, he'd be absolutely right."

"But I thought ..." started Jud, before being stared down by Sam.

"But you thought. You thought what? That this was some game? That we had an ironclad case against this guy? That we were pleading for your help just for the hell of it?"

"I just thought ..." Jud tried again.

"Listen, whatever you thought, you were wrong. Just flat out wrong." Sam stopped pacing and slid back into one of the conference room chairs as if exhausted from the two minutes he'd spent circling the room.

Ski attempted to clarify the situation for Jud. "Look, all we have is speculation at this point in time. We don't have any hard evidence. We don't even have any good circumstantial evidence. We think Terrance <u>planned</u> these murders, at the very least, even if he didn't personally execute them. And we suspect he flipped the switches that sent 34 unsuspecting individuals to early graves.

"But this is America. We can't just pull this guy in off the street, railroad him through the system, put him away forever, and everyone lives happily ever after. We have to have evidence that will stand up in court. Evidence that can withstand the kind of attack that a team of $1,000-an-hour lawyers would mount. Evidence that would convince a jury beyond a reasonable doubt that

Terrance Newberry, successful investor, big-time philanthropist, is a cold-blooded killer.

"Without being able to trace Terrance's finances offshore and back to the short sales," Sam added, "we ain't got dick."

Summarizing the situation, Ski concluded, "And Terrance has to be pretty confident that, as Sam said, 'we ain't got dick', because, with all his resources, and with the tip he must have gotten from Elizabeth, if he was the least bit concerned with our investigation, he'd already be so lost we'd never have a chance to find him."

Jud started to speak again, but this time he was cut off by Kate. "OK. OK. I agree that this looks bad, but just because Terrance obviously thinks we're out in the cold, doesn't mean he's right. Does it?"

Kate now had everyone's attention. She just wasn't sure what she was going to do with it. "OK, so maybe we can trick Terrance into thinking we have more than we have. Maybe, we can set him up to make that mistake you keep talking about, Sam."

This time Sam was about to speak but was interrupted by Jud. "Let me get something in here, OK?" Jud almost pleaded.

"A big part of my job here is to serve as a sounding board. I don't get involved in the day-to-day trading. I don't manage any client accounts. But when one of the brokers gets stuck ... When one of the recommendations that comes out of

New York doesn't make sense ... When someone hits a wall out there, they come to me. They come individually. They come as a group. They come to me and we talk about the situation. We talk about options and solutions. I never make a decision. I never have to tell one of my people what they have to do."

After a deep breath Jud carried on, "Most of the time, they already know what needs to be done. They just want some validation. When they are really lost, just talking through the situation seems to clear things up, so a course of action becomes obvious."

Sam was about to say something when Jud continued on. "Maybe you guys are all just too close to this. Maybe Terrance is so arrogant because he's too close to it as well. Maybe there is something out there. Some evidence, what'd you say, some mistake, that we can find by taking a fresh look at everything."

Without pausing long enough for Sam or anyone else to get a word in, Jud concluded, "Here's what I propose. I don't really know anything about this situation. So, pretend I'm a judge, pretend I'm the jury, pretend I'm your boss, it doesn't matter. Just pretend that you need to give me all the evidence you've got. All the facts and the speculation, everything.

"Everybody participates. We'll see what we've got. We'll see where the holes are. We'll see what mistakes you may have made and what mistakes

Terrance might have made. Maybe we come up with some fresh ideas. Maybe we find a way to make Terrance pay for not pulling a disappearing act when he had the chance."

With that, Jud folded his arms across his chest and leaned back in his chair.

Slowly, they all took turns endorsing Jud's game plan. It was, they agreed, at least something to do to get them started again.

IV

Ian Proctor had done the evil things he did because he felt he could get away with them. He wanted to experience murder firsthand, along with torture, rape, and a litany of other crimes from the horrific down to the petty.

Ian Proctor, in Sam's opinion, got caught because he wanted to experience getting caught. Ian had experienced life outside a prison and, Sam thought, he wanted to experience life inside a prison.

Sam was convinced that incarceration was not society's solution for dealing with Ian Proctor. Incarceration, whether in a prison or a mental hospital, wasn't punishment. Life 'inside' was just an opportunity for Ian to find new, fertile ground for experiences he couldn't possibly find on the outside.

Maybe Terrance Newberry, like Ian Proctor, wanted to get caught. Maybe there was more in his return to L.A. than his knowledge that they 'didn't have dick.'

If that was the case, there was hope. But they'd still have to find the way to nail him. He wasn't going to just turn himself in.

If Terrance Newberry consciously, or subconsciously, wanted to get caught, he would provide the clues. But they'd have to find them.

Jud was right. They needed to review everything. They needed a plan, and the only way to develop a viable plan was to develop a clear picture of where they'd been, where they are, where they're going, and what they still needed to do to get to that destination.

They had a lot of ground to cover. And Sam declared that it was time to get started.

Chapter 41

Jud ordered in sandwiches and caffeinated soft drinks for everyone. As they were finishing their lunch, Sam began to relate what he knew about Terrance's life. Jud cut him off and stated, "I think if we go at this chronologically, we'll have a better chance of not overlooking anything. Rather than start with Terrance, why don't you start with the incident that first led you to the larger case."

Sam rolled his eyes, took a deep breath, and then stated flatly, "This guy, Henry Watson, gets himself blown up. Ski and I are up, so we draw the case. No leads, no clues, no nothing. Just this guy who gets toasted."

As Sam starts to perfunctorily move on to the next case, Jud again cuts him off. "Come on Sam.

This isn't Evelyn Wood's here! We've got to take a serious look at <u>all</u> the cases. Talk about <u>all</u> the evidence. We won't have a chance at uncovering that one percent of new information without going over the ninety-nine percent of what's already known. So slow down and tell me exactly what you know about this first case."

Sam tried a second time to relate the details of Watson's car bombing, but quickly got on a roll, picked up speed, and started blurring through details and rushing to conclusions.

"Look," stared Jud. "You think that you have the inside on this case because you have all the information. But if something was going to jump out at you, you'd already have seen it, wouldn't you?"

Sam nodded his agreement.

"I really have the advantage here, because this is all new to me. So tell me the complete story. Tell me everything you saw, everything you felt, everything you wondered about. Every detail, every sight, every smell. And not just you, Sam. I need everyone to tell me their stories, because each of you will have a different take.

"If we find a flaw in Terrance's actions, it'll be in some small detail, not in some major action. And spotting that flaw will likely result from how two of you saw, or interpreted, that small detail. So, slow down. I'm not going anywhere. Tell me the story."

Before Sam could start up again, Ski stood up for effect, began pacing around the conference room table, and started relating the events of the evening he and Sam first went out on the Watson case. Ski's remembrances were in such detail that even Sam was impressed. As Ski continued, Sam began to add additional details he suddenly remembered or impressions he carried away from the crime scene that differed from Ski's.

Even Kate interjected comments on points where her memory of what she had been told differed from what either Ski or Sam were describing to Jud. "Didn't you tell me that the security guard didn't actually see Henry Watson get in his car? It's probably not important, but you just told Jud that Watson had stopped to say 'good night' to the security guard, who watched him walk to his car, which would have meant that he saw the explosion. But he didn't. Right?"

Jud chimed in with positive reinforcement, stating that Kate's comments were the kind of interaction that would get them somewhere.

Sam acknowledged that the security guard had not, in fact, seen the explosion. Ski half expected an explosion of his own, from Sam's being stopped, mid-story, and corrected. But surprisingly, Sam not only took the interruption in full stride but, as he continued on, his recollections were in greater and greater detail.

After a couple of hours, two things became clear. The first was that this case had become like the game of 'telephone.' The game where you line up six or eight kids, whisper a simple phrase to the first child who passes it on to the next and so forth, until the last child has to repeat the phrase. Invariably, the last phrase has little, if anything, to do with the original.

The basic facts in this case weren't in dispute. But it was clear that there were several different interpretations of the circumstances surrounding those facts.

The second thing that became clear was that this was going to be a time-consuming process. After several hours, they had covered just the Watson and Newberry bombings. Terrance hadn't even been introduced into the cast of characters yet.

Checking his watch, Jud offered to order in some Chinese. Donny, who had been absorbing details as if he were a sponge, volunteered that he thought Philly-Cheese-Steak sandwiches were called for, along with baskets of fries and onion rings, and a round of beers down at Ted's.

For the first time since Kate corrected Sam's recollection about the security guard, the group found something they could all agree on. It was time to introduce Jud to Ted's.

II

The case review went on for three days, taking up every free moment Jud and the others could spare. Breakfasts at IHOP, lunches at Jud's, dinners and drinks at Ted's. Every detail, every development, every discussion was hashed and re-hashed. Every loose end tied into a tight knot.

Donny hadn't been privy to the details of the car bombings and was equally drawn to, and repulsed by, the descriptions of the actual crime scenes. He had somehow assumed that the car bombings had been neat and tidy affairs. He wasn't prepared for vivid descriptions of the destruction each bomb left behind.

Jud seemed to be fascinated by the details of the bombs themselves. He took notes throughout the discussions to help keep remembrances consistent and the conversation on course. But he took unusually extensive notes whenever Internet sites about bomb making, lunatic fringe organizations, or Waco, Texas were discussed.

Kate sat silently through the discussions concerning the victims and the bombings, interjecting only a comment here or there when the conversation stalled. Clearly she was following the regurgitation of facts and impressions but didn't have much to contribute. Not until attention was finally directed to Terrance.

Once the discussion focused on Terrance, Kate became very animated and, at times, agitated. Katherine stayed out of the discussion because this was no place for a lady, but there was clearly a battle going on between Kate and Kat.

Kate had clear opinions on Terrance. What kind of monster he'd have to be, to be able to inflict the horror and physiological devastation he'd inflicted on both his supposed relatives and total strangers.

Kat had clear opinions on retribution. Kat desperately wanted Terrance to pay for his sins and had some graphic suggestions as to how payment was to be rendered.

Ski displayed a remarkable memory for details that impressed even Sam. Ski added colors, smells, even textures to every scene described. At first his observations seemed extraneous. But they always helped evoke richer recollections from the others and he was encouraged to continue his color commentary.

Ski was especially detailed in his personal recollection of the initial interviews with each of the victim's next of kin. Ski had clearly been moved by not only the tremendous sense of loss each individual felt but by how the nature of the murders devastated them even more.

Everyone dies someday. But none of these victims deserved to be murdered. And no one deserved to be so cruelly executed that the next of kin didn't even have their remains to bury.

Through his murder-for-profit scheme, Terrance left a legacy of friends and families who couldn't answer the basic question, WHY? He deprived them all of any hope for closure.

III

Once he got past the concept of talking rather than doing, Sam reveled in recounting the investigation. He relished the opportunity to put forth his deductions.

Unfortunately, every time Sam would get on a roll and his spirits would rise with the thought that they were finally onto something, his subconscious would flash an image of Ian Proctor just grinning to beat-the-band. Then his mood would take a turn for the worse. Sam was repeatedly tempted to relate his Ian Proctor story to the others, but he knew he couldn't and wouldn't.

Sam knew by now that if they were going to <u>nail</u> Terrance, it would only be because Terrance really wanted to get nailed. Terrance wasn't going to make any silly mistakes, but they were doing the right thing looking for any clues Terrance might have left for them.

The more they organized, dissected, and re-assembled the material they had on each case, the more Sam became convinced that Terrance wasn't going to provide them any clues. Sam began to suspect that Terrance had returned to Los Angeles, not because he wanted to provide one last opportunity for Sam and the others to solve his puzzle and bring him in, but because now that his social aspirations had been dashed, at least he could flaunt his guilt, his wealth, and his untouchability in front of the small group of people who still had an interest in him.

IV

By putting every aspect of their case under the microscope, everyone was now in agreement as to what had transpired over the course of Terrance's crimes. The evidence was consistent with the story that had unfolded.

There was also a new sense of family within the group, which had expanded to include Jud. But they still didn't have a case that would lead to an indictment, much less a conviction. The circumstantial evidence was overwhelming. They were individually and collectively convinced that Terrance Newberry was guilty as sin. But they didn't have any hard evidence to tie Terrance to the murders. Terrance could flee, or Terrance could stay. It didn't really matter.

"We can't just give up," Kate stammered, unsure whether to cry or scream.

"But we can't just make stuff up." Sam put his arm around Kate when she made her choice and began to cry. "We've got to face the facts. If they called the game today

... he'd win."

Sam hadn't wanted to be the one who stated the obvious, but after Kate had started to cry he'd opened his big mouth, and now he had to go on. "Terrance Newberry can pack up tomorrow and leave the country and there's nothing we can do to stop him. Worse, he can sit up there in his fancy mansion and we can't touch him. He's won." With his voice trailing off, holding Kate as tightly as he could, Sam whispered, "There's nothing we can do."

Without another word being spoken, the individuals who, moments before, had been like family, gathered their files and, wrapped in their own personal thoughts, slowly drifted off into their separate worlds.

Chapter 42

"**F**letcher here," Fletch answered after picking up the receiver. "Who's this?

"How'd you get this number? ... No, I don't have a few minutes to talk ... How'd you get this number? It's unlisted, you had to get it from someone ... Listen, I don't know what you're talking about ... I don't have time for this crap ... Now hold on just a minute ... OK, OK, I'll give you exactly 30-seconds to make your pitch."

Fletcher listened intently. When the caller was finished he replied without emotion, "I don't know why you think I can help ... Well, you're wrong about that. Let's say, just for argument's sake, your information is correct. What makes you think I freelance? ... OK, let's say, just for argument's sake, that I do occasionally freelance, what makes you think I'd have anything to do with you? ... You don't seem to be getting the point. There's no way I'd get mixed up with you on something like this ... No I'm not going to get together to discuss this with you further."

Fletcher was about to hang up when the caller made the suggestion that set the hook. "Run that past me one more time ... You can do that? ... What kind of guarantees? ... Why in the world would I not think this is a setup? ... Well, that's a point ... Yeah, I hear what you're saying ... Let me sleep on it. Call me in a couple of days and I'll give you an answer. You've obviously got the number."

II

Elizabeth Rockwell, or Amy Adrian, as her newly minted passport said, wasn't particularly happy about the situation. Stuck in Bangkok with no prospects except a trip to Singapore ... alone.

She'd always thought of herself as self-sufficient, kind of a loner. But now that she really was alone, she realized how much the passing interactions she had with clients and co-workers meant to her, even her superficial friendships. She was alone and lonely, and it pissed her off.

She'd wait this mess out for awhile. But if Terrance thinks he can just cut her loose, ditch her in the Orient, well he's got another think coming. There was always Slip.

Elizabeth knew how Slip spent his money. She knew of his obsessions. She knew she could tap into his connections if necessary. She'd delivered more than just hefty returns on his settlement funds, and she was confident she could call in a favor if needed.

Right now, though, Singapore was a must. Cash, better papers, a chance to shop.

Elizabeth wasn't really a shopper. But she hadn't grabbed much when she left. She wasn't about to shop in Bangkok. And she could already tell that, by the time she arrived in Singapore, even idle chit-chat with a store clerk would be a pleasure.

III

Kate couldn't stop crying. While they were 'on the case,' there was some purpose to her life. She felt like there'd be some answers. It looked like there'd be some resolution. While all that was going on, she was OK.

She knew the tell-tale signs of depression. She had them all. No appetite. Hadn't been out of bed in days. Hated sunlight and kept her curtains drawn. She knew the symptoms but didn't have the energy to do anything about them.

Ski had stopped by a couple of times, bearing Campbell's Chicken Noodle Soup and a cheery attitude. She'd pretended she was asleep.

Donny was sweet enough to send flowers. She didn't have the energy to put them in water and they wilted overnight.

If it wasn't for Sam, Kate might still be locked in her house. Locked in passivity. Locked in her thoughts. Sam just wouldn't take no for an answer.

"I know you're in there ... I know you're not asleep ... I know how to pick this lock and I'll be inside in about 15 more seconds ... You have the choice of freshening up or going as you are ... the choice is yours, but going you are."

Kate let Sam in, plopped herself on the couch and declared she wasn't going anywhere.

"So then it's go as you are," Sam declared.

Kate instantly realized that Sam meant business and the only thing worse than her depression would be to go out in public looking the way she did. If Sam had done nothing more than force Kate to take a shower and wash and dry her hair, his visit would have been a success. The walk, the fresh brewed coffee, the cranberry scone, and the company were a bonus.

Sam and Kate walked and talked for two hours. It was the most open and engaging Sam had ever been. As they chatted about the case, as they chatted about things other than the case, Kate began to notice that Sam was expressive as long as they were walking side-by-side.

When they stopped for their coffee and pastry, were seated across from each other, and forced to make eye contact, Sam slid into his old, abrasive, obtuse self. Kate began to wonder if all males were more communicative when they weren't forced into face-to-face discussions.

As the day wound down, possibilities were discussed, pledges made, promises exchanged. By the time they returned to her home, Kate was starting to feel like her old self again. And Sam was exhausted.

IV

There's a reason why the French Impressionists spent time in the south of France. The atmospheric conditions haze the sky, mute the colors. Even to the naked eye the Provençal countryside is Impressionistic.

The hill country in Provence is dotted with castellated villages, most of which date back to the 15th and 16th centuries, if not before. One of the most picturesque of these is Moustiers. That's where Mary Louise Richter traded in the hassles of New York for the serenity of the French countryside.

Mary Louise took up residence in a cozy apartment above the small shop where she set up her gallery. Located on a narrow cobblestone side street between a boulangerie and a boutique chocolat, Mary Louise's gallery drew only intermittent foot traffic since the town was known for its hand painted ceramics, not for the paintings and small sculptures Mary Louise preferred.

Mary Louise Richter didn't mind that business was sparse. She was comfortable mingling with the villagers and chatting with tourists. She was comforted by her daily climb up the thousand step walk, under the Cadeno de Moustie, to the chapelle Notre-Dame-de-Beauvoir, the 12th-century parish church perched on the hill above the town. And she was now financially comfortable.

There was no longer anything in America but her past. France was her future.

Chapter 43

Neither Terrance nor Oscar had called to set up the appointment that Sam had requested, and Sam hadn't initiated any contact while the others were dissecting the case. But now that they'd finished that exercise, it was time for Sam to arrange one last audience with Terrance. He needed to see Terrance's eyes ... to see just how cold they really were.

Oscar answered the call and, without apology, stated that neither he nor Mr. Newberry had called to set up an appointment with Detective Siemen because Mr. Newberry had apparently picked up some kind of "bug" and had been sick in bed since his return. Oscar offered that "Mr. Newberry seemed to be feeling better recently," and that he thought it would be "safe" to schedule an appointment for some time during the middle of the following week.

Sam said it was important that he speak to Terrance before Terrance did any future traveling. Oscar assured Sam that he wasn't aware of Mr. Newberry having any travel plans and that if Mr. Newberry did schedule any travel that would take him out of the city, he, Oscar, would inform him.

Sam asked Oscar to set an early morning meeting, if possible. Sam felt he could 'read' people better before they got distracted by the day's activities. Oscar offered an 8:30 a.m. time for the following Wednesday and Sam accepted. "Of course, I'll have to confirm the time with Mr. Newberry," Oscar added. "If there is any problem with the time or date, I'll let you know immediately," he concluded.

"And you'll be sure and let me know if Terrance plans to leave town?"

"Certainly, Detective Siemen. I'll let you know if Mr. Newberry can't make next Wednesday's appointment, or if he plans to travel."

"Thank you, Oscar."

"See you next Wednesday, Detective Siemen."

II

Sam was actually relieved that he had a few days before he'd have to confront Terrance Newberry with his allegations. Maybe over the next few days he'd come up with a better plan.

As it was, his only thought was that he needed to see firsthand Terrance's reaction to the mountain of circumstantial evidence they had gathered. Maybe he'd flinch. Maybe he'd give something away. Maybe Sam could pick up some vibe that indicated Terrance was another Ian Proctor, who was going to help get himself caught.

Then again, Terrance might not feel the need to get caught. Maybe Terrance's evil hadn't developed a fascination with what it was like on the inside.

For the first time, it struck Sam that all Ian's crimes had been up close and personal. Ian got his thrill from being intimately involved in his crimes. He was in the moment. He <u>was</u> the crime.

Terrance, on the other hand, committed his crimes from a distance. Terrance heard the blasts, but he didn't hear the screams. Terrance saw the devastation, but he didn't see the eyes pop, the flesh tear, or the blood spill.

Sam suddenly realized that Terrance had chosen car bombs for his crimes specifically because they allowed him to keep his distance. Terrance got his thrill from the results of his crimes, not the crimes themselves. Terrance wasn't a bomber, he was a stock manipulator. He wasn't in it for the moment. He was in it for the money.

Sam wasn't sure where this new revelation would take him. Maybe it made Terrance more vulnerable. He feared it made him less.

Over the next couple of days, Sam began to formulate his strategy. Terrance had committed his murders from a distance. If Sam could pull Terrance into the actual crimes, if he could make the tragedies real, if Terrance possessed any sense of humanity ... maybe, by removing the sense of distance, Sam could get to Terrance. Faced with the collective human carnage of his scheme, maybe Terrance would do the only conscionable thing and seek forgiveness.

Sam knew it was a long shot. But it was the only approach he could think of that had any chance for success.

Chapter 44

Sam had been distancing himself from the others after the final round of drinks at Ted's. Now that they had completed their exhaustive review of the case for Jud, it was clear that they hadn't uncovered any apparent gaps, mistakes, or missed leads.

No one was ready to throw in the towel, which was fine with Sam. But, he'd run out of patience with investigating. He knew it was time to act.

Ski and Kate had decided to rework all the physical evidence that had been collected. Maybe there was a thumb print here or a palm print there that had been overlooked. Something that could tie Terrance to the bombs.

Donny and Jud teamed up to take another look at what they knew about Terrance's finances. Maybe they could piece together something that would fill in the blank spaces left when Liz deleted all of Terrance's records ... records that would tie Terrance to the offshore accounts and the short sales transactions.

Sam was pleased that the others had renewed their efforts. He knew from experience that it was impossible to just walk away from a case like this. He knew that Ski would work this case, at least during his spare time, for the rest of his career. He knew that Donny and Jud would pursue new interests in international finance, always with an eye to finding the link that tied Terrance to the short sale murders. He knew that Kate's obsession with trying to solve her grandfather's murder would taint all her relationships in the future.

But most of all, Sam knew he had to act. He had to confront Terrance Newberry one more time, or this case would finish what Ian Proctor had started.

II

Even though he and Kate were engrossed in their re-investigation of physical evidence, Ski was hurt when Sam informed him he was going to interview Terrance ... alone. Sam had waited until the last minute Wednesday morning to make this announcement, not wanting to give Ski any time to stew over his decision or try and talk him out of it.

"This has nothing to do with you as a partner. I just think that I have a better shot at getting inside this guy's head if I'm there solo. If it doesn't work, we go back in as a team. Swear to God! We go back as a team."

Frustrated as he was with his partner, Ski was actually more interested in the IHOP meeting Kate had called for that morning.

Ski and Kate knew that, while Donny and Jud were supposed to be trying to reconstruct Terrance's financial accounts, they had gotten sidetracked by a newfound fascination with explosive devices. Neither Donny nor Jud even owned a handgun, but once they had been drawn into this case, they developed a ferocious appetite for information on making bombs. They collected stacks of survivalist magazines and pulled reams of information on homemade explosive devices off the Internet.

Ski and Kate had also been focusing on the explosive devices used in the car bombings, since they were the one common element that could tie all the murders together. They had inventoried all the items that had been recovered from the blasts and, while they hadn't discovered any latent fingerprints, they couldn't help but feel that reconstructing and understanding the bombs could be a lever to opening up the case.

Based on their investigation of the physical evidence and the explosives team's reports, Ski and Kate felt they knew how the bombs were built. But they didn't know how they worked. Ski knew that Sam had a working knowledge of explosives and could probably save them a lot of time and effort, but Sam obviously had his own agenda.

Besides, Donny and Jud could fill in the blanks. They could figure out how these bombs were made on their own. They didn't need Sam.

III

Sam arrived at Terrance's estate at 8:30 sharp. He was as prepared to face Terrance as he'd ever be.

Oscar invited Sam in, offered him coffee, which he declined, and asked him to take a seat in the foyer. Returning from Terrance's office, Oscar motioned for Sam to follow him down the long hall for his scheduled meeting.

Terrance was seated behind his huge desk, looking pale enough that Sam concluded he really had been sick. Sam once again declined Oscar's invitation for coffee or tea, and likewise declined Terrance's admonition to "Please, have a seat."

Sam stood his ground until Oscar had backed out of the massive door. He slowly walked toward the chairs in front of the old-world desk, set his satchel on one of the available chairs, placed both his hands on the desktop, leaned part-way across the desk, which had to be at least four-and-a-half feet deep, and, holding back as much emotion as he could, stated, "I know what you've done ... you fuck."

Terrance had recoiled as Sam leaned across the protective desk, but he stopped at Sam's exclamation. "Excuse me, detective ... It is detective, not officer? ... I want to have this right ... detective. Isn't it a little early in the morning to be in someone's face over something they ... something I ..." Terrance half stammered, "something I have no idea about."

"No idea, my ass!"

"No idea, whatsoever."

Sam realized he just lost the battle over physical intimidation and that further demonstrations would only get him thrown out even faster. So he retreated from the desktop, turned on his heels, and retrieved his satchel.

Inside the satchel were the 8x10 black and white crime photos Sam had gathered. He pulled them out and began shoving them, one by one, onto Terrance's desktop.

"What's all this supposed to mean?" queried Terrance in an inappropriate, almost sing-song tone.

"This is Henry Watson!" exclaimed Sam, as he slid the photo of the blown-out-remains of Henry Watson's Mercedes across the desktop, so that it nearly fell into Terrance's lap.

"Looks like a bunch of twisted metal to me," Terrance responded flatly.

"And this is Watson's family!" Sam bellowed, as he tossed the photo from Watson's funeral at Terrance.

"Don't know those people," Terrance yawned.

"How about <u>this</u> job you pulled!" Sam exploded as he forced another picture of a burnedout hulk under Terrance's nose.

"Just more twisted metal to me."

As he continued flashing pictures of grieving families and destroyed automobiles in front of Terrance Newberry, it became clear that Sam wasn't having any success in personalizing the crimes or drawing Terrance into any place where guilt, sorrow, or regrets could take root.

Sam had seen inside the cars. He knew firsthand the destruction caused by the car bombs. He thought that the horror of the situation would be obvious to anyone seeing these stark black and white images.

But now, in Terrance's massive, cold office, on Terrance's massive, cold estate, Sam could see how someone — especially someone who didn't really want to deal with the horrific reality of the photos — could see nothing but a pile of cold metal, strangers at some unfortunate but unknown soul's funeral. No loss of life. No abandoned families. No guilt. No remorse.

If he'd had full color glossies with someone's brains splattered all over the sidewalk, maybe he could have personalized the crimes for Terrance. If he'd been able to force Terrance to attend one of the funerals, see and hear the anguish of the bereaved families and friends, maybe he could have drawn Terrance into recognizing the personal consequences of his crimes.

But while the crime scene and funeral photos spoke volumes to Sam, they failed to kindle even the smallest spark in Terrance.

Sam's number one game plan had failed. He had just one last gambit to play.

"Liz didn't get all your records," Sam muttered as he began stuffing the black and white photos into his satchel.

"Excuse me," responded Terrance. "I didn't quite hear what you said."

"I said, Liz didn't get all your records," repeated Sam.

"Liz ... you mean Ms. Rockwell."

"Yes, Ms. Rockwell."

"I don't know what you're talking about, records. But, have you seen Ms. Rockwell recently? She hasn't returned my calls to her office for weeks," continued Terrance as though he and Sam were old buddies.

"You know full well that she's fled the country."

"Detective, you come in here shoving photos of people and piles of ... mounds of ... debris ... that I don't know anything about into my face, accusing me of some kind of crimes. Now you act as if I have some knowledge of Elizabeth Rockwell's whereabouts, which I don't. What's next, detective. Am I somehow responsible for the loss of belief in Santa Claus?"

"Cut the crap, Terrance," exploded Sam. "We know you're smart, but we also know you murdered all those people so you could profit from the short sale positions you took through your offshore corporations. We know Liz was in on the scheme. We know that Liz tipped you off, cleaned out your files, and left the country. We know all about you ... your fucked-up sense of your place among the social elite. We know it all ... and we're going to nail you."

During his rant, Sam noticed that Terrance's eyes showed no sign of anger or remorse until he said that Terrance had a 'fucked up sense of his place among the social elite.' Sam suddenly realized that, while this guy was a monster, a true monster, he still harbored images of being accepted into high society. That thought would drive Sam crazy, if he let it.

As Sam was steadying himself following his last outburst, Terrance rose from his chair, leaned part way across the desk, and in a near whisper stated, "You come into my house and accuse me of terrible crimes. Crimes for profit. You insult me to my face. You and I both know that if you had any evidence other than your wild accusations, you'd be here with a warrant, not tabloid photos.

"So, detective, this interview is over. You are no longer welcome in my house.

"Now, you'll have to excuse me. I have a meeting with the Getty Museum's Board of Trustees. Seems like there's been a recent opening on the Board, and they'd like to have another Newberry fill the position."

IV

Sam had remained calm as he retreated from Terrance's study. He'd steadied himself as he traversed the long driveway. But as soon as he had turned onto the main street, he pulled over, rushed to the nearest bushes, and threw up.

Still shaking, Sam needed a cup of coffee and a place to think. Instinctively he headed for the IHOP. Inside, he encountered an impromptu bomb-making symposium.

Sam slid into the booth with the others and ordered a cup of coffee. He half listened as Donny finished describing the similarities and differences between the detonating devices used in the car bombings. As soon as Donny concluded, Ski tried to bring Sam up to speed.

Ski told Sam that by pooling the information they had gathered on the various explosive devices, they felt that there were enough similarities to link all the bombs together and tie them to the same designer. If they could connect Terrance to any of the components, they could connect Terrance to all of the bombs.

By the time Ski finished, Sam had consumed his first cup of coffee and had regained some sense of his bearings. He took a deep breath and related the events of the morning.

Everyone sat in stunned silence. Sam knew in his heart that the others would continue to look for bomb components or any other shred of evidence that would pull Terrance into their case. He knew in his heart they'd never succeed.

Ski was concerned for his partner. He'd never seen Sam so devastated by a case.

Kate longed for her grandfather and grappled with the thought that Terrance would be taking Jonathan's place on the Getty Board. Would his social resurrection follow? For some reason, Kate had found comfort in the picture of Terrance on the run. Now, she found the thought of his surfacing in her social circles to be totally unacceptable.

Donny and Jud didn't know quite what to think. They were innocent bystanders. They were not really involved in the crimes or the investigation. Yet here they were. They didn't know what to do. They just knew their lives had been changed.

Chapter 45

Sterling sensed he was losing control of the meeting. Why was it always so hard to keep these old fools on point?

Weren't they titans of industry, scions of family fortunes, leaders of institutions of higher education? But Christ, just trying to keep them from bickering amongst themselves was the best he could hope for.

Sterling Hatcock was Executive Director of the Getty. The museum was his show. But this was a Trustee's meeting. That was Winston Wainwright III's show. At least when he was coherent which, unfortunately, he wasn't this evening.

How can I make this any clearer? Sterling thought to himself. We're talking about finances here, not pedigree.

Sterling's mind wandered as he searched for a hook to get the discussion back on track. He'd laid it all out for them as clearly and concisely as possible.

Captains of industry? You'd think he'd been eavesdropping in on a clique of junior high girls talking about the new boy over lunch. You know, the boy they suspect, and hope, has a 'bad' reputation.

It was all there in black and white. Tours and admissions were at capacity. Gift shop sales were up seven percent. And, even at that, revenue from operations only covered forty-two percent of expenses.

Grants, corporate giving, and donations from individual patrons had been flat for years. Endowment funds were strictly controlled.

Continue to bicker and they'd lose this opportunity. And having just spent six months getting his Board to approve his budget, the last thing Sterling Hatcock wanted was to reopen that painful process.

No, he had to regain control of the meeting. He had to play his trump.

"Gentlemen ... gentlemen ... I think we've strayed a little from the topic at hand here." As he continued, Sterling slowly raised the volume of his delivery. Not to make a particular point, but to make sure all the hard-of-hearing Board members got the message.

"We can continue to debate the necessity of an Ivy League education or the benchmark for minimum years in the community all we want. But that discussion won't solve our funding issue."

Sterling sensed he had about two seconds left before he was put back in his place and the meeting would again degenerate into rantings on inconsequential, tangential issues. He had to strike, and strike fast.

"Here's the bottom line, gentlemen. Newberry's executor is holding up what would have been Jonathan's annual gift. There's no telling when, or even if, it will be forthcoming."

Now for the zinger, "So you have two choices, as I see it. We can either extend an invitation to Terrance to assume Jonathan's vacant position and allow him to assist us with our shortfall. Or, gentlemen, you can each increase your annual gift by $15,000."

Now he had their attention.

"But, he's ... he's just ... so ... so ... so ..." Justin Sample stammered, finally giving up, unable to find the right words.

"And that mess with Jonathan," added Max Adler. "It just feels unseemly to offer him Jonathan's seat on the Board. Maybe another time. But now?"

"I have tried ... we all have tried," Sterling stated, standing for the first time that evening to make his point. He added a broad sweeping gesture with his left arm to emphasize they were all in this together. "We have all tried to come up with an alternative. I personally visited with every person this Board could think of.

"Your friends, business associates, club members, they're all tapped out. Everyone is already on so many Boards, Commissions, and Advisory Panels that they can't keep up.

"Their charitable giving is committed. And in most cases, the individuals I talked with are already on our Patron's list.

"Shifting funds from the Patron's category to the Board category doesn't solve our challenge. That just moves money from one pot to another.

"As you're all well aware, the annual meeting is next month. We either have to nominate a new Board Member, disclose an anticipated funding shortfall, or announce increased pledges from the Board."

"Gentlemen," Sterling concluded as he resumed his seat. "What I see here is a need for new money. But, as always, the choice is yours. Now, do I hear a motion?"

II

Terrance was carefully positioned at the wrought iron settee that was tastefully situated in his most impressive formal garden, when Sterling Hatcock and Winston Wainwright III arrived to pay their personal visit. Oscar served tea. The setting couldn't have been better.

Why, Terrance was both surprised and flattered to be considered for a Trustee position at the Getty. Terrance had always been an admirer of fine art, but the Getty? Well, he'd be honored to even be considered for the position.

Certainly, Terrance was aware of the duties and responsibilities of a high-profile Board membership. He'd been there. And he must have been a good representative of those organizations; otherwise why was he being courted by several other foundations and arts organizations as they spoke?

Of course Terrance understood the financial strain on the arts these days. He was certainly prepared to assist certain organizations.

"Just as a point of reference," Terrance inquired. "What would an individual like Jonathan Newberry have pledged to the museum?"

"Well, there's no set amount," Sterling responded.

"Oh, I know there's no set amount." Terrance probed, "Just for a frame of reference."

"Most of our board members generously donate in the neighborhood of $150,000 annually," Sterling offered.

"Would that be in the ballpark of what Jonathan had been giving?" Terrance asked.

Sterling glanced about and then acknowledged, "That'd be in the ballpark."

Winston Wainwright III seemed to be lost in thought, but was really just lost. On the other hand, Sterling Hatcock was attentive and all smiles as Terrance said, "Well, I'm such a fan of the museum that I think a $200,000 donation would be more in order."

The sun shone on Terrance's formal garden that afternoon. A pleasant breeze carried a pot-pourri of scents from the roses, which was much more noticeable once the business of the day had been concluded. For vastly different reasons, all three men smiled as they sipped their tea.

III

Aside from Kate, the Newberry clan was too busy litigating Jonathan's will to take much notice of Terrance's reemergence on the social scene. He wasted no time in repurchasing his "A" list status, including a membership on the Getty Museum's Board of Trustees.

During his first Trustee's meeting at the Getty, Terrance didn't say more than four words. He actually felt a little intimidated by the other Board members. He was sure he'd get over that.

What Terrance didn't realize was that, not only was he considered an outsider, he would always be considered an outsider. And to make matters worse, his magnanimous pledge had now upped the ante for the rest of the Board.

Now they <u>all</u> needed to pledge at least $200,000, just to stay in line. Sterling was thrilled. The Board members weren't.

To think, they could have each kicked in an extra $15,000 and not had to let this black sheep into their fold! But they'd miscalculated, and when it was time to make their pledges next year, each was going to have to pony up an additional $50,000 to keep pace. There would be no statute of limitations for the grudge that little bit of showboating had created.

But insider or outsider, Terrance couldn't have been happier. His first meeting as a Getty Trustee!

He'd finally made it. He'd finally arrived.

It was all worth it. Everything. He'd do it again. In a heartbeat.

It was worth it. He'd arrived.

IV

Terrance lingered after that first Trustee's meeting at the Getty, hoping to engage in a little small talk. But the cliques formed without his being included and he was left to chat with Sterling Hatcock.

They would come around. He had time. He had patience. He knew he could, and would, get the treatment he deserved.

After a few awkward minutes spent with Sterling, Terrance announced that he had some unfinished business he needed to attend to. He hated to have to leave without having a chance to chat with some of the other Trustees but this matter just couldn't wait.

With that, Terrance circulated from Trustee to Trustee offering his hand and a genuine, "Good evening." He received a series of icy stares in return.

Terrance Newberry, alone and somewhat embarrassed, took his leave. He slowly crossed the Museum's parking lot, slid into the front seat of his Bentley, turned on the ignition, and was instantly consumed by the fire ball that ripped through his automobile.

Even after an exhaustive investigation, this car bombing, like the others before it, remained unsolved.